Christoph Ransmayr was born in Austria in 1954, and studied philosophy at Vienna University. He has worked as a journalist for several years, and since 1982 has been a full-time writer. He lives in Vienna. *The Last World* is his second novel.

CHRISTOPH RANSMAYR

THE
LAST WORLD

With an Ovidian Repertory

*Translated from the German
by John Woods*

PALADIN
GRAFTON BOOKS
A Division of the Collins Publishing Group

LONDON GLASGOW
TORONTO SYDNEY AUCKLAND

Paladin
Grafton Books
A Division of the Collins Publishing Group
8 Grafton Street, London W1X 3LA

Published in Paladin 1991
9 8 7 6 5 4 3 2 1

First published in Great Britain by
Chatto & Windus Ltd 1990

German title *Die Letzte Welt*
Originally published by
Greno Verlagsgesellschaft m.b.H., Nördlingen, 1988

Illustrated Roman numerals drawn by Anita Albus

ISBN 0-586-09123-8

Printed and bound in Great Britain by
Collins, Glasgow

Set in Bembo

For Andreas Thalmayr

A hurricane – a swarm of birds high in the night, a white swarm rushing ever closer, cresting suddenly into a monstrous wave that lunged for the ship. A hurricane – screaming and weeping in the dark below deck and the sour stench of vomit, a dog gone mad in the pitching seas and ripping at a sailor's tendons, spume closing over the torn flesh. A hurricane – the journey to Tomi.

He tried by day as well to flee from his misery into unconsciousness or at least into a dream, sought out every nook of the ship, each a further retreat, but Cotta found no sleep on the Aegean, nor later on the Black Sea. Whenever exhaustion gave him hope, he pressed wax in his ears, bound a blue woollen scarf over his eyes, sank back and counted the breaths he took. But the surge lifted him, lifted the ship, lifted the whole world high above the salty foam of their course, held it all suspended for a heartbeat, and then let the world, the ship and the exhausted man fall back into a trough, into wakefulness and fear. No one slept.

Seventeen days – Cotta had to ride them out on board the *Trivia*. When, one April morning, he at last stepped from the schooner onto the jetty washed sleek by breakers and turned toward the walls of Tomi, moss-grown walls at the foot of cliffs, he was so wobbly that two sailors lent a hand, laughing, and then left him behind on a heap of frayed rigging at the harbour-master's door. There Cotta lay amid an odour of fish and tar and tried to calm the sea still raging inside him. Moulding oranges, cargo from the *Trivia*, rolled across the dock – memories of Italy's gardens. It was cold, a morning without sun. The Black Sea, churning sluggishly toward the Cape of Tomi, broke on the reefs or pounded booming against the rock of steep walls that jutted from the water. In many bays, the breakers hurled ice onto shore, floes spattered with debris and bird droppings. Cotta lay there and stared and moved not a hand when a gaunt mule began to gnaw at his coat. As the sea inside him flattened, wave by wave, he fell asleep. He had arrived.

Tomi, the backwater. Tomi, the middle of nowhere. Tomi, the town of iron. Hardly anyone here took notice of Cotta's arrival – except the ropemaker who rented the stranger an attic room, unheated and with garish wall hangings. It took a while before rumours began to follow the stranger. They lacked the customary exaggerations, but at some other time they might have stirred up bad blood: the stranger who stood freezing under the arcade there, the stranger who copied the schedule off the rust-eaten bus stop and would talk to yapping dogs with inexplicable patience – the stranger came from Rome. But these days, Rome was farther away than usual. Because in Tomi, people had turned from the world to celebrate the end of a two-year winter. The narrow streets were noisy with the din of brass bands, and the nights with the bawling of revellers – farmers, amber-hunters and swineherds who had come from scattered farmsteads and remotest valleys high in the mountains. And the ropemaker – who went barefoot even on icy days and only on special occasions slipped his grey feet into shoes that squeaked as he walked through the silence of his house – was wearing shoes these days. Bread sweetened with saffron and vanilla was baking in the dark, slate-roofed farms among the terraced fields outside the town. Processions moved along the paths that followed the line of coastal cliffs. Thaw. For the first time in two years, the gravelled slopes that poured out of the clouds and down between crags, spines and ridges were without snow.

Of the town's ninety buildings, many stood empty at the time. They were falling into ruin and vanishing beneath vines and moss.

Whole rows of houses appeared to be slowly reverting to mountainous coast. And yet, through the steep streets smoke still drifted from the ovens of the smelters who gave the city low-grade iron – the only thing that had never been in short supply here.

The doors were of iron, the shutters were of iron, the fencing, the figures on the gables and the narrow footbridges that crossed the torrent dividing Tomi into two unequal halves. And all of it was corroded by the salty wind, devoured by the rust. Rust was the colour of the town.

In the houses women toiled, prematurely ageing and always sombrely dressed, and in the mine shafts high above the roofs, high up the slopes, dusty, exhausted men. Whoever put out to sea to fish cursed the empty waters, and whoever tilled a field cursed the vermin, the frost and the stones. Whoever lay awake at night was sure he sometimes heard wolves. Tomi was just as desolate, as old and stripped of hope as a hundred other coastal towns, and Cotta thought it odd that in this place – pressed hard by both sea and mountains, trapped tight in its customs, in the torments of cold, poverty and hard work – anything could ever happen to set people talking in the faraway salons and cafés of Europe's great cities.

Cotta had been stalking the rumours from the town of iron for a long time now. Other people were sure to trace them down as well. They had first reached him in the conservatory of a home on Rome's Via Anastasio – small talk among begonias and oleanders. On that winter evening, the images of Tomi – of its narrow smoke-filled streets, overgrown ruins and packed ice – had served to add some authenticity to news that might have sounded too skimpy and unconvincing without embellishment. The rumours then spread, like the spillway plunging down the street to the jetty, fanned out, here and there moving more swiftly and forming new branches, elsewhere coming to a standstill and drying up – wherever people did not know those names: Tomi, Naso, Trachila.

And so the rumours were transformed, further embroidered upon or attenuated, sometimes even refuted. Yet they persisted as the cocoon for a single statement, concealing its larva within, and no one knew what might yet come creeping out. The statement was: *Naso is dead.*

The first answers Cotta got in Tomi were muddled and often no more than recollections of everything odd and strange that had ever happened here. Naso . . .? Wasn't that the crazy man who occasionally turned up with a bouquet of fishing rods and sat out on the rocks in a linen suit, even in driving snow? And come evening, he drank in the cellars, played the harmonica and yowled in the night.

Naso. . . . Of course, that was the dwarf who came to town in his covered wagon every August and, once it was dark, showed his films – love stories booming across the white rear wall of the slaughterhouse. Between shows he sold enamelled pots, stone alum for stanching wounds and Turkish delight, and the dogs all bayed to the music from his loudspeakers.

Naso. Not until the second week after his arrival did Cotta chance upon recollections that had a familiar ring. Tereus, the butcher – he outbellowed even the bulls when he bound their eyes with a leather blindfold, depriving them of their last look at the world. And Fama, the grocer's widow – she was forever nailing nettle garlands to the shelves of her store to prevent her epileptic teenage son from grabbing at soap in red wrapping, pyramids of tins and mustard jars. Whenever the epileptic stung his fingers on the garlands, his scream was so shrill that the neighbours would bang their shutters closed. . . . Tereus, Fama or even Arachne, a deaf-mute weaver, who read the stranger's questions from his lips and either nodded or shook her head in answer – they did in fact recall that Naso was that Roman, the exile, the poet, who lived with his Greek servant in Trachila, an abandoned hamlet four or five hours' walk north from the town. *Publius Ovidius Naso*, the epileptic reeled the name off several times, mimicking the solemn way his mother had spoken it, while Cotta stood there in the grey shadow of Fama's store one rainy day.

Right, Naso, the Roman. Was he still alive? Where was he buried? Ah, had they passed a law now that forced you to worry about some Roman rotting away in Trachila? Some law that said you had to answer a stranger asking the whereabouts of somebody else? The people who lived on this coast lived and died hidden beneath these stones like wood-lice. All in all, Cotta learned little more than that here, at the end of the world, people didn't want to talk to anyone from Rome. Lycaon, the ropemaker, kept his own counsel as well. A letter, which arrived months later at Via Anastasio, said: People don't trust me.

Cotta set out for Trachila on one of the last days of April. On a beach strewn with shells that crunched under each step, he crossed paths with a procession that was appealing to an Almighty – whose name he did not recognise – for fertile fields, swarms of fish, veins of ore and peaceful seas. The procession pulled him along for a while, and he recognised several of the worshippers under ashen masks that distorted their features. The ropemaker was among them. Then Cotta turned off and, taking a serpentine path bordered by wormwood and blackthorn, climbed along the slopes. When for a moment he halted high among the boulders and gazed below, the procession was only a tangled line of faceless creatures. They crept silently along the beach. Their tiny banners fluttered – tiny, too, the canopy over the cart dragged and shoved by a black horde. Gusts of wind silenced their chants, the lament of their entreaties and the clash of their cymbals. There below, the inhabitants of Tomi were trying to make peace with a heaven that had never shown them mercy. In the haze they became one with the grey coastline. Cotta was alone at last. He crossed the narrow moor of an upland valley, stumbled over the rubble of old, caked snow in the shadow of the cliffs – and still he had the sea, deep and silent, below him. Here Naso had walked. This was Naso's path.

Now the ravines prevented him from looking anywhere but to his next step. They were so steep that at times Cotta had to move forward on all fours. And then suddenly before him stood a stone dog, a crudely hewn, battered statue, its hind legs missing. Breathing heavily, Cotta pulled himself up. He was standing amid ruins.

Trachila: collapsed limestone walls; bay windows through which firs and stunted pines stretched their branches; roofs of reed and slate, splintered and sunk into soot-blackened kitchens, into bedrooms and living rooms; doorways left standing in empty space, only time passing through them now – there must have been five, six houses at some point, stalls, barns. . . .

And up out of the desolation, jutted stone markers, dozens of slender cairns, the largest tall as a man, the smallest barely reaching Cotta's knee. At the point of each cairn, small banners fluttered – tatters in all colours, clothing cut or torn into strips. When Cotta walked over to one of the smaller markers, he saw that the banners bore letters of the alphabet. Each was inscribed. Gently he pulled at a strip of pale, bleached red. The fabric was entwined between the stones, so that when he took hold of the banner to decipher it, the cairn toppled. The stones rolled down several steps that the roots of a pine had burst apart, and Cotta read: *Nothing retains its form.*

In the wake of the stones sand trickled, compacted, stopped. It was silent again. But amid the devastation, Cotta saw the one roof still intact, jackdaws perching atop it, saw the house among the ruins. He made for it, for the remotest spot, and began to shout as he walked, to shout his and Naso's names, over and over, shouted that he was from Rome, had come here from Rome. But all remained silent.

The door to the inner courtyard was ajar. He pushed it open and a moment later, his arm still reaching out, he stood as if struck by some geat horror. There – in a bright corner of the courtyard, in the cold of these mountains, among patches of snow and frozen puddles – stood a mulberry tree, soft and green. Its trunk was limed to keep animals away, and the snow in its shade was dotted blue with the juice of fallen berries.

Just as someone afraid of the dark begins to whistle and sing in the dark, so Cotta began to call out Naso's name again, crossed the courtyard under the cover of his own voice, entered an arbour, and finally the poet's house. All doors stood open. The rooms were void of human life.

Linen curtains billowed at the small windows and to the rhythm of the breezes disclosed the view across the thicket of a garden, down into the milky white depths. The sea must lie beneath the white. From Naso's table one could see the ocean. The stove was cold. Ants were marching among crusted pots, tea glasses and bread crumbs. On the shelves, on the chairs, on a bed – a layer of fine, white sand that was gritty underfoot and trickled from the ceiling and walls.

Cotta wandered through the stone house twice, three times, examined the mildew stains on the plaster, a Roman street scene under glass in its black wooden frame, trailed a finger along spines of books, read the titles aloud, but called out no more names, went back to the stairs leading to the floor above – and still he held carelessly to the cloth banner. But a gust of wind snatched it from his hand and promptly dropped it. Cotta bent down for it. Suddenly he was staring face to face with a man. In the darkness under the stairs an old man squatted, knees pulled up. He pointed to the banner and spoke into Cotta's own breathlessness: Bring that back.

Cotta felt his heart seethe. Naso, he stammered. The old man made a hasty grab for the banner, crumpled it, threw it back into Cotta's face and giggled: Naso is Naso, and Pythagoras is Pythagoras.

An hour after being discovered, Pythagoras was still crouching under the stairs. Cotta spoke to him to no avail, repeated his questions to no avail. Pythagoras, Naso's servant, was no longer responsive to words spoken to him. But at times he would begin talking to himself, rapidly, softly, without gestures, railing then at Cotta as an eater of carrion who fed on his relatives' corpses and slaughtered his most faithful servants. He giggled, fell silent, began anew, at random, this time cursing a dictator in the Aegean, who copulated with goats before breaking their backs with his bare hands. But he could turn affable, too, once even clapping his hands in delight and praising the miracle of the transmigration of souls. He had himself resided in the bodies of a salamander, a cannoneer and a swineherd, was also forced for years to be a child with no eyes, until that incurable little body finally fell from a cliff and drowned.

Cotta made no more objections, listened, kept quiet. No path led, it seemed, into this old man's realm. But much later, sometime during the long silence of pauses when Pythagoras said nothing, he began to speak again – at first halfheartedly, the way one speaks to idiots, thinking he might stir the old man's trust after all. But at last Cotta realised that he spoke to challenge these wild rantings from the darkness with the order and the reason of a familiar world: Rome against the impossibility of a mulberry tree in the snow outside the window, Rome against those cairns squatting in desolation, against the forsaken world of Trachila.

He described for the servant his stormy journey and his sadness in the days of farewell, spoke of the bitter taste of wild oranges from the groves of Sulmona and strayed ever deeper into time, until at last he was standing once again before the fire he had seen burning in Naso's house on the Piazza del Moro nine years before. Thin smoke drifted from a balconied room into which Naso had locked himself. Flakes of ash flew from the open windows, and in the entry hall, amid luggage and the pattern of light cast by the late afternoon sun on the marble floor, a woman sat and wept. It was Naso's last day in Rome.

Just as death sometimes opens the most inaccessible houses to admit not only relatives and friends, but also those obliged to mourn, the curious, even indifferent strangers, so in those days the house on the Piazza del Moro, hidden by cypress and stone pine, had been burst open by the news that Naso was to be banished. And although the timid were frightened off by the calamity and kept their distance, the press of people on the staircases and in the salon was that of a house in mourning. Those saying their farewells came and went, and with them came and went lottery vendors, beggars, and ragamuffins, hawking bouquets of lavender and stealing the glasses from the tables and the silver from the vitrines. No one took any notice.

Pale, but with black hands, Naso opened the door to his study that day only after many soothing words. A blue carpet lay under a snow of ashes. The draught riffled a charred stack of paper on a table whose intarsia had been rolled into wooden curls by the heat. Books and notebooks lay bundled and smouldering on shelves and in corners. One pile was still burning. Naso must have moved along his books, flame in hand, the way a sexton moves with his wick from one candelabra to the next. He had simply set fire to his notes and manuscripts wherever he had laid them – always after much careful thought – in gentler days. Naso was unharmed. His work, ashes.

Pythagoras had laid his head on his knee and seemed neither to hear nor understand anything of what Cotta told him. Cotta shoved a chair up to the darkness under the stairs, then sat there without a word and waited for the servant to look him in the eye.

To be sure, the fire on the Piazza del Moro had consumed only Naso's manuscripts. Those elegies and stories that had been published, celebrated and denounced, long since lay secure in the stacks of public libraries, in the homes of his audience and in the archives of the censor. In a commentary appearing in a Padua newspaper (seized that same day), it was even said that Naso had set the fire merely to serve as a beacon protesting the suppression of his books and his banishment from the Roman world.

But there were so many explanations. A book burning – a desperate, enraged man acting without thinking. A matter of insight – the censor was right, and he laid his own hand to the ambiguities and blunders. A precautionary measure. A confession. A deception. And so on.

Beyond all such conjectures, the bonfire remained as puzzling as the reason for the banishment. The authorities were silent or fell back on empty phrases. And because as years passed there was no trace of a manuscript that people had long thought to be in safe hands, the suspicion gradually grew in Rome that the fire on the Piazza del Moro had not been set out of despair nor to serve as a beacon, but indeed to destroy.

Cyparis, the Lilliputian, came at noon out of the dust clouds of the coastal road, out of the year's first cold dust. As in every year before, Cyparis drove along the shore, two duns harnessed to his covered wagon, and with his whip he traced menacing, mad figures in the air, screaming at Tomi the names of heroes and beautiful women. This was how, still from afar, the dwarf announced pleasure, pain and grief and all the passions of the films whose light he would beam on the peeling whitewashed walls of the slaughterhouse in the darkness of the days ahead. Cyparis the projectionist was coming. But it was spring. In the brandy cellar or in the hot glow of a forge, in Fama's grocery or in the twilight of a storehouse – there, everywhere in Tomi, people stopped what they were doing, stepped outside or opened the window and looked in bewilderment at the dust drifting slowly toward them. The projectionist. For the first time, Cyparis was coming in spring and not in August.

This time too, as every year before, a stag – tired, emaciated and bound to the wagon with a long rope – trotted behind the team. In all the villages along the coast, the Lilliputian showed this stag as the Royal Beast of his homeland, which, as he told it, lay somewhere in the shadow of the Caucasus. He would make the animal dance on its hind legs to the tune of jingling marches. After the stunt, he often pulled the stag's massive head down to him, whispering in its ear in a strange, tender language. And every year he sold the moulted antlers to the highest bidder in the villages, to some trophy collector or other, for whom the cast-off rack served as emblem and skeleton of a frustrated passion for the hunt – for there were no stags in the impassable, thorny woods of this stretch of coast.

In the square outside Fama's shop, the old and the idle – as well as several of the ashen-faced people from the beach procession and sooty, bashful children – gathered around the projectionist's team. Battus, Fama's son, sniffed the horses' steaming flanks and with the flat of his hand brushed the foam from their nostrils. Why so early, the people in the crowd remarked, asked, while Cyparis unharnessed the duns. Why not at his regular time of year? And the saddle blanket there, the beautiful pictures on the canvas and the brass of the bridles, all so different and new? All so beautiful.

Cyparis led the horses to a stone-rimmed pond, from which coots flew up, threw the stag some chestnuts and a handful of dried rosebuds and, as always, went about his chores chatting quietly in a tone of voice alien to the town of iron. Why should a man such as he, Cyparis, submit to the dictates of the season and wait till summer to make his appearance? On the contrary, it was summer that was waiting for him. Wherever Cyparis appeared, it was always August. And he laughed. The bridle? He had got that in exchange for three shows at the Byzantium Fair – a gem. And it was there, too, that a scenery painter had decorated his wagon's canvas with *The Death of Actaeon* – a Greek hunter, an idiot, who had met his idiotic end in the fangs of his own bloodhounds. This deep red here, the splash across the draped canvas, that sheen – all hunter's blood. And he laughed.

This was typical of the Lilliputian, the way most of the inhabitants of Tomi knew him. Everything he said was a story, whether the topic was his whence and whither or the delicate mechanism of his projector shimmering dull black in the tulle-lined crate where he kept it. His machine – Cyparis could hitch human destinies to it and transpose them whirring into the bustling world, into life. And so each year, under the dwarf's deft hands there appeared on Tereus's wall a world that, to the people of the town of iron, seemed so distant from their own, so unattainable and magical that for weeks after Cyparis had disappeared into the vastness of time, their only stories were versions and recountings of the films whose light had now gone out for another year.

Cyparis loved his audience. When, after tedious preparations, the projector magnified the face of a hero to gigantic size and the slaughterhouse wall became a window onto jungles and deserts, the Lilliputian would sit hidden in the darkness and watch the spectators' faces in the blue reflected light. At times he thought he recognised in their pantomime the power of his own unrealisable longings. There in the dark, Cyparis – even when standing, he gazed face to face only with the cripples, with people stooped low or forced to their knees, and for him a watchdog was as big as a calf – yearned to be slender, tall and majestic. He wanted to stand tall. And Cyparis – who had driven his team through more towns and across high moors and desolate wastes deeper into stranger lands than a smelter in Tomi could possibly imagine – longed for the depths of the earth and, at the same time, for the heights of the clouds, for some immovable spot beneath an immovable sky. During the show he sometimes fell asleep over such longings and dreamed of trees, of cedars, poplars, cypresses, dreamed that he bore moss on his hard, fissured skin. Then his toenails would crack open, and roots would creep from his crooked legs and, quickly growing strong and tough, begin to bind him deeper and deeper to the spot. The protective rings of years formed around his heart. He grew.

And when the rattle of an empty reel or the flapping of a torn strip of celluloid would awaken him with a start, Cyparis could still feel the fine creaking of wood in his limbs, that last, slight quiver of a tree with a gust of wind trapped and dying in its crown. In those confused moments of awakening, during which he could still sense the earth's solace and coolness on his feet even as his hands were reaching for reels, wing nuts and lights, Cyparis the Lilliputian was happy.

In Tomi the only large buildings were the slaughterhouse and a gloomy church, a stack of sandstone blocks. Its nave was decorated with damp wreaths of paper flowers, mildewing pictures, statues of saints contorted as if numbed by dreadful tortures and an iron figure of the Redeemer, which turned so cold in the winter that the lips of the desperate worshippers who kissed its feet sometimes froze fast to it. Except for the slaughterhouse and the church, however, there was no hall, no room, that could have held the projectionist's audience, let alone his splendid, enormous images.

And so on the evening of this unusually mild April day – a time of year when an ice storm might just as easily have come out of the northeast to rip at the shutters and set glass rattling far into the depths of their houses – the people of Tomi sat outside on wooden benches behind the slaughterhouse and waited for the start of the first of the dramas that Cyparis had been advertising all afternoon. The noise of cicadas crackled from a loudspeaker tied with wire to the branches of a pine tree. The spectators sat pressed tightly together. Many of them were wrapped in horsehair blankets and, as in winter, the breath fled from their mouths, cloudy and white. But around the projector panicked moths swarmed as they had on the summer nights of years past. When one of them met its death on the hot glass, a ringlet of smoke rose up. And Fama the grocer thought she spotted a summer constellation in the chaos of the sky. Finally there was light on Tereus's wall. It *was* indeed August. . . .

Panning slowly, the camera glided deep into the countryside, brushed above pine forests, across black hills rolling into the distance, the roofs of farms, then across long crests of surf, swung to follow the crescents of beaches and now, gliding again under the deep shade of a boulevard, closed in on a palace that lay in the night like a festive, illumined ship – domes, arcades, sweeping staircases, hanging gardens. The focus became more precise for a leisurely inspection of the pilasters and cornices of a façade, when a narrow open window suddenly appeared at its fuzzy outer edge. As if caught by a riptide, the camera flew toward this window and came briefly to rest in a dimly lit chamber on the countenance of a young man, on a mouth. And the mouth said: I'm leaving. Now the camera lowered, swung to one side, where a woman stood leaning against a door. She whispered: Stay. Battus moaned when he saw the tears in her eyes. Fama pulled her son closer to her, laid a hand on his brow, calmed him. In the palace gardens the cicadas were loud and the lemon trees heavy with fruit. But the heat from basins of glowing coals that had been carried out behind the slaughterhouse was gradually assuming the smell of blood and sewage. Those sad figures on Tereus's wall, they must be noble people. Twice Fama asked their names, although they had been mentioned some time before amid the crackle and gurgle of the loudspeaker. She was named Alcyone, and he Ceyx. And the tender and sad farewell they took of one another was unlike any a man had ever taken of his wife here in the coastal town of iron.

Why was that gentleman up there leaving? – this evening's audience only grudgingly tried to understand. They grumbled and signalled their displeasure to the projectionist. They watched the lovers embrace, hold one another, watched them there on the whitewashed wall, in loose attire and then naked as well, and they comprehended only that there was great pain in that chamber muffled by tapestries. Then they realised they were just as perplexed as Alcyone that a man could leave when he loved.

To be sure, Ceyx, who ruled over this palace, over this land of night and the watch fires burning behind stockades and in courtyards, did speak of his own great confusion and of his hope of a consoling oracle, spoke of a pilgrimage to Delphi . . . or was it a crusade, a war? In any case, he spoke of having to journey across the sea. He was leaving. All the rest was of no significance.

As news of Ceyx's departure escaped the narrow chambers and corridors and reached the courtyards, things got noisy. Drunken stableboys chased women whose soup and hot spiced wine they had first laced with hippomanes, in the belief that this aphrodisiac brew would at last drive into their arms by night those who had fled them by day. From the ramparts could be heard the laughter of the guards, who were flushing every threat from their minds by taking long, burning pulls on a demijohn passed from trench to trench. At midnight, fire broke out in one of the stalls. The flames were just barely kept secret from the palace and smothered by the swineherds. The servants, the whole court, had begun to free themselves from their lord, his laws and ordinances – as if he had left long ago, had disappeared.

The splendour of Ceyx's power had reached deep into that August night. The mere dazzle of the splendour had sufficed to hold together the framework of his rule. His guards had watched in silence, his servants had obeyed in silence. But now that framework began to turn brittle, indeed to collapse, as if in every trench, on every rampart and battlement the flag of premonition had been planted: This time the lord is departing for good.

Ceyx did not seem to have energy left even to comfort his wife. Six, seven weeks perhaps, he whispered drowsily and hid his face on Alcyone's shoulder. A few weeks, then he would return a happy man, happy and unharmed. And Alcyone nodded in tears. Black and beautiful and light as a feather, a brigantine rose and fell in the shimmering water of the harbour. Torches smoked along the railing, and sometimes, below deck, the chains of sleeping animals rattled. Exhausted, Ceyx fell asleep in Alcyone's arms.

Into this peaceful scene Tereus bawled a filthy remark, which failed to gain approval. No one laughed. But neither did anyone tell him to be quiet when he bellowed a litany of suggestions to the unhappy pair. Tereus had a nasty temper and brooked no opposition. They had watched him today – it was killing-day – working for hours in the bloody foam of the stream. Standing in its shallows, he smashed open the skulls of bulls. When his axe landed with a crack between the eyes of the fettered beast, every other sound was so inconsequential that even the rushing torrent seemed to halt for a moment, transformed into silence. When at day's end, filthy and befouled, he loaded his lorry with neatly hacked carcasses while his dogs scuffled by the brook for scraps of offal, Tereus was so weary, unpredictable and irritable that anyone who could avoid him, did. And on this evening, too, fat and pale, lost in watching these farewells, Procne sat beside him – his wife. The butcher would sometimes disappear from Tomi for days on end, and it was a poorly kept secret that he was cheating on his wife with some nameless whore or other, though only a shepherd had heard her screaming, just once, high up in the mountains. Only Procne seemed to suspect nothing. Sickly, but uncomplaining, she accompanied her spouse through their ugly life and did what he demanded of her. Her only protection against Tereus was a growing corpulence. This once slender woman seemed to be gradually disappearing into fat that she pampered with salves and essential oils. Tereus beat her often, without a word and without anger, as if she were an animal entrusted to him for slaughter, as if the sole purpose of each blow was to numb what scant will she had left, to numb the disgust she felt for him. On the very day of their wedding, the people of Tomi had seen portents of evil. On the top of their roof had sat – large, immobile and fearless – an owl, the bird of ill omen, boding a dark future for any bride and groom. At last Tereus fell silent.

Alcyone lay as if lifeless beside her sleeping husband. She watched with eyes open and risked no movement that might give the sighing and dreaming sleeper cause to turn from her. Now she was alone with visions of her fears. And Cyparis's projector made visible each vision that she had conjured up herself all evening long in hope of persuading Ceyx to stay or at least to gain his consent to accompany him and perish with him. Alcyone beheld a sea by night and a sky in ruins, waves and clouds jumbled in uniform rage, rising up like mountains, then tumbling to the rhythm of her breath. Then spindrift avalanches roared down the steeps. Alcyone saw sails ripping apart, heavy with rain, each seam strangely precise, each thread of canvas. A mast split in silence. Then a torrent as violent as the brook cascading through Tomi broke over the gangway into the darkness between decks. Through the hatches, arms of water thick as tree trunks reached inside the ship. A gust of wind flung an albatross far above the doomed ship, broke its wings somewhere on high and tossed a mass of flesh and feather back into the water. When, in a flash of lightning, the horizon reappeared for a moment or two, its former gentle, peaceful line was jagged with crests of waves, like the blade of a saw ruined by a nail concealed within the wood. Above the sawteeth rose the smoke of a new black sky, approaching in frenzy and finally closing over everything that had not belonged to the sea from the very beginning. The ship sank. And whatever had gone overboard or had been able momentarily to save itself, followed in slow, then ever more rapid spirals into the deep. In the end all that was left spinning in the whirlpools and waterspouts was sand from the sea floor. It was grandiose, and ridiculous.

The audience on the wooden benches knew about storms on the Black Sea, and as the catastrophe unfolded they were all quick to agree that the scene blustering across Tereus's wall was a poor fake, that the ocean up there was in fact probably only tepid water churned in a tub and the sunken ship no bigger than a toy. The people of Tomi were, to be sure, familiar with fakery of this or other sorts, knew about trick photography, and during the tedium of the year often longed for such deceptive variety. But what Cyparis was showing this evening dealt with something they could verify, their own life, the calamities of the coast and the sea

. . . why, even dim-witted Battus could see that there was nothing believable about these storm scenes. Toy masts were broken, toy sails rent. Even the great stormwind had probably come from a windwheel, like the fan that the dwarf used to cool the blazing lamps of his apparatus. Last year, Tereus's son Itys had mutilated a finger by sticking it into the whir of that fan. The blades had dispersed his blood over the dwarf's projector in a thousand tiny droplets.

The disaster was unmasked. When Cyparis realised that his drama was in danger of running out of steam, he turned up the volume on the music and the howls of the storm – and drowned out his audience's coarse jokes.

Only now,in the midst of this new outbreak of fury, did Alcyone discover her beloved. Clinging to a scrap of lumber, Ceyx was drifting alone in the spray. In his hair seaweed glistened, on his shoulders sea anemones and mussels perched. He stretched out one bloody hand to Alcyone and opened his mouth to scream. No sound came. And so Alcyone screamed for him. And awoke. And saw Ceyx, breathing deep and calm beside her on the bed. But it was no consolation to see him lying there.

The next morning, flags swung their weary way to the harbour. They halted at the gangway of the brigantine. Ceyx went on board, turning around again and again on the short, steep gangway, and then stood for a long while leaning at the railing as the brigantine glided through a thick, sighing forest of masts and yardarms toward the open sea and out of sight.From this point, everything happened as it had been dreamed, but now in deeper, more lustrous colours.

The evening of the third day after setting sail, the storm arose out of the dream. Ceyx's comrades worked like madmen against their terrible end, grew desperate, hurled ballast and, at the last, offerings into the waves, but the ship was a wreck before it sank. The first to die was a sailmaker, who took his own life before the storm could. Others fought for their lives for an hour or more, and died as well. Finally Ceyx was indeed as alone as Alcyone had long since seen him. He was still clinging tight. And with each cough and gasp, her name and every hope drained from him. Then he perceived, or thought he did, that every solace lay in Alcyone's arms alone – not in Delphi, not in any shrine. How he longed for her and the ground on which she walked, for firm ground. Then he too went under. On the plank were flecks of blood and bits of tattered skin, which the water quickly rinsed away. Sea birds alighted on the wood and pecked at the scraps with their beaks. In the meantime the sea had grown calm.

Now it turned cold after all. The veil of fog that rose each evening from the shore got caught in the black trees of Tomi, in the labyrinth of its streets and in the wrought-iron ornaments. It would turn to hoarfrost during the night. The first ice crystals glittered on the canvas of the projectionist's wagon. The coals in the basins still glowed, but weakly, and were not replenished. The audience knew the usual length of Cyparis's dramas, and surmising that this one was drawing to a close, they began to call out to each other how they thought it was going to end. Acknowledging defeat, Cyparis turned down the booming loudspeakers.

Alcyone's dream had come true. But still the widow sat with two women friends among laurels and tree roses on a veranda of the palace and sewed a dress that she hoped to wear at the celebration of Ceyx's return. Her thoughts raced far ahead of her handwork – she twined garlands, saw Ceyx coming up the steep avenue toward her and spread her arms wide.

Dead! Battus yelled now and laughed, happy that it was he, he, who knew so many important things well before that beauty up there did, before all the others. Dead! He's dead.

Every morning, every noon and every evening Alcyone walked and ran along the coast, searing her eyes on the gleaming distance, and did not believe her own dreams. Her hopes waned, but very slowly, as slowly as life itself. And then came the day when a Spanish galley entered the harbour with five castaways on board. Like a fury, Alcyone pushed her way through the crowd that thronged the docks. Howling, she shoved aside whatever stood in her way, as if there were still something to be saved – although the decision whether they were to drown or be saved had been made long ago. The faces of the shipwrecked men were ravaged by sun and salt. Their lips were white and their shoulders so raw that they wore no shirts but were simply swathed in broad, light-coloured strips of linen that was slowly beginning to stain from their seeping burns. For twenty-three days – word spread on the dock – they had drifted on a flooded raft, had had almost nothing to eat the whole time and water to drink only twice, after cloudbursts. The rescued men staggered through the rows of the curious and did not respond to their shouts. One of them appeared to have gone crazy. He burst into laughter, then barked like a dog, flung his arms wide and sprawled out on the cobblestones. They pulled him up, dragged him along. And suddenly Alcyone thought she recognised Ceyx's features in that bruised face – there amid the sores and gashes Ceyx's eyes burned. Alcyone threw herself on the castaway's breast, felt his sweat on her brow, heard him groan and saw at last that this was not Ceyx's face, but rather the face of death. The shipwrecked men were strangers. They knew nothing about a brigantine. They remembered no other disaster except their own sinking ship.

Alcyone did not return again to the palace. She stayed close to the sea, close to the breaking waves and her faith that a gracious current would at least lay Ceyx's corpse at her feet. In the next days, her servants hauled furniture, clothes, baskets full of bread, dried meats and fruits into a cave whose entrance was between two towering cliffs feathered with gulls and pelicans. After performing this last duty, the servants ran off. Alcyone was left behind in the dark of the cave with only her friend, a maid, while outside, all along the coast, the domain of the missing lord went to ruin. Dressed in Ceyx's clothes, stableboys reeled along the quays and through the markets, aped his gestures and voice and threw bottles and stones at his statue. The poor rampaged in the halls and arcades of the palace. Horses and swine, doves, peafowl and even the lapdogs ran from their open cages, coops, stalls and pens, and fled into the wilderness. What remained behind was dragged off or slaughtered. Alcyone took no notice of it all. She would sit huddled at the entrance of the cave or on the beach, staring out to sea, and suddenly leap up and run in the shallows at the edge of the surf, weeping and gasping for breath, until her maid fetched her and held in her arms the raving woman, no longer responsive to words of reassurance or comfort. Then the sea rolled grey and peaceful toward the two women – grey under a sky that at times turned high and huge, only to sink abruptly again and lie cold and impenetrable upon the water. Winter came on.

Several of the spectators, impatient or suddenly chilled, had got up from the benches and were warming themselves, stamping feet and flailing arms in front of the basins of dying coals, when one young woman in the front row let out a terrified scream. It was Proserpina, a woman with a reputation in the town of iron for being man-crazy. Lets the cattle dealers leer at her like a cow, lets the amber hunters ogle her like a gem – Fama would comment, behind her hand, behind her grocery counter. And hadn't she been making eyes at the stranger from Rome? Even though Proserpina had been engaged for years now to Thies – a German tossed up on these shores from some forgotten war. In Tomi he was known only as Moneybags, because twice a year the ship's mail brought him money, a disability pension. But the worst illness that Thies the German suffered from was an all-consuming homesickness for the marshes and low-lying forests of Friesland. He spoke often of Friesland when he was shearing sheep. Thies could also trim hair and beards, sew up wounds, mix salves, and he sold a medicinal green liqueur that he claimed came from the Carthusians of Switzerland. When such remedies proved futile and all other healing arts were exhausted, Thies then buried the town's dead as well and built little stone domes over the graves. This evening Proserpina was sitting at a quarrelsome distance from her fiancé. She was still holding one hand pressed to her mouth and staring, through a hole in a fog bank that drifted slowly across Tereus's wall, at a long white stretch of reef off the coast. There, laved only by delicate waves, lay Ceyx's corpse.

As if Proserpina's terrified cry had frightened her, Alcyone, sitting as every day on the beach, now lifted her head and saw the dead man too. Suddenly, how close and clear her memory of his face – of every trait, every feature. Did that stranded corpse out there still resemble the portrait she wore on a medallion around her neck? As if demented, she stood up and began to run along the cliffs, the reefs. At last her mad racing had a goal. She leapt, she bounded, skipped from stone to stone and over the crevices in the rocks, flew past the shore boulders. And then the fog bank drifted farther and clouded the view. The audience lost sight of the frantic woman for one gasping moment and in the next saw only a bird launching itself above the cliffs, a kingfisher that hovered above the breakers, gave several graceful flaps of its wings, was above the corpse now, and eased down upon the breast torn open by scavengers. Ceyx. His closed eyes bore rings of salt, and petals of salt had formed at the corners of his mouth. The kingfisher's pinions seemed to caress the ragged cheeks, the brow, the face that blows from beaks had slashed. And suddenly something small and glistening sprang to life in that ravaged face, suddenly the purple and black of corruption faded, the putrid foam in the hair was now only a wreath of downy feathers – white, fresh down. Pearl eyes sprang open – eyes. From the surface of a sea engraved by a gentle breeze, a dainty head lifted, jerking to gaze about as if in amazement. A small, feathered body sat up fluttering its wings and shook off the water, the petals of salt and the scabs. And the audience, seeing neither corpse nor mourning wife, but only two kingfishers soaring aloft, understood. Many of them laughed in relief, too, and clapped their hands. Titles appeared and faded. Names of actors, composers, make-up men, acknowledgements. Then Cyparis heard the clatter of the reel and reached for the switch. Tereus's wall went dark. It was night in Tomi. From the sea a raw wind was blowing and carried with it, high onto the slopes, the barking of dogs, the noise from the brandy cellar and the chatter of the audience on its way home. As it reached the scrubwood along the path to Trachila, however, the wind seemed to slough off the last noises from the town of iron, turned blustery and empty.

While storms raged on Tereus's wall and the slaughterhouse was lashed by waves, high in the mountains Cotta was trying to light a lamp without success. Darkness reigned in the poet's house. After each of Cotta's attempts, the petroleum lamp hanging from a brass chain above the stove gave only brief, inconstant light and then, spinning a thread of soot, went out again. Like two night watchmen, they were back to holding their positions – Cotta a black figure outlined only dimly against one of the windows, and Pythagoras motionless and invisible now in the impenetrable darkness under the stone staircase. Only the irregular asthmatic seething of his breath revealed the continued presence of Naso's servant. Neither spoke. They had sat like this for hours, and Cotta perceived the silence and the inertia, this total retreat into himself, to be, in the end, the only mode of existence suitable for this spot here in the mountains. And now the stillness of Trachila seemed immense enough to absorb all the noise of the outside world until it died away – the rumble of falling rock in the high ravines, the toppling of walls and trees, the pounding of factories in subjugated provinces. And the voices, the numberless voices of malice, of gentleness or fear, and the clicking of the ivory balls on the billiard tables in the game room on the Piazza del Moro . . .

In these mountains, the world faded – and Cotta remembered it. Just as air bubbles lurch and climb out of watery depths, so images rose from within him, out of oblivion, only to reach the surface and become nothing again. The images achieved clarity as they made their lurching ascent, as if for him to remember them they needed the cold of these mountains, the ruins of Trachila and the presence of a crazy old man. What Cotta had told the servant hours ago, conjuring it up in speech, now became wordless history in the hush. Yet it seemed as if Pythagoras were listening to the inaudible voice as well, as if each of these silent memories were caught in an undertow that carried it into the darkness under the stone stairway. And so the glory of Rome appeared and vanished – the June sun in the windows of the palaces; the restless shadows of cypresses on Naso's house, its windows nailed shut now; then the stream of evening traffic creeping along like glistening insects on the march under the plane trees of the boulevards.

Pythagoras's breathing passed into a long, stifled cough and the cough back into silence. Then a shadow shuffled toward Cotta, the shadow of a stooped man, Pythagoras's shadow. Unapproachable for so many hours, the servant now rose up out of his distraction, came over to the Roman, laid a gentle hand on his arm and whispered: What do you want?

For a moment Cotta felt the same panicked helplessness that had always gripped him whenever a meteor drew its brief blazing streak across the night sky of Sulmona and he was required by the rules of superstition to think of a wish before the shooting star burned out. Now the meteor's fire drove him back into the house on the Piazza del Moro. There Naso's books were burning – no, one single book was burning in the flames of the manuscripts. In the capital city of Emperor Augustus, the very title of the book had been presumptuous, a provocation to Rome, where every edifice was a monument to authority, invoking the stability, the permanence and the immutability of power. Naso had named his book *Metamorphoses*, transformations, and paid for it with the Black Sea. Cotta watched the book burn and once again could feel the draught as it leafed through the glowing pages. At last he turned to the shadow of the servant and replied: The book.

The book. As if driven back by a magic charm, the shadow pulled away from Cotta. Then there was light. Naso's servant was standing bent over the stove. The lamp, which he had lit with a few deft manoeuvres, swung lazily back to rights. Shadows squirmed along the walls. The book.

How long had Naso worked on the book he had burned? Four years? Five? Cotta could remember a time when the *Metamorphoses*, known as *Naso's Project*, was a constant topic of discussion, as enigmatic as it was inexhaustible, in Rome's literary circles and in the arts sections of the major dailies. Naso, it was said, was working behind closed doors on his masterpiece. At the time, a tragedy he had written was a hit in the most fashionable theatres of the empire, even in provincial houses. In the display windows of the bookshops, Naso's books lay arranged in pyramids and mosaics beneath posters with his picture. The whores in the capital's brothels adopted their professional names from his erotic poems, which had already gone through several editions. Even the love letters of the better set were often simply copies of his wonderful elegies. But Naso's name was also mentioned whenever the conversation turned to scandal, to lawn parties, banquets, the latest fads of luxury, or the intrigues of power. . . . No doubt of it, Naso was famous. But what, after all, did a famous poet amount to? Naso had only to sit down with working men in some suburban brandy cellar or with the cattle dealers and olive farmers under the chestnuts of a village square an hour or two's walk from Rome – and no one recognised his name, had even so much as heard of him. What was the elegant little audience for poetry compared to those enormous masses that screamed themselves hoarse with excitement at the circus, in stadiums and grandstands at the racetrack? Naso's fame counted only where the written word counted, but was worthless wherever a long-distance runner panted toward victory down the cinder track, wherever an acrobat crossed a wire stretched high above the canyon of a street. Indeed, compared to the rustle of cloth when the emperor took his place under the canopy and a hundred thousand of his subjects rose from their seats in the arena, applause in a theatre was a relatively modest, silly noise. Although Naso must have known that the ovation of the arena was a kind of acclamation unattainable through poetry, he sometimes seemed to be consumed with a craving for such triumph. Then he would linger in the vicinity of the great stadiums for days on end, sit in the shade of an umbrella and listen to the surge of excitement as it ebbed and flowed. Indeed, his desire to appear before the masses himself was probably one of the reasons behind his misfortune. Because the frenzy there in the stadiums, the howl of docile submission – one man alone could lay claim to that: Augustus, Emperor and Hero of the World.

The book . . . Pythagoras said and pointed at Cotta with a poker he had just used to shove an empty ashpan back into the stove . . . that fellow wants our book. How spry the old man was now. He had lit the lamp, made a fire, closed the windows, filled a stone basin with water – and amid all these chores had resumed his low conversation with himself. That fellow there, what does he want, let's give him onions, we'll give him some bread, and water to wash his hands. He wants a book? Maybe he's thirsty, and let's close these windows too. . . .

Cotta was a courteous guest. He sat there shivering, for despite the crackling fire in the stove, the room was still ice-cold. With a slight, absentminded bow he accepted an onion from Pythagoras's hand, a slice of black bread, then a carafe filled with vinegar. He obediently rose when the old man took back the carafe with one hand, picked up a hurricane lamp in the other and, kicking the door open, motioned for him to follow.

The light from Naso's house fell far out over the old snow in the courtyard, even grazing the mulberry tree, from which the wind picked the berries, rolling them across the icy crust like black beetles. Then a bank of clouds ripped open, as if the time had come to display for the Roman visitor to the mountains what had so often been shown to Naso and his servant, comforting the exile perhaps as much as it reminded him of his abandonment: the night sky above the ruins of Trachila, the constellations of Lyra, Draco and the Crown, and a scarred moon rising behind a ridge and making the firs high atop a crag look like silhouettes cut in paper. The moon, said Pythagoras, without lifting his eyes from the steps hewn in stone and leading from the courtyard down into the garden, into the wilderness that lay beyond Naso's windows. The moon, Cotta repeated, as haltingly as if this were his first word learned in the servant's language. *Luna*.

Cotta stumbled along behind the old man and sensed the plants pressing in upon him, until at last they brushed against him and struck him. Branches, leaves – were they ferns, great fronds of fern like the ones he had seen in the deserted olive groves of Sicily and Calabria? Now the wilds closed behind and over him. The servant was up ahead with his lantern – keep moving, come on.

In the afternoon, from Naso's windows, this had been merely a dense garden. Cotta had observed only some sort of thicket, an indistinct, dark green foreground to the blue of the sea, more surmised than seen in the misty depths beyond. But now – the thicket had swallowed Naso's house, the mountains, even the moonlight and seemed to open by itself, bit by bit, before the steps of the servant and the shine of his lamp.

Pythagoras stopped and with his lantern inscribed a slow arc in the darkness. The two men had reached the end of the short path and were standing in a narrow opening, virtually roofed by the thicket, and with all its vegetation apparently withered. At the edges of this dark green room the plants closed in, all but impenetrable. Cotta stood in the lamplight, turned around and saw only his shadow cast against the leafy wall, but he could no longer tell at what spot they had emerged from the thicket. Pythagoras went on inscribing the arc with his lantern, completing the circle, and by its skittering light Cotta saw stones, granite slabs, menhirs, slate tablets, columns and crudely dressed, massive blocks, some erect, others toppled and sunk deep into the earth as if strewn over the clearing by brute force, overgrown with lichens and moss – a ravaged sculpture garden or a cemetery. No, that wasn't moss, those weren't lichens on the stones. Those were hundreds, thousands of little slugs, creeping in layers, in tangles, enveloping the stones in many places – long, shimmering cushions of them.

Pythagoras walked about among the stone columns as if among men or their graves, stopped at one and muttered several unintelligible words, cast the next stone only a fleeting glance, nodded to a monument, put the carafe of vinegar on the ground and took hold of a blanket of slugs as if it were a shoulder, clutched the slimy mesh. He had already moved a step away when Cotta felt nauseous. They were in Naso's garden. The servant turned now to a megalith towering grimly above him and casually reached out to pour a stream of vinegar over a colony of slugs.

And in that same moment, the silence of the clearing gave way to a high, many-voiced and delicate whistle, hardly louder than the faraway sound of a wind harp, its fading tones almost inaudible in the distance, and Cotta realised that this was the noise of dying, the terror and the pain of the slugs . . . and saw how the motion of death entered into the tough, moist webwork of feelers and bodies – hasty, twitching life. The slugs squirmed and twisted under the dreadful effects of the acid, and with their dying whistles they spewed little clusters of foam, blossoms of foam, glistening, tiny bubbles. Now the animals fell away, died, embracing as they plunged, slid, ran down the stone and left it exposed. And then, on one of the spots now freed of life, the word FIRE appeared. Cotta saw that the stone bore chiselled lettering. The servant went about his business of exterminating slugs. The darkness was filled with the delicate song of their pain. The servant moved from stone to stone with his carafe, carefully dispensing the vinegar over the slug pads as if by some plan, and on the barren surfaces more and more words appeared, sentences, many unreadable, others clumsily chiselled, as if by a mason making his first try at it – letters, big as fingers, big as hands.

Thirteen, fourteen, fifteen chiselled stone columns, Cotta counted in all, and read the words FIRE or WRATH here, POWER, STARS and IRON there and began to understand that he was standing before a chiselled text spread over fifteen menhirs, a message in basalt and granite under a blanket of slugs. And then it was Pythagoras who stood still and watched as Cotta, who had taken the lantern from his hand, walked about among the stones with growing haste and impatience, eager to discover the meaning and syntax of the sentences – one fragment per stone.

Cotta unriddled and whispered the words like someone learning to read, tearing a blanket of slugs away with his bare hands wherever he suspected new words. He patched together what was revealed, checked it for sense and syntax, discarded it, once, twice, began the game anew elsewhere, until at last it seemed to him that he had exhausted all the possibilities for combining and connecting the fragments into a single message:

I HAVE COMPLETED A WORK
THAT WILL WITHSTAND FIRE
AND IRON
EVEN THE WRATH OF GOD AND
ALL-CONSUMING TIME

WHENEVER IT WILL
LET DEATH NOW COME
HAVING ONLY MY BODY
WITHIN ITS POWER
AND END MY LIFE

BUT THROUGH THIS WORK
I WILL LIVE ON AND
LIFT MYSELF HIGH ABOVE THE STARS
AND MY NAME
WILL BE INDESTRUCTIBLE

Although Cotta knew only one man in all the world capable of such a vision, he called in the darkness to the servant. Who wrote this? Pythagoras was standing at the edge of the circle of light, scraping pieces of slug with a dry stick from the deep groove of the chiselled *I*. He said what he had to say: the name of his master.

But where was Naso? Was he alive? Was he hiding in this wilderness? Gone, was all Pythagoras said, he's gone. What did *gone* mean? Gone meant that Ovid had got up one morning as always and opened the window, that he had used an axe to break the ice in the big stone trough in the courtyard and had scooped a pitcher full of water. Gone meant that one winter morning everything had been as always and Naso had gone into the mountains and not returned. How long ago had it been, that morning, that winter? A year? Two years? And had anyone looked for him after he vanished? But the servant simply shrugged and fell silent. The *I* was smooth and shiny now, as if freshly chiselled on the menhir. Satisfied, Pythagoras tossed his scraper away, stepped back and gazed at his labour: I HAVE COMPLETED A WORK.

Completed. In Rome they knew only fragments. In his craving for applause and acclamation, Naso had demanded that his public give attention and approval not only to his completed works, but also to his intentions and unwritten fantasies. So that finally it became routine in literary quarters of the capital for Naso occasionally to offer – in overcrowded, stuffy rooms – readings of widely divergent examples from his budding transformations, without once betraying the total design of the work. The readings were followed with predictable regularity by conjectures, protests and everything from curious to reverent anticipation, all of which Naso appeared to enjoy as special, playful forms of an ovation. When he gave readings, he usually sat bent low over pages scribbled full in his tiny hand and spoke without gestures or pathos and so softly that his audience was forced to pay strictest attention. If he paused, suddenly a great, breathless silence reigned. Breaking into such a silence at the end of his reading, Naso would express his almost inaudible thanks to his audience and leave the podium, without ever responding to questions or even waiting to hear them. This brusqueness stood in strange contrast to the openness and ease with which he wrote and read aloud about love and war, even about the difficulties of telling a story. It was as if with time he had transposed *everything* he was capable of saying and writing to the realm of his poetry, to rhythmical language or perfected prose, and in the process had turned mute in the world of everyday speech, of dialect, of screams and fragmented sentences and phrases.

In his readings from the *Metamorphoses*, Naso introduced characters and landscapes cut adrift from every context – human beings who turned into beasts, beasts who turned into stone. He described deserts and primeval forests, summer parks and the scene of battlefields after the slaughter. But only seldom did he read self-contained episodes, whole stories. His inventions seemed a numberless legion. Enter resplendent heroes, and villains, the vanquished in their chains, gentle people, cruel people, whose genealogies reached back through the kingdoms of animals and plants and down into the crystalline world; dogs and cows appeared, speaking and grieving, fabulous beasts and forgotten gods. . . . The public could make nothing of the great design according to which Naso arranged his fragments. Was Naso writing a novel or was it a collection of smaller prose pieces, a poetical history of nature or an album of myths, legends about transformations, his dreams? Naso kept silent and entertained all the guesses, denying none, fostering none, and so fed the bewilderment that was slowly growing about his work. People took to calling it his *masterpiece*, although no one has seen more than a few pages filled with his cramped hand or heard more than these public readings.

Whenever the pace and progress of the rumours slackened, however, Naso would himself rekindle interest with a new reading. Every thread of this web of speculations and expectations always led back to the man who surrounded his work with all these riddles and secrets – not only making the truth hidden behind them that much more precious, but also placing that truth beyond all criticism and control. Metamorphoses: through all the hearsay, only the title of the work remained beyond doubt – a title that ultimately became a clue for the fateful conjecture that Naso was writing a *roman-à-clef* about Roman society. In it many citizens of rank and wealth would recognise themselves, with all their secret passions, business dealings and bizarre habits – masked and unmasked by Naso, the subject of gossip, the object of ridicule.

None of his readings ever gave grounds for this suspicion. But the poet – trotted out at so many parties and invited into so many houses – indisputably knew that society, knew its salons and its cellars, was qualified in every respect to write such a novel. Not that he was actually writing such a book, but one reason people in Rome gradually began to mistrust, avoid and, finally, hate the poet was the sudden and terrifying knowledge that he *could* write it. But for a long time, Naso's star shone unassailable, went on climbing at a period when the mistrust that greeted him in many homes was undisguised. Indeed, as the result of a scandal, his fame increased to a level of celebrity that put his name in headlines as big and bold as the name of any victorious athlete or movie star.

The scandal began on a hot September evening. A comedy was opening at one of the capital's smaller theatres. The play, a loose series of scenes, was called *Midas*, and according to the posters the producer had had pasted to the trees along the great boulevards, it was yet another excerpt from Naso's mysterious work-in-progress. It dealt with a Genoese shipping magnate, an absolute fanatic about music, who was so mad with greed that everything he touched turned to gold. At first it was just the pebbles of a garden path, plaster roses and a sheaf of straw that turned solid under the magnate's hand, but little by little it was his hunting dogs, too, the fruit he reached for, the water in which he wanted to bathe, and finally the people he caressed, held tight or beat. At the end, the unhappy man sat caked in filth, an emaciated skeleton in a golden desert, surrounded by the dull shimmering statues of his loved ones. And from his metal world he delivered a ringing monologue in which he not only cursed money, but also wittily taunted everyone who hungers for it. In the course of his monologue, interrupted constantly by laughter and applause, names known all over town were dropped as well, hidden within palindromes and spoonerisms – of board chairmen, congressmen and judges. . . . The magnate finally rescued himself from the curse and starvation by exchanging them for a fate only somewhat less awful. His ears grew hairy and long, and his voice cracked as mournfully as an ass's. With that, he exited. The audience yowled with pleasure and threw velvet pillows and flowers at the stage. That evening, and the two following, the theatre was sold out, and the air was so heavy with the sweat and perfume of the many spectators that the ushers had to spray pine scent from squat little bottles even during the performance.

On the fourth evening, a troop of mounted police wielding steel truncheons and long whips prevented the audience from entering and the actors from leaving the theatre. Both actors and members of the audience were injured. They lay, bleeding and moaning, in their golden costumes and evening finery on the steps and along the colonnades of the theatre until they were dragged away. A senator from Liguria, who owned docks in Genoa and Trapani and – it was later learned – maintained a large private dance orchestra at his summer estate in Sicily, had had the comedy closed down.

Reacting to the public outcry, and in particular to protests in the newspapers, which apparently passed the censor unobstructed, the senator justified the closing and the use of mounted police in two long speeches. These were printed up as flyers and pasted over the theatre posters. Naso was silent about this, too. The scandal then reached its high point when, early one morning, one of the senator's bodyguards was found on the banks of a large reedy pond near Rome – chained, his knees and wrists smashed and so confused that for ten days he was incapable of offering an explanation, indeed of saying anything at all. The man merely stared back in absolute terror and stupefaction into the faces of his questioners and remained so totally bereft of reason and speech that, as interest in his maiming waned, he was locked up in an asylum, where he rotted. True, no stratagem proved successful at establishing a connection between the closing of the comedy and the bodyguard's troubles. Nevertheless, the memory of that maimed man in the reeds and of the swish of steel truncheons outside the theatre became associated with the comedy, and so with Naso. What sort of literature could provoke such violence?

Naso broke his silence only once, when he let it be known in a newspaper article that the figure of *Midas* had been travestied beyond recognition on the stage of the wrecked theatre. The scenes he had written did not refer to a shipping magnate or any other living person, but solely to a Greek king, the prototype of avarice and foolish wealth. He had in fact never attempted to dramatise Roman reality by trite analogy. The suppression of the piece could therefore have nothing to do with him, but rather, with a false interpretation of his work. . . . But because this remained the only explanation Naso ever provided, it was dismissed as conventional caution and hardly noted. And because the scandal also had such fully unexpected consequences for him personally – even lottery vendors, fish and soft-drink dealers, money changers and illiterates now knew his name – the poet no longer resisted the course of events. And so he became *popular*.

Naso moved in different circles. His name appeared in gossip columns. Whether as court jester or the final malicious touch of the guest list at a banquet, he was now invited into homes in which there were, to be sure, hardly any books, but plenty of marble statues, electric eyes, silver-plated fountains and jaguars in cages. The people who lived in such homes were members not simply of society, but of the society of power, families whose pomp and luxury – safeguarded by dogs, glass-studded walls, armed sentries and barbed wire barricades – reflected the splendour of the emperor. Late one night in one such home, amid the applause and laughter of drunken costumed guests and by the gossamer light of a fireworks display, someone made a suggestion. Why not have that poet, the provocateur from Sulmona, give one of the speeches at the opening of the new stadium. According to news that had only briefly interrupted the evening's gala, the orator chosen by the municipal senate had died late that afternoon of internal haemorrhages.

A sudden death, the turn a garden party had taken, and a rare unanimity of mood among several of the invited dignitaries – these were the events to which Naso owed the commission that reached him next morning, only forty hours before the stadium was to be opened. He had opportunity neither to reject nor accept, but only to obey: Publius Ovidius Naso is to give the eighth of eleven speeches concerning the blessings of the new stadium. It is to be ten minutes in length and will be delivered before two hundred thousand Romans within the stone oval – and before the Exalted One in their midst, Emperor Augustus, who will personally introduce each of the eleven orators.

The stadium, a tower of limestone and marble, rose up out of a moor – drained at great cost of human life – south of the valley of the Tiber, and because the emperor had had a dream and because his will was unbending, it was to be named the Seven Refuges. For centuries, only buzzing, swaying columns of fever-bearing mosquitoes had risen up out of this moor and only vultures had ruled its skies, circling above the carcasses of goats and sheep, or more rarely, above the corpses of shepherds and moor dwellers, who had wandered away from the corduroy path and died choking in the morass. The Stadium of the Seven Refuges was the crown of the epochal draining of the swamp, and during the ditch-digging years was lauded as the emperor's greatest gift to Rome.

Here inside this mighty cauldron of stone, where on opening night, under the command of scores of ceremony monitors, two hundred thousand people lifted multicoloured torches like blazing gems while music surged from the Army Band in parade formation along the cinder tracks – here amid this dreadful splendour, as the people of Rome were transformed before the eyes of their emperor into a single mould that burned and raged – here Naso's journey into total solitude, his journey to the Black Sea began. At the signal from the emperor, looking bored now after seven speeches and giving his nod for the eighth orator from a distance so great that Naso could see only the depth of pallor on Augustus's face, but no eyes, no features . . . at his weary, indifferent signal, then, Naso stepped foward that night to a bouquet of shiny microphones and with that one step left the Roman Empire behind him. Because he did not mention – because he forgot! – the one directive more important than all others, forgot the litany of greetings, the genuflection before senators, generals, before the emperor himself beneath his canopy, he forgot himself and his own fortunes. He stepped up to the microphone without the slightest bow, and simply said: Citizens of Rome.

Naso spoke softly as always, but this time the enormity of his words was amplified a thousand times over. They echoed through the black velvet arena studded with flames and stars, rushed past the boxes, the railings, protective walls and ramparts and up the cascades of stone, only to break somewhere up there in that endlessness and fall back from it in distorted, metallic waves. Under the canopies of the court all whispering and chattering was suddenly hushed, yielding to a silence that for several breaths interrupted every motion, even the dancing eyes and the fluttering peacock feathers on the fans. Only the emperor still sat leaning back in the shadow of his guards, staring absently into the fiery display, as if he were deaf, as if he did not comprehend that Naso, the gaunt hunched figure there in the distance, had just broken the first law of the empire and denied him due reverence. And that wasn't all. For, apparently unaffected by the dismay behind him, Naso now raised his voice and began to conjure up the horrors of plague. He told of an epidemic that had raged in the Saronic Gulf, on the island of Aegina, told of a drought, of a summer when as harbinger of the coming calamity, millions of snakes had crept through the dust of the fields, told of the poisonous mist that had followed in the vipers' wake. He told of oxen and horses collapsing suddenly in harness and at the plough, perishing before a farmer could even lift the yoke from them. He told of cities where death erupted from the inhabitant's bodies in black boils.

Finally the sky darkened and rain fell. But it was only hot, foul-smelling water that carried the plague into the last refuges of the island. A great languor settled over the land. Battered by sudden fever, masses of people began to stagger and sink down beside livestock already blanketed with flies. In vain the inhabitants of Aegina tried to cool their burning skin with stones, pressed their brows to the ground and embraced the rocks.

But the fire, Naso said, was not to be cooled. The very stones and the soil, Naso said, warmed themselves on the fever. And now the sick and dying crept from their houses as the snakes had crept from cracks and holes in the earth. They stammered with thirst and crept behind the vipers to the banks of the rivers, to the lakes and wells, and lay in the shallows and drank in vain. The thirst of the plague could be quenched only by death. And so they died as they drank, and the mirrors of the waters went dead.

Those whose strength had held until now, Naso said, slew their neighbours out of pity and then themselves – with a thrust of the knife, with a leap into the noose or from the chalky cliffs, or with the last medicine of slivered crystal and glass. Aegina perished. Soon there was no longer ground enough to bury the corpses, no wood with which to burn them, and no hand left able to hold shovel or torch. Only the flies received the carcasses and the dead. Shimmering emerald green, blue with their swarms, Aegina lay humming in the sea beneath clouds.

On the slopes of Mount Oros, Naso said, stretched the largest of all the charnel fields. There the desperate had died trying to flee into the mountains from the heat and putrefaction of the lowlands. Most of the dead lay in the shade of an oak, the only tree for miles. This oak was as old as the oldest trees on the island and massive as a fortress. In the scars and fissures of its bark and in the forests of lichen and moss in the forks of its branches, colonies of ants scurried in shimmering streams, numberless insects that gave the tree its dark hue and a veneer, it seemed, made of millions upon millions of glinting scales.

When the cries of the last human beings on Aegina had ceased, the ant colonies left their oak, flowed down the trunk like water from a cloudburst, spread out in many veins across the charnel fields and, defeating the superior numbers of the flies, took possession of every empty spot, conquered eye sockets, open mouths, bellies, ear chambers and the shallow pits left by the plague boils. In troops that grew ever denser, they ran to close ranks in these cavities, clotted to form new twitching muscles, eyes, tongues and hearts, and where limbs had rotted and were missing, they replaced arms and legs with their own bodies. They *became* arms and legs and, at the last, formed facial features, for expression and pantomime. From their own mouths, which had begun to disappear, they spat white slime that froze as human skin over their sculpted mass, and so they became a wholly new race on Aegina, a people who stood under the sign of the ants. They arose, silent, left the slopes of Mount Oros *en masse* and moved forward only *en masse* in the future as well. They were docile and asked no questions and followed their new leaders, who were of the same descent, into the triumphs and miseries of time – without complaint, through the ice of the Alps, across seas and through deserts, into war, even into fire, a conquering army. They were a strong people of few wants, who became an army of workers wherever ditches were to be dug, walls razed or bridges built. In times of war, they were a nation of warriors. In time of defeat, they were slaves, and in victory, masters. And yet through all these transformations, they proved more tractable than any other race.

And just as the oak of ants proved a blessing for the island of Aegina, Naso said into the bouquet of microphones as he closed his speech, so now and in the future shall this edifice upon the swamps, the Stadium of the Seven Refuges, be a blessing for Rome – a place of transformation and rebirth, a stone cauldron in which from hundreds of thousands of the abandoned, the subjugated and the helpless, a new nation will be cooked, as changeable and tough as the new race of Aegina – as unconquerable. And he fell silent.

Nothing happened. The Venetian Guard raised neither rifles nor billy clubs against the speaker. The weapons and eyes of the court were kept lowered. The fiery display inside the oval yowled and clapped the same applause that had swelled up after the other speeches – perhaps because in the emperor's presence, applause and approval were obligatory, but perhaps, too, because something had been said about being strong, being unconquerable. Then the roar ebbed, and Naso stepped back unscathed into the row of orators, rejoined the extras. Nothing happened. Because Augustus lay sleeping, snoring under his canopy in his heavy ornate robes, while a thin man, a gymnastics trainer from Abruzzi, kept the flies from him with a parchment fan dipped in eucalyptus oil.

And so that night, along with the other speakers, Naso received a token of the emperor's thanks, a silver-trimmed bridle, and as ceremony required, he walked down the steps to the cinder track, very slowly. There a court groom took the reins from him. Eleven white horses were harnessed and handed over to the speakers, who then had to mount them. On the backs of their horses, stiff and swaying like eleven metronomes out of synch, the honourees disappeared into the splendour of the parade, a clattering torrent that marched past the masked court and the common folk with their torches, through the north gate of the stadium and into the night, toward Rome.

Perhaps at some extravagant moment in life, Naso had imagined his triumph like *this*: in the saddle, beneath the gaze of the whole imperial court and the assembly of the mighty, on horseback before the emperor, moving hoofbeat by hoofbeat through the ecstatic roars of a hundred thousand, two hundred thousand. Perhaps the stage-set for this opening night was indeed the realisation of some extravagant fantasy, and into the daydream Naso had now stepped, apparently impassive. But that night, as always, entering a daydream had meant no more than stepping through a picture frame the way a trained animal leaps through a flaming hoop, only to discover that there, too, on the far side of the fire, someone is standing whip in hand. The emperor had slept and snored. The faces of the court were chalk-white, their eyes set fixed with rage. The people howled, but their enthusiasm was mandatory and intended neither for the poet nor his fading words. Fine, Naso was mounted on horseback. But people near him in that moment saw the white knuckles, saw how tightly the rider had to hold on, how when the horse did a charming curvet he was closer to the dust of the cinders than to triumph.

Next morning a flock of pigeons darkened the sky above the cypresses and stone pines on the Piazza del Moro. Memnon, a refugee from Ethiopia, who was grafting a wild cherry tree in Naso's garden and trimming hedges, interpreted the flock as an omen of good luck. No one paid any attention to his talk. The Ethiopian thought all flocks of birds – starlings, daws, even crows – were messengers of good fortune. In truth, this flock of pigons, their shadow whisking over the house, the gardens, the whole neighbourhood, embodied the colour of the Black Sea.

At the stadium that morning, three hundred thousand convicts from Trinità dei Monti were set to work carting away the trash of opening night. Under the curses and blows of their overseers, they collected the fag-ends of torches, bottles, debris and the charred frame casings of the Bengal lights – burned-out mementos of Saturn suns, diamond fans and broomtail stars. The stoutest of the convicts festooned themselves with torn garlands and stuffed scraps of beef from the garbage into their pockets, while the timid used scrapers and wire brushes to scour the excrement from the marble galleries. Then a long column of dung carts crept along the corduroy lanes of the Seven Refuges to the garbage heaps of the capital.

At the imperial court that morning, however, an equally polymorphous, though practically invisible, mechanism was set in motion – an apparatus of whispers, dossier entries, hints and recommendations. Among its many functions, it was also assigned the task of gradually awakening Augustus to matters he had failed to hear or see, had slept through in the night, or whenever. Naso's speech now belonged among the materials from which, as every morning, the apparatus constructed and interpreted a view of reality for its sovereign lord.

Concerning speaker number eight at the opening celebration of the stadium, the apparatus not only remembered words of deference neglected, genuflections omitted and humility disdained, but also recalled whatever had made Naso so conspicuous over the years – poems and coiffures, voyages, changes of residence and both the bravos of a certain theatre audience and the blackouts of the censor. The apparatus's memory retained elegies and flyers verbatim, the sneers of a comedy, the sight of ass's ears on a shipping magnate, and above all the impertinent title of a poem, which, so it was said, remained unpublished because no printer would risk a project that had degenerated into an exposé of and insult to Rome: *Metamorphoses*. And the eighth speaker yesterday, this long-nosed fellow from Sulmona, the apparatus remarked that morning with one of its many voices in one of its many locations (it was on a footbridge, overgrown with iris and willow, that led across one of the rivulets of an imperial garden) – this Naso . . . had, to cap it all, actually provided occasional lodging to whores, to whores, in his villa on the Piazza del Moro, despite the untiring appeals by Emperor Augustus in his messages to the empire to honour the sacredness of family and the precious jewel of decorum.

At the Stadium of the Seven Refuges, for the first and only time in his life, Naso had appealed to the people, to a huge audience ready for anything. But even on the first day after his appearance, it was clear that all he had been able to move with his speech was the open-eared, many-voiced and infinitely fine-tuned apparatus of state. He had moved a gesticulating secretary on his long walk through a suite of rooms, who got angry all over again as he passed on the description of the island of Aegina and its dead. He had moved a department head, who drafted his daily report and sent it on its way. He had moved a voice on the telephone that spoke of poems and hymns as if they were pamphlets . . . and had moved several messengers who had to deliver the circular mail, letters that some overworked general in civvies now had to read just because the file bore the name of the eighth speaker. And after the scandalous parable of ants and plague one's way to the top might possibly be opened – so much was quickly understood in these offices – in the ruin of that name.

To be sure, the movements of the apparatus were slow, dispassionate and with none of the anger mirrored in the faces of the court. But whereas the anger might have been allayed and dissipated, the apparatus was not to be placated, nor could it be shut down. And so information concerning the poet Publius Ovidius Naso, verified now in files, gradually began to flow, sweeping with it patience and sympathy from the channels of bureaucracy, rising like flood waters to the top of the dike, to the threshold of the emperor's audience chambers. There the news, the reports, the expert opinions sloshed, until the first catchword leapt the threshold in white-capped waves, spilled over the dam and rushed down over the land below: Metamorphoses – the work of an enemy of the state, an affront to Rome, the document of a deranged mind, but likewise proof of the turpitude and ingratitude of a man ennobled by an invitation to speak at the opening of the Seven Refuges.

On a stone bench by the window, an immobile Augustus sat watching a rhinoceros, secured behind its stockade, take a mud bath in the courtyard. A gift of the procurator of Sumatra, it wallowed in its bog and made no sounds of pleasure. Rusty-red tickbirds that usually scuttled back and forth on the beast's back, keeping watch and living from the vermin among the wrinkles of its plated hide, now squawked and fluttered in a rain of sludge. The emperor did not lift his gaze from the scene when the informant entered and, waved on by a nervous secretary, began to speak.

Read? Had the emperor ever once read an elegy by this Naso? a poem? one of his books? Augustus seemed spellbound by the agile movements of the primeval beast under his window. The rhinoceros flung fountains of mire into the air and used its horn to tear deep furrows, semicircles and wavy lines into the soft earth. The mighty of this world did not read books, nor elegies. As with everything else that occurred in the world out there beyond the bog, books reached the emperor only by way of the summaries and descriptive reports of his underlings. If Augustus could be informed of a retaliatory expedition or the construction of a dam without tiring his eyes on clouds of dust, chains and scaffolds –

was that not all the more reason, then, to lay before his feet the contents of whole libraries without his ever having so much as to crack a book? But whoever had access to the chambers of Augustus was himself powerful enough to command a host of informants to mediate between himself and the world. Whoever was a confidant of the all-powerful did not first have to feel against his own skin the lava of Sicily or the ashes raining upon Naples to know more about the fires of a volcano than any of its scorched victims. No, in the heart of the palace, no one had read elegies. Books were as far from that heart as the world itself was.

The layer of mud with which the rhinoceros clad itself twice, three times a day, protected it only briefly from the horseflies and swarming gnats. When that coat broke under the heat of the sun and slid from the animal in great plates, the insects seemed to fall upon the unprotected hide with even greater fury, sometimes setting the beast into such a frenzy that it would suddenly charge, stomping and ploughing to pieces everything in its way, until finally it would rub violently against the piles of the stockade and the trees around the pond as if hoping to rid itself not just of the flies and vermin in general, but of its own mighty grey body. Bark had been stripped from many places along the wooden stockade, and the trees were smooth as polished stone.

But enough now. Not another word. Not this morning. Not here at the window. Later perhaps. Go. Get out.

Without a word, with just an abrupt, curt motion of his hand, hardly more vigorous than if he were shaking off a housefly, Augusus interrupted the informant and then sank back again to gaze at the rhinoceros. A cursory motion of his hand. That was enough. The court needed neither complete sentences nor final judgments. In their council chambers, at their desks and in the filing rooms of the archives, they now had a sign. Whatever was lacking for a final judgment could be appended with no difficulty. He was a poor servant of Rome who did not know to interpret an abrupt motion of His right hand as a sign of the greatest displeasure, indeed of wrath.

Just as the image of the poet and the content of his works had been disfigured and transformed on their way upward, so now the sign from the emperor, the deeply engraved memory of a cursory motion of His hand, was sent on its way back downward and subjected to the same laws of distortion. Prison, someone in the conference room said and reached for the water carafe, Trinità dei Monti, minimum of three years, perhaps four. Labour camp, whispered someone else, Castelvetrano, off to Sicily and the stonecutters. Wrong: the sign had certainly been nothing more than an injunction against all literary activity for one year, at most a forfeiture of royalties, maybe only the suspension of travel privileges until fall. Merely a warning.

As so often in the history of executive action, this time too it was left to the fantasy and imaginative powers of subordinates to construe and execute the will of the emperor, who was not particularly interested in this or similar cases of no consequence. A motion of the hand. The sign was passed on and sank only very slowly down through the levels of government. By way of precaution, the apparatus embraced all interpretations. The poet no longer appeared in public. The court was silent.

Naso's white horse prospered without saddle and bridle and raced about the garden on the Piazzo del Moro, a mere ornament to the estate. The speech at the Stadium of the Seven Refuges seemed almost forgotten when the emperor's sign finally reached the bottom level – where the blows were actually inflicted and not simply decreed, where the cell doors really clicked shut and a year in prison was not simply the flourish on a court sentence, but time taken from life. Somewhere in those depths, then, somewhere very close to real life, a presiding judge *rendered* an opinion. It was shortly before his lunch break, and he dictated it to an apathetic clerk in the presence of two witnesses. A motion of His hand meant *begone*. *Out of my sight!* Out of the sight of the emperor, however, meant to the end of the world. And the end of the world was Tomi.

IV

The stones were unriddled. Smooth, still shiny with vinegar and the slime of slugs, they mirrored the flickering lantern. Only now did Cotta feel his weariness and the cold. Night's frost moved over Naso's garden. Thorns, needles and bristles of ice grew on the leaves of the thicket, on strands of bast, on fern fronds. Crouched before a blank menhir, Pythagoras seemed to have relinquished, abandoned, the wilderness to his Roman guest. The servant's face was veiled by the misty vapours and thick clouds of his breath. While Cotta still wandered reading among the stones, Pythagoras had begun to speak again in the darkness – soft, unintelligible, unremitting words, like hoarfrost falling on the world. As he spoke he took back the lantern from Cotta's hand and walked ahead toward the green wall of the clearing. The slugs' bodies, frozen fast to the ground where they had fallen, crunched and crackled under their steps. In the cold, the path over their cadavers was a path of glass. Once past the crackling and splintering, Naso's servant and the Roman entered the dark green of the thicket.

Cotta followed the old man through the labyrinth of tree trunks and branches, was too tired to defend himself against the lashes of the shrubs. Whipped and bloody at the temples, he followed him – still muttering away – up the stone steps and at last into the courtyard, white beneath the moon. The wind had subsided. The leaves of the mulberry tree jingled metallically. The poet's house was only a shadow against the pale vastness of the mountains, still clad in glistening rags from two winters of snow. The small shadow took them in. But then Naso's house began to resist the stranger as violently as the garden thicket had. As he stepped over the threshold behind the servant, a hook in the wall ripped Cotta's coat, then the handle of an axe propped against the wall struck his knee. He buckled in pain. And when Pythagoras threw a log on the dimly glowing fire, a swarm of dark red sparks leapt at the Roman, singeing his eyebrows and hair. The servant took notice of this swift succession of mishaps, but went right on talking. He pointed with the poker to a bedstead between two bookcases in one sooty corner of the room, to a matted sheepskin and a crumpled blanket of horsehair that stank of soot and grease. Then he turned toward the steep staircase leading to the upper storey, stood for a long time on the first step peering up as if weighing yet once more the torment of the climb and summoning all his energies for the effort. Cotta suddenly saw the servant – in that pose, bent over, holding the lamp above his head and hesitating before that first step – as an ancient creature of inhuman age that had reached the outer limits of life. It frightened him. Gasping, yet still talking as if his stammerings were bound inseparably to his heartbeat and breath, the old man climbed the stairs at last, peered back over his shoulder through the black hole of a trapdoor, snuffed out his lantern and, rumbling across the plank floor overhead, disappeared in the darkness. His conversation with himself could still be heard as a distant murmur once the noise of his steps had faded away. It was the dead of night.

Cotta groped his way through gloom softened by a few cracks filled with moonlight and found the bed by the glow from the stove. He sank back into its stench of grease and smoke and hides and fell asleep before he could pull the horsehair blanket over his shoulders. Staring out at the sleeping man through a barred mica window cut into the door of the stove, the flames at length settled back deeper and deeper into their ashes, finally consuming the last annual ring in the log. Only a slowly cooling, soundless darkness remained. The room turned cold – on the window the sleeper's breath was gradually turning into promenades of tiny frosted palms, into delicate jungles, rose gardens and thistles of ice. At some point the door to the courtyard flew open with a crash. A torrent of icy air surged toward the bed, waking the sleeper with a start. Now the gloom melted and in the strange silvered light, Cotta saw a monstrosity cross the threshold, a brutish herdsman wrapped in a coat of pelts, whose head was not a head, but a glistening, skull-sized mass much like the foaming clusters of slugs perishing in vinegar. But what shimmered atop the herdsman's shoulders were not bubbles or blossoms of foam filled to bursting with delicate cries of pain – those were eyes, dozens, hundreds of eyes. On his shoulders the herdsman bore a clump – of eyelashes, lids, tear ducts and eyeballs that mirrored and refracted the silver light like stars – a blinking, staring, watching clump gawking in all directions, a skull of irises, beautiful and dreadful.

Without a word, the monstrosity walked over to the stove and squatted there on the floor as if before a campfire, paying no attention to the sleeping man. Cotta felt terror seize him, felt how a long, hollow scream started deep within – a strange animal sound that filled his throat, his sinuses, set his whole head vibrating – and exploded at last in a bellow from both mouth and nose at once. It was the bellowing of a cow.

Frightened, transfixed by this voice, his own voice, Cotta sank back onto the horsehair blanket. As if with shattered bones, he lay there twisted and twisting in the embrace of a merciless world. The herdsman's skull shimmered now as a single eye composed of countless facets – the silky head of a fly, yet not one of those many eyes appeared to see the man, lame and lowing, on his bed. The herdsman squatted before the cold iron of the stove and began to tug at a rope stretched taut through the open door and out into the night. He pulled and jerked until the exertion spread a delicate red filigree of veins over the whites of his many eyes – until a cow, a snow-white cow appeared in the doorway against the backdrop of the moonlit mountains. The herdsman's efforts were in vain. Shying at this stall, the animal lowered itself ponderously onto the threshold of Naso's house. It began to chew and grind its cud, staring into the corner where the sleeper lay. Suddenly it stopped, listening. Now Cotta heard the music too. A moment before, he had thought he heard the soughing wind, a bass tone rising and falling, but now he caught the slow rhythm of a melody coming from far away, across the rubbled slopes, or from some high valley perhaps – music so gentle it reminded Cotta of the lullabies of Sulmona, of caresses and the odour of warm skin, of a safe haven long since vanished. Was that the sound of an oboe? of a flute?

The starry skull held its eyes fixed on the white cow, but it began to rock listlessly to the rhythm of the melody while gazing through the open door, beyond the animal and into the mountains, as if listening to emerging memories, to the stanzas of songs that taunted a monster. And the herdsman was touched. His blinking eyes watered, and tears began to trickle into the fur of his coat. The distant tune evoked not only scenes and feelings long since vanished, but even more, a great weariness. The melody transformed each glance into weariness. Entire rows of the herdsman's eyes had closed now, and sleep scurried across a hundred eyes like a gull's shadow over a school of fish, their scales flashing silver one last time before the headlong dive into the depths. Where, moments ago, eye after eye had stared alert, now only lids lay closed. But glistening rows of black pupils opened to replace them at other spots on the skull. The blinking eyes moved in rolling waves, wide with fright, then dozing, struggling against dreams – until sleep gradually began to grow stronger and star after star went out and no new light appeared. By now the herdsman was only dreaming his cow, and the Roman was dreaming the herdsman, and moon and mountains were mere chimeras – when the music suddenly broke off and a shadow appeared at Naso's door, glided over the threshold, reached for the axe lying on the floor, leapt at the sleeping monstrosity. And struck.

Under the savage force of the axe's blow the herdsman's eyes fell away like scales, scattering into the corners, drops of quicksilver. The starry skull burst. Blood boiled up out of its gaping wounds, washing away eye after eye, carrying with it retinas, tear ducts and lashes. Long after the shadow had withdrawn without a sound into the courtyard and the night, the cow, spattered with its herdsman's blood, got up and tugged the rope free from the slain man's slowly opening fist. And escaped. Cotta screamed a second time. He had his voice back, his Roman voice, but still he went on dreaming – he saw the floorboards move, saw the rough nail-studded planks as long bird feathers, saw the floor of Naso's house as a peacock unfolding its tail feather by feather. And saw the eyes that had burst from the monstrosity's skull stick to the peacock's train, embedding themselves in a downy wreath. When not a feather tip lacked for an eye, the peacock snapped the rustling fan of its tail shut and giving the plaintive cry of its species, disappeared into the night.

At last the Roman awoke. He sat up, bewildered. Morning was breaking over Trachila. No, it was only the moon. A gust of wind had opened one of the shutters. It was only the moon hanging there among the frost patterns on the glass. The iron hinges of the shutters screeched in peacock voices, and upstairs Naso's servant was still droning on. The women of Sulmona droned like that, monotonous and incessant, beside the biers of drowned sponge divers who lay soldered inside tin boxes that were borne to their home village from the coast. Priests leading prayers droned like that at every funeral in Italy, beside catafalques fringed with flowers and rows of candles. And Cotta thought he understood that those mutterings – seeping downstairs from the floor above, unintelligible, unremitting – were meant for him. Those were dirges mourning his death. His bed was a catafalque.

Sleep and another dream almost overwhelmed Cotta before he finally struggled to his feet, reaching for his coat and shoes like someone with barely enough time to flee. He dressed hastily. He had to return to Tomi this very night. He had to get away from this madman and Naso's house before the ruins of Trachila and its terrible desolation confounded him by day as well, before they embraced him, never to let go. In this forsaken and abandoned place, here in the mountains, Tomi seemed so distant and so comforting – a human place, a safe haven, indeed the only refuge from the perils of sleep, of phantoms and of isolation. The moon was still high. His path was not yet a day old. Surely he could find it by moonlight.

And so Cotta left the poet's house without looking again for Pythagoras, closed the door as carefully as he had opened it on arrival the afternoon before – so long ago now. He ran across the courtyard and hurried down among the stone markers waving their unread banners at him. He banged and cut his shin on a window frame lying across the path, but with each step he could feel a vice loosening, giving way to the familiar anxiety he often felt alone at night in open country. At last the ruins of Trachila lay behind him.

The descent to the coast was more difficult than the climb had been, and full of uncertainties. Was this mound of scree in the deep shadow of a crag the same he had crossed in the afternoon? Didn't his way lead, rather, across that hillside bleached by light? And there, opening up before him, was that the ravine he knew or an abyss into deepest night? Cotta found many parts of the descent so unfamiliar that he was sure he had lost his way and was prepared to wait for morning in some niche in the rocks, when at last he found tracks in a field of old snow, his own footprints, and he followed them to the crest of more gentle slopes. There he set his mind at rest. In the depths below, he saw the wedge cast by the moon on the lightly scuffed expanse of the Black Sea, and where the light tapered and lost itself in the darkness of the coast, he saw a few flickering golden sparks – the lights of the town of iron.

As Cotta descended the serpentine path to the beach where he had watched the procession of ashen faces, he suddenly heard a noise that sounded like naked feet slapping on cobblestones. He thought of Lycaon the ropemaker, of his landlord's chapped, naked feet. And at that moment he saw the outline of a man leaping from one slab of slate to the next, panting straight uphill toward him. Lycaon. Cotta recognised the runner, knew it was the ropemaker. Barefoot, the full moon at his back, he was heading into the mountains, scrambling up the glimmering slate that lay strewn over the gorge like a huge, fragmented roof.

Startled, but at the same time relieved to see a familiar figure, Cotta called to his landlord, who sped past him, very close, without even turning his head. How could anyone run like that in this steep bowl? High above him now – at the spot where Cotta had seen the sparks of the town of iron – the ropemaker halted to catch his breath. He gasped for air, as if trying to breathe in the whole expanse of the night sky, wheezed as he pushed the air out of his lungs again – and the sound was like a howl. Then he turned back toward the mountains and scampered on, up a stony gully, across the gorge bathed in light. Cotta thought he saw saliva frothing and trickling from the ropemaker's mouth. Lycaon charged off across the rubble, blindly, never hesitating, as if in a towering rage. Suddenly he stumbled, fell flat out, or so it appeared. But what happened next thrust Cotta back to the edge of his nightmares in Trachila. The ropemaker did not trip, did not fall, he *threw* himself at full speed over the stones – did not lie there or get up again either, but ran, sprinted off on all fours, ever higher and deeper into the night on all fours.

Cotta heard nothing now but the ripple and roll of stones loosened underfoot and the startled cry of daws taking wing. He was struck by a memory from the day he arrived in the town of iron, from his first hour in the ropemaker's house. Lycaon had demanded a month's rent in advance, a small sum for someone who came from Rome, but then carelessly tossed the handful of money into a cast-iron safe that stood, streaked with broad bands of rust, against one wall of his workshop. The ropemaker had all he could do to pull open the strongbox door, which was fitted with heavy steel hinges. He tried to close it quickly again when the Roman walked up behind him. A brief glance sufficed for Cotta to make out the curious jumble inside the unshelved safe: tangles of leather thongs, a scattering of blackish silverware and coins, crumpled paper money and letters, an army pistol. But at the very bottom lay a bristly, stone-grey hide, a moth-eaten pelt, kept in the safe as a memento perhaps of some hunt whose hounds had been called off decades ago, the trophy of some splendid adventure. All that was left were these bristles, a string of mothballs and the cold oily smell of a gun in its case. The day he arrived Cotta had recognised the pelt lying in the open safe as the skin of a wolf – and now he saw its dull sheen again, on the ropemaker's back, high above him on a moonlit crag. He used his coat sleeve to scrub the sweat from his temples, as if to remove the fresh, warm, filthy slobber of a beast of prey – and began to run.

Without regard to the path, Cotta leapt, plunging down the slope toward the sea, while around him flowed rushing rivulets of gravel and sand. Only when he had almost reached the crescent of the beach did he realise that the path of his flight had been Lycaon's as well – the wolf's path.

Mussels crackled underfoot at last. His sore ankles ached. He stood by the sea, panting. The water was calm. No sound reached him from the mountains now. Ice patterned by the talons of gulls glistened in puddles left on the beach by the spraying surf. The moon was setting. But to the exhausted man, the town of iron – coming closer now, but more and more slowly and reluctantly, until at last it seemed to recede from him – promised no rest. Tomi was a frenzy of light. Cotta could now hear the brass bands of previous nights, the caterwauling, the kettledrums and cymbals, the drunks banging on shutters and gates. Two years of winter had ended, and exhilaration was still rampant in the narrow streets of Tomi. The town of iron was giddy with relief, with a violent joy that had already wreaked more havoc along this coast than the winter storms, ice or mud slides it had survived. It was carnival in Tomi. The glittering streaks and sparks, which had looked like dotted lights of refuge in the distance, now blazed as the bonfires and torches of a berserk and yowling village.

Following a wagon trail to the harbour – its mole had long since collapsed under the pounding surf and become a heap of rubble, a breakwater in the bay for the town of iron – Cotta now heard the slapping of naked skin on stone and turned to look for the wolf's skin of the ropemaker – and instead saw two half-naked bodies on the massive hewn block at the end of the mole. There on the icy stone two figures were writhing among their discarded clothing, clinging to each other as if drowning, babbling and moaning with lust. Moist vapour formed a faint, rainbow-coloured corona above their bodies steaming in the cold. It was Procne, the butcher's stout and sickly wife, and in her white arms was a scrawny, whispering man – Thies, the mixer of salves, the German. The couple – Tereus's wife and Proserpina's fiancé, still homesick for the forests of Friesland –were like a monument set atop the hewn stone platform of the mole to commemorate what was happening in the tumbledown streets and on the sloping squares of the town of iron in the small hours of this spring night. Masked figures had burst from all the houses to enjoy the license of carnival until the onset of dawn and exhaustion. Each of them was changed into his or her secret, and opposite. Smelters became lords, fishermen became Chinese warriors. Those who spent evening after evening howling obscenities in the brandy cellar, now fell mute in drunken silence. Those who held their tongue now screamed. And those who all year long cringed and cowered in fear of blows, now struck them. Numbed with schnapps and fearing no punishment, using rods and whips, they indiscriminately drubbed anyone who failed to escape in time. Each became – if only for a hundredth part of the year – whatever he was permitted to be. These were the final hours of their yearly freedom, and Thies the German spent them atop a stone, caressing the huge body of the butcher's wife, writhing between her breasts, in her blubber, as if he hoped to drag her from her refuge, to liberate this gentle creature, who had fled the world's violence and Tereus's hate and withdrawn deep into her own fat. To whom else could Procne have surrendered herself in this night of bewitchment except to this melancholy man who had lingered here after the war? Whom else could she embrace except a man tormented by yearnings? He would safeguard her secret lust in his jars of salve and in his memory, just as she kept it safe inside her fat for fear of the butcher's rage. And so they pressed against each other, and Thies whispered shocking, obscene words in his beloved's ear and hair, still fragrant with the gentle perfume he won from tiny blossoms of purple moss and the salt of his tears. Procne gave a fragile cry, finding at last abrupt release from her lust. She stifled it when Cotta stumbled in the shadow of a harbour wall. The German, too, was suddenly like the stone their bodies warmed. There the two remained, sculpted lust and terror. In his embarrassment Cotta moved cautiously off, kept close to the wall and out of sight until he reached the torchlit square outside the harbour-master's office.

There he ran into the arms of a pack of drunks clad in hides and oxhorns. The masked figures surrounded him. When he tried to flee up one of the flickering, steep streets, they dragged him back into their yowling midst and bellowed slogans and questions in a language he did not understand. Then a hand, a claw grabbed him by the hair, another sprang at his throat, and a third and fourth held his head in a vice, forced his mouth open and with laughter and shrieks poured it full of schnapps from a canteen – ice-cold, red-hot, stifling schnapps. Cotta tried in vain to twist his way out from under the pounding fists and shaggy arms that held him. He fought for air, coughed, swallowed, drank, felt the canteen's cold tin screw threads between his teeth, and watched the starry sky dissolve beyond the horned heads of his tormentors. Then the claws released him. The Roman slumped to the pavement. His clothes sucked an oily puddle dry, while boots and heavy shoes stamped off out of view. Tomi, the town where for days he had made futile inquiries about Naso, where he tried in vain to gain the attention of these taciturn, ponderous people – the town had taken him in hand now for the first time.

Short of breath, his heart racing, he lay there for several minutes before getting up again. He was drunk. He crossed the square, staggering, but no longer avoiding the fools, some of whom were pelting one another with torches and bottles, others merely reeling along just like him. Dirty and numbed, his clothes shredded to rags by mountains and cobblestones, he was one of them now. He turned up a street that dilapidation had widened. It led, past cracked façades and black courtyards, to the ropemaker's house. But he found himself in the middle of the night's main carnival parade, in a straggling throng of trolls, bird-people, stones come alive, men riding donkeys and chain-swinging warriors, all accompanied by a brass band that had lost every sense of rhythm and order. They were now near the end of an arduous path spiralling through the town, and many of those in costume shuffled wearily and silently in procession. Whenever someone fell, so drunk he could not get up again, the band played a lame flourish. It was shortly before dawn. The parade threatened to drag Cotta with it back to the sea. It took all his energy to struggle against the hands, the shoulders and the kicks of the mummers. Drunk and fighting the inertia of the throng, he was hardly any closer to the ropemaker's house. He marked time, tramping his feet, while mask after mask lurched past him. A general with broad epaulets made of pig's ears held the end of two strings in his mailed fists. If he pulled on them, the wings of his helmet would beat and rattle. A gigantic woman, her torso made of wood and straw and splattered with red paint, used the two thin arms sprouting from her gut to fling a cardboard skull high into the air, again and again, and gave shrill shrieks each time she caught it. A bishop spent perpetual blessings on every step he took. A phallus shoved two balloon testicles along in front of it. It was followed by a man bent low under the weight of his vendor's tray. On it he carried an electrical device, a battery encrusted with saltpetre petals feeding the wreath of light bulbs that encircled him. And here came a whitewashed oxcart lumbering over the cobblestones. The driver up on the box was having trouble sitting upright. He was swinging a burning whip – Tereus. Cotta recognised the butcher under the trappings of gold confetti and chrome chips. Tereus was wearing a birdcage tied to his head with leather pigtails. White flakes flew like dust through its latticework. The cage, filled with fine down, was the prison of two rats. Enraged and terrified by the flames of the whip, they kept leaping, banging against the wire mesh, pouncing on each other and covering the butcher's head in a blizzard of down. As Cotta tried to catch his breath for a moment when the wide cart forced him to step back flush against a wall and the band struck up a flourish for another casualty, he heard only the whip, the scraping of rat claws and the little cries of the animals as they fought for their lives. And he began to understand what, in its final hour, this carnival parade of brutish figures was meant to represent. It was a disfigured, crude caricature – but nevertheless Tereus's costume called to mind weathered reliefs on the façades of Roman temples, ministries and palaces, called to mind a depiction of the sun god and his fiery chariot. The butcher was trying to be Phoebus. This was the hour when the herdsmen from valleys high up in the coastal mountains and the smelters and miners of Tomi were free to mimic the splendour of the Roman heavens. The highest of the gods was dragging a battery in a vendor's tray through the streets of town – Jupiter's nimbus and his bolts were the glowing tungsten filaments inside the vacuum of light bulbs. The general tugging like an imbecile at those pull-strings was war's divinity, and the red woman was blood-spattered Medea, who had slaughtered her own brother, dismembered his childish body and hurled the chopped-off head against the rocks of a coastal cliff – a gory, hairy ball. Medea, the title figure of Naso's tragedy, which had been acclaimed and applauded in all the theatres of the empire and had made a celebrity of the poet. Medea, a sullied scarecrow of rags and straw tottering along in this parade of fools.

Wedged among Rome's reliefs and statues now come to life, the drunken man strained his way toward the ropemaker's house. Images from the crumbling stone of the metropolis filed past, each more distinct than the last. Who was that hunchback there with the tin boat on his head? – And the fellow in black sackcloth with a lyre under his arm, an Orpheus . . .?

To be sure, this parade of fools could only be a pale shadow of the myths in which Roman imagination had rioted and spent itself, until under the rule of Emperor Augustus it was trimmed to reason and transformed into mere duty, into obedience and loyalty to the state. This procession was only a wretched relic, but even a drunken man could recognise ancient Rome's image mirrored in this carnival – images of gods and heroes, whose mighty and wondrous deeds now seemed forgotten forever in the emperor's capital. And had it not been Naso, with his elegies, his tales and dramas, who had stirred forgotten memories and reminded Rome, now a pallid body politic, of its archaic and wild passions? Naso, whose writings – denounced in the empire of bureaucrats, generals and magistrates – were the last beacons of a waning creative energy, phantoms of a dying world.

As if his ripped coat, bruised hands and scratched face were only another costume, the drunken man now joined in the yowls of the other mummers shoving their way toward him. This parade of fools – was it not proof that the people of the town of iron had known the exile much better than they were inclined to admit to the suspicious stranger, possibly a spy from Rome? Was it not proof that Naso had brought the characters of his poetry into exile with him, that he had not fallen silent in the town of his misfortune, but had gone on telling his stories? How else had the butcher in this godforsaken hole come up with the notion of transforming himself into a carnival sun god, his oxen into fiery steeds? Like the primal rhinoceros in the emperor's gardens, something was wild and alive in Tomi, something that now belonged to the past in the capital and the empire's other great cities, that had frozen into monuments and museum pieces, petrified into reliefs, equestrian statues and temple friezes beneath the creeping moss.

Sluggish, but as irresistible as migrating lemmings, the trooping fools weltered toward the sea, turning from the Roman and leaving him behind. Only a few stragglers still lurched out of side streets to follow the main troop. Cotta was painfully groping his way along the wall of the ropemaker's garden, when one of the last stragglers blocked his path, then moved aside the moment he saw that his victim was the Roman. But Cotta grabbed the fool – a shape that threatened to dissolve before his eyes, that twisted under his grip, straining its neck for some way to escape. Its head had a large hooked nose and resembled the portrait one of Naso's admirers, as fearless as he as wealthy, had had stamped on silver coins and distributed among the poet's closest friends after his banishment from Rome – a medallion in his memory. They were conspirators in a secret society, who, even after Naso's fall and exile, met to read aloud from his forbidden books, from transcripts of his speeches, and treasured like precious jewels the notes that had been kept at readings from the *Metamorphoses*. To whoever was hosting one of their secret gatherings, this last intrepid audience would show their silver medallions, the badge of

a harmless cabal that did no damage to the emperor's authority –
nor helped the exile for that matter – but gave the admirers of his
poetry the illusion of being comrades in a cause both dangerous
and momentous. With almost derisive precision, the struck
medallion reproduced the unhappy poet's unusually big nose, a
nose of such striking and impressive shape that during one of the
more carefree periods of his life it had earned him a nickname,
sometimes used affectionately, sometimes ironically: *Naso*. This
was how friends greeted him and how opponents insulted him.
The hastily scribbled notes people left for him in the billiard room
when they found it empty, or pinned to the door of his house on
the Piazza del Moro if it was closed – all were addressed to *Naso*.
And this head now wrenching away from Cotta with such fury,
trying not to show its face, bore that same big, unmistakable nose
– of cardboard on a rubber band that snapped and broke when
Cotta made a rough grab for the flailing figure's face. And
suddenly before him stood a terribly frightened Battus, the
epileptic. Squealing like a piglet, the idiot son of the grocer slipped
from the Roman's arms and giving his cardboard nose up for lost,
ran off into the darkness.

May arrived, blue and gusty. A warm wind, redolent of vinegar and hellebore, gnawed the last crusts of ice from the ponds, swept the smoky fumes from the streets and drove torn garlands, paper flowers and greasy scraps of lanterns along the beach. After the fervour and mortification of their penitential processions, after the exhausting abandon of their carnival, the inhabitants of Tomi returned to their work in the mountains – to ore, stony fields, anvil and sea.

The aged and infirm, who had hoarded all their energies in the cold and were kept alive only by hope of a thaw, could breathe easy again at last. In their infinite relief, they let go the reins and sank back – and so death took many of them. During that first week of wind from the south, Thies the German dug three new graves, four in the second week, and over each he erected an intricate dome of stone.

Until deep dusk, the call of birds returning to the Bay of Tomi could be heard above the surf's thunder – and in the houses the sound of prayers for the dead, the carpenter's hammer, animals bellowing before slaughter. All the windows and doors stood open. During the day, the wash was spread out over the ivied gardens, where it fluttered and billowed, and carpets were laid out to dry on the flat stones of the beach. It was spring.

During those weeks, Cotta was recovering from a fever he had taken in the heat of carnival or in the cold of Trachila. Encircled by the garish scenes of the wall hangings in his room, he shivered with chills, fighting off the ornaments and figures that loosed themselves from the stitches of Arachne's tapestries and swooped down upon him. No one tended him. But with the grey light of dawn, he would calm down and then fall asleep until afternoon. When his eyes had grown clearer and his blood cooler, he saw the ropemaker standing at the foot of his bed with a tin pail and a plate of milksop. He sat up, drank and ate and noticed that Lycaon was barefoot again, saw the bruised feet, the hands with their cracked nails and could no longer believe his own memory. The hands of an old man, the feet of an old man – those had once been claws? limbs of a wolf?

The ropemaker was as taciturn as always during those feverish days. One Friday morning, however, when Cotta had regained some strength and left his chamber to descend the spiral staircase, he saw Lycaon smile for the first time. The ropemaker was perched on a three-legged stool, picking oakum from old ropes. He was not alone. A woman clad in black was kneeling on the wooden planks of the workshop floor, using soft soap and a brush to scrub away a strange pattern that reminded Cotta of the tracks left by dirty or bloody paws.

Wolves, Cotta said. I saw wolves in the mountains.

The ropemaker slid a piece of silvery, bleached rope through his hand, said nothing.

The woman in black stopped scrubbing and sat up, a young woman. Cotta instinctively took a step back. The handsome face of the woman kneeling there and looking up at him now, was covered with layers of scales, with white flakes of dead skin, as if she had dipped her face and hands in lime that hard work had then dried, cracked and chipped loose.

Wolves, she whispered, *in the mountains?*

The rope fell from Lycaon's hands and slapped the floor. With a groan the ropemaker bent down for it. Apparently he had heard neither Cotta's voice nor her whisper.

Wolves, Cotta said, turning now to the woman in black. Who are you? And getting no answer, asked Lycaon, who is she?

Now the kneeling woman laid a hand flat to her mouth, as if trying to stop herself from speaking. Flakes of skin fell like snow over her chest. She stared at Cotta and repeated, *who are you?*, then stretched her hand toward the ropemaker and asked him in Cotta's tone of voice, *who is she?*

Lycaon smiled.

Confused and embarrassed, feeling he was the victim of a word game these two were playing for the hundredth time, Cotta fled into helpless chatter. Does she work for you? he asked Lycaon, who did not look at him. What's her name? And then introduced himself to the woman as he would to a simpleton, pointing to his chest and saying: Cotta.

Cotta, the woman in black repeated, refusing to take her eyes from him, *does she work for you? What's her name?*

Echo, the ropemaker said at last, her name is Echo. She cleans my house.

House, Echo whispered, bending deep over the pattern of tracks again, *my house.*

Echo did not know where she had come from. The people of Tomi had discovered her one summer at the house of Arachne the weaver, and they thought she was the deaf-mute's relative or ward. She lent a ready hand, enduring the old woman's moods and gout attacks with what the infrequent visitors said was admirable patience. Arachne's gentle servant came from Troy – so said the rumour from Fama's shop at the time – and was the child of the weaver's brother, who had turned her out, but Arachne had taken her in and disguised her as a maid. Because the weaver was so unapproachable and gruff, other versions were also cultivated in Fama's shop over the course of the summer: Echo had come from Colchis with a troop of knife grinders; no, Cyparis the projectionist had brought her with him, a floozie who had ditched her showman.

Troy? people had asked Echo, you come from Troy? *From Troy*, Echo had replied with the same unflappable composure with which she later also said *from Colchis, from Petara* or *from Tegea*. Arachne's boarder was feebleminded, that was the final version. But that autumn the weaver accused her maid of stealing, barred her from the house, and gave a neighbour to understand that she had booted out neither relative nor ward, but only a stranger, a vagrant.

Echo stayed on in the town of iron, sleeping in the open air until late November, when she took refuge from the storms of winter in the innermost chamber of some ruins that lay under the shadow of a rocky overhang – in a dark, indestructible room, half of it hewn from the bedrock, more cave than room. From that point on, its damp, soundless seclusion was her home. She would sometimes lie there for days, motionless, afflicted with raging headaches that only the cool twilight of these ruins could ease and make bearable. Even worse, however, than this periodically recurring pain – which was perhaps only the reverberation of the world's noise in her head – was another illness from which Echo suffered, one that no silence or twilight could relieve: a disease of her skin, which, because it lacked the top protective layer, was so delicate that a single ray of sun or a dusty gust of wind would leave its mark behind. Even in the mildest light and in the fragrant, dry air of spring, her skin would crack, break and scale, falling like snow from the wretched woman's body.

Cotta was to learn only later that Echo's disease was always confined to a limited area of her body. The scales formed a large oval patch that wandered restlessly and slowly over her slender form, a compact flaky mass that at times would attack face and neck and then move on across her shoulders and arms to breast or belly. Whenever this patch would at last migrate from her face and disappear under her clothes, Echo would be – for a week, for a month – a woman of captivating beauty, her skin flawless. But once the scales returned to her face, any touch, indeed a simple gawking stare, would often cause her such pain that those who loved her withdrew and avoided her.

And Echo was loved, though in secret, by many inhabitants of the coast. By cover of night, both herdsmen and smelters sometimes sought her out in her cave. There, in Echo's arms and far from their hard, harried wives, they could be transformed into babies, into lords or animals. Her lovers knew that Echo's impenetrable privacy protected them from any reproach, any shame, and in exchange they left amber, hides, dried fish or pots of oil behind in the debris of the ruins.

Echo visited the ropemaker's house at irregular intervals and then only to collect, remove or scrub whatever Lycaon suddenly declared was trash or garbage – it was something different every time. The ropemaker would take an impulsive dislike to all the plants within his walls, and Echo would have to scrape moss from the stones, uproot ivy and grass, even toss out pots of dahlias and orchids, or get them out of the house. The next time the ropemaker could no longer stand the rust, and Echo had to use files and glass-paper to polish all the gratings, hinges, tools and iron ornaments, then seal them with a transparent varnish to keep them from soon losing their white sheen again in the damp sea air.

Very rarely, however, was the ropemaker bothered by dust. Little furry pelts of it mingled with tiny wood chips, hair and hemp fibres, scurried like nimble, protean animals across the floor of the ropemaker's house and rope-walk. . . . Like the world in its last formless state, dust lay over the ropemaker's solitude, on the yarn bobbins, punch plates, cablets, lines, cords and hawsers, rose up in the least draught, at times became rich and radiant when struck by sunlight, then sank back down in melancholy swaths and eddies.

Echo came when the ropemaker sent for her. She asked no questions, obediently repeated all instructions, threw away what she was told to throw away and gave lustre to what was kept. Since that Friday when the fever had loosed its grip and Cotta had seen the woman in black kneeling on the floor of the workshop in the morning light, the town of iron seemed less cold and desolate to him. It was not only that Echo's face – and its beauty was visible even under the white, flaked skin – had awakened in him memories of the slow, soft hands and caresses of Rome's women, but it also seemed as if Rome itself had drawn nearer again in Echo's eyes, in her glance and graceful movements.

On the morning of Cotta's recovery, Echo had cleaned his room as well, had washed the dingy windows and polished them with doeskin, had rid the tapestries of a whole year's dust, restoring to the hangings colours so dazzling and intense, that Cotta thought it was the power of those colours even by candlelight that kept him from feeling tired and falling asleep that night.

Cotta touched Lycaon's maid for the first time on the same afternoon that the projectionist left the town of iron. Cyparis walked slowly on his bowlegs through the streets, once again chanting singsong praises of his thrilling shows. In one hand he held the reins of his team of duns – monsters tottering behind him – and in the other, the rope with which he pulled his stag along.

The animal had struggled against the rope so violently when they had started out that before it was subdued it struck the soft, velvet-covered tips of its newly regrown antlers against the edge of a stone gateframe. During pauses in his chant, the dwarf tried to calm the animal. Blood dripped from two fractures in the antlers, ran in fine, intricate lines down over the skull and sprinkled the cobblestones of the town of iron. An evil omen, Fama said, who stood, her arm around her son, in the group of onlookers who were watching the projectionist get underway and called to him how sorry they were.

Cyparis's last show had been disrupted the evening before by the angry, shrill outcry of Lichas, a missionary of the Old Believers of Constantinople. Every year around Easter, Lichas arrived from the Bosporus aboard a fishing cutter. He came to Tomi, to the twilight of its neglected, mildewed church, to read out an endless litany of tortures endured by members of his sect slain under Roman rule. Among the remote farmsteads and ruined villages of this stretch of coast, a missionary who cursed the cruelty of Rome and invoked the splendour of some God or other had nothing to fear from officials or their informers.

On the previous evening, the missionary had stormed out of the church, fists raised against the slaughterhouse wall ablaze with pictures, railing at the Lilliputian's startled audience, screaming that even a place as forsaken as Tomi should remember the sufferings and agonies of the crucified Lord of this world on this holy day, Good Friday! The audience laughed, and he started to pound the sides of the covered wagon where Cyparis had set up his humming projector. Finally, when all entreaties proved in vain, he rang and rang the single bell in the steeple until the dwarf stopped the show and the slaughterhouse wall went dark.

And so the people of the town of iron were kept from seeing the bloody end of the last of the three films that Cyparis – out of reverence for the many deaths and funerals that spring – had shown on three consecutive evenings. The films were tragedies, bombastically flamboyant versions of the fall of three heroes whose names until then had been unknown in the town of iron: *Hector*, *Hercules* and *Orpheus*.

For Cotta, who joined the others on the wooden benches in front of Tereus's wall each evening, those were names from his youth. He remembered Hercules and Orpheus, they made him think back to afternoons spent languishing in the study halls and library of San Lorenzo boarding school, where he was asked over and over to recount the fates of these and other heroes: Life and death of Hercules! Life and death of Orpheus! From memory and in hexameters!

The mention of Orpheus's name also brought to Cotta's mind the branches of a wild orange tree and some oleander bushes reaching through the wide-open windows of San Lorenzo. Driven to desperation on occasion, the most daring of the pupils would drip the bitter sap of these plants into their eyes, so that for a few days an inflammation of the retina – as painful as it was irrefutable – would excuse them from exams that required them to recite the fates of the heroes.

Cyparis had shown the fall of Troy to the town of iron: fields ablaze with plumed helmets and swaying plantations of bristling spears as far as the horizon, fire carried on the wind, clouds of smoke larger than the sky above the city. Against this background, he had shown the mutilation of Hector the Trojan, who was dragged around the walls of his own fortress until his gruesome death became evident from the trailing pack of dogs tussling over the wide-strewn scraps of his flesh.

The second evening, Cyparis introduced Tomi to the fate of Hercules, who had to bear all the world's hardships, endure and conquer all its dangers – only to tear himself to pieces in the end with his own hands. To the amazement and horror of the smelters, Hercules was slain by a magic shirt he had slipped on in all innocence, its poisoned fabric immediately fusing with his own skin, burning on his body like boiling oil. He could not cast it off again except at the price of his very life.

Groaning, roaring, and finally mad with the pain, this invincible man tore his own skin and flesh from his bones along with the shirt, laid bare his bleeding sinews, his shoulder blades, the red cage of his ribs, and inside it, lungs burning out, his heart. He fell. And the light from that day gathered in seven ponds, into which the wretched man's blood and sweat dissolved, seven mirrors that bore the image of the sky – clouds, shadows, emptiness. Then it was night. But the light of the seven ponds remained and rose up, stars among the stars of the firmament.

And for the final day, this Good Friday, Cyparis had announced the martyrdom of a poet named Orpheus, who, he said, was stoned to death by women wrapped in the hides of panthers and deer, then was skinned and hacked to pieces with axes and sickles. He had just shown the first sequence, the victim fleeing through a forest of holm-oaks, when the missionary came rushing out of the church. . . .

During those three evenings, however, Cotta recalled – even more clearly than the death of the heroes, than the lessons and the discipline of San Lorenzo – the whitewashed walls of its echoing corridors, the windows open to the afternoon, beyond which lay, forbidden and inaccessible, fish ponds and overgrown meadows, and he had glided back through time and deep, shady courtyards until he saw Naso, the guest of honour, striding along the arcades of San Lorenzo, a crowd of nervous prefects and local VIPs crowding around him – the celebrated poet, entering the assembly hall at the side of the rector one May evening, or perhaps it was June. The prominent visitor.

Naso's appearance for a reading was to be the crowning event commemorating two hundred years of San Lorenzo's existence, to be yet another illustrious moment in the institution's history. The murals in the hall, titanic pictures of saints, had disappeared beneath all the banners and the floral array of garlands and wreaths. When Naso began to speak the heavy scent of lilacs lay over the assembled pupils and faculty. But despite the flashes of magnesium set off by the school photographer and the menace of leaden solemnity on the rector's face, what the pupils recognised in several passages of the reading that day were verses and words with which they had been tormented in their classes:

> The straw gave the Roman
> The gift of a sleep without dreams.
> And when he awakened he rose
> From the chaff to the stars overhead,
> Flickering high above earth now,
> A starry red form.
> Purple with lustre of blood,
> The scars of the moon.

Numb with awe, Cotta compared Naso's features that day with the coarse-screened photos of newspaper clippings that a school employee had tacked to the San Lorenzo notice-board a few days before the celebration. There in the auditorium, however, he hardly recognised the poet – the distracting size of that nose, those restless eyes, which at the beginning and end of the reading, swept out over the heads of the assembly, along the garlands and into infinity, then returned to the pages of the book open before them. To Cotta, a schoolboy in a front-row seat, the poet Publius Ovidius Naso seemed so removed, so untouchable that he hardly dared a steady look at the man as he read, not even for the space of a breath, for fear that some sudden, casual glance from those moss-green eyes would meet his own and shame him.

For years after the convocation at San Lorenzo, Cotta preserved in his mind this strangely transfigured image of a poet, a crystal memory, unalterable and removed forever from time, and against it he secretly measured the gradual decline and transformation of the living, ageing Naso, the waning of his glory and then the depths of his fall. If a man so revered could fall from inaccessible heights into contempt, be chased to the rockbound coasts of the Black Sea, if every image of him could disappear from the framed memorial photographs at San Lorenzo and the notice-boards of academies, be airbrushed away, transformed into milky or silver-grey splotches of fog – if all this was so, then shouldn't you also be able to recognise the contours of the rubble to which even the most splendid palaces of the capital would some day be reduced? To see the hard glow of future deserts in the blossoming clouds of its gardens and parks, the pallor of death in happy-go-lucky faces enthralled by a comedy or a circus?

And when Naso did fall, Cotta saw the marks of passing time in the very stones. When he compared that crystal image from San Lorenzo with the sobbing man who left his home on the Piazza del Moro forever one cloudless Tuesday in March, he was aware for the first time that the world is built with a feathery lightness, that mountains are prone to become drifting sand, that the ephemeral sea evaporates into spiralling clouds, that stars burn like straw. . . .

Nothing retains its form: In the end, it was this awareness – even in his San Lorenzo days it filled Cotta with a *Weltschmerz* as deep-felt as it was adolescent – that established his kinship with the poet's circle of friends, who marvelled at Naso in his fall and persevered after his disappearance, faithfully reading from his forbidden books until hundreds of the phrases and verses were indelible in their memories.

Cyparis the projectionist left the town of iron that afternoon just as Naso had once left San Lorenzo and Rome: eyed by rows of the curious, eclipsed by his fate and with that unmistakable, distracted look on his face of someone who knows he will never come back.

Once the projectionist had left the narrow streets behind, he tied the stag's long rope to a strut of his wagon, climbed up onto the box with a groan and used his whip to scribble little spirals and loops in the air just behind his horses' manes, as if to describe the labyrinth of his future path to both the duns and that part of his audience that had followed him this far. The covered wagon began to lurch over the potholes and rocks, down the road connecting Tomi with the deserted town of Limyra.

A rust-eaten bus, its windows broken long ago by flying stones and never replaced, travelled this road sometimes during periods with no snow, after the morass of the road hardened and crumbled to dust. Three or four days on that bus, and the passengers who arrived in Limyra to dig in its time-ravaged ruins for bronze buckles, ornaments and bracelets looked like the miners of the town of iron when, exhausted and caked with dust and mud, they emerged from the tunnels.

Cyparis was no more than a hundred yards down the road, but the spectators only heard the dwarf's cajoling shouts as he began his journey into the future, because such a huge flurry of dust was roiling in the wagon's wake, stinging their eyes with ochre and grey, that they had to put their hands to their faces as protection against its sandy whirlwinds. It was as if all the dust of the coast were rising up against the town of iron to prevent a last look at the departing projectionist and his team as they slowly grew smaller and disappeared, taking with them any hope of consolation from the Lilliputian's stories and pictures.

Like the inmates of a penitentiary who have just accompanied a pardoned man to the gate, Cyparis's audience then made their way back to the centre of town. The timid and superstitious scattered onion peels and dried, plaited campions over the slender trail of blood left by the stag: a charm to bind misfortune – for that was Fama's prophecy – to the earth once it took the bait of the blood and rose up from the depths.

Cotta, too, had followed the band of curious onlookers to the farthest edge of town that afternoon. He had moved to its head as the band slowed its pace, but he did not turn back with the others once the cloud of dust closed behind Cyparis. His eyes burning and blinking, he followed the team as it became invisible in the sandy whirlwind, so that at first he was aware of only a slender, faceless shadow moving towards him. It was Echo. Seemingly undisturbed by the dust, not holding her hand up to protect her face, she came toward him, and Cotta felt – more than he actually saw with his watering eyes – that she was staring at him. The nearer Echo came, the heavier was the burden of her gaze, so heavy that Cotta stepped off into some bottomless depth – actually only a shallow hole washed out by melting snow – staggered and would have fallen if Echo had not held out an arm to him.

She was still a heartbeat too far away for Cotta actually to grasp her arm, but the gesture alone, Echo's willingness to hold onto him, restored his security even as he lurched. He caught and righted himself. They were alone now in the dust cloud, inside a sudden calm like that at the centre of a tornado. Cotta's eyes gradually began to clear. He felt steady on his feet now, and gazed into Echo's face – flawless, with only a hint of pallor – and took her hand.

When the Roman and the ropemaker's maid stepped out of the dust that afternoon, they looked like ashen-grey passengers on a trip to Limyra, and as the cloud slowly drifted away, it seemed to turn the wormwood bushes along the road to stone. By now Cyparis's farewell audience had already dispersed in the alleys of the town, and when Fama turned around for one last look at the Lilliputian's track before entering the darkness of her shop, all she saw in the distance was the Roman and Echo, a lingering, suspicious couple.

The hesitant conversation Echo and Cotta had as they walked back into town was broken by many silences, but they were so good at disguising their mutual embarrassment that they seemed to be two friendly, dusty travellers with at least a long journey in common. The ropemaker's bruised feet, Cyparis's gloomy films and his sudden departure, about which they also spoke – there was little to distinguish the things they talked about from the daily, matter-of-fact gossip dispensed at any corner in Tomi or among the shelves and molasses barrels of Fama's shop. And Echo's answers always corresponded to what Cotta already knew – in fact, Echo told him about the town of iron in his own words. But despite all the repetitions and trivialities, Cotta sensed a shared osmosis of tangled emotions, a puzzling, tacit understanding. He hardly recognised Echo as the distraught, intimidated housekeeper he had seen kneeling on the floor of the ropemaker's workshop – indeed, by its end, the conversation with this woman seemed to him to be his first encounter with a human being since his departure from Rome.

When Echo started down the path that led to her dwelling between overgrown walls, Cotta found a pretext to stay at her side and to keep asking new questions, trying to delay the moment of parting. But as he vainly attempted to halt time's progress that afternoon, a warm spring rain began, at first tapping, then drumming and finally sweeping in a heavy rush that drove all the dust back to earth and sent water shooting in loamy yellow cascades down the stairways and through the gutters of the town of iron. The two hurried through the cloudburst, leaping over puddles and rivulets, and were soaked and out of breath when they reached Echo's ruins. There they stood, protected from the sheets of water by an overhanging rock that seemed to grow out of what was left of the walls. They stared at one another, panting.

Above the swell of the rain, and without even the hope of an answer, simply to put off their farewell one last time, Cotta gasped out two or three of his tired questions about Naso, questions he had forbidden himself to ask as they walked, for fear of forcing the woman back into the same standoffishness that had so often been the response to similar inquiries in the town of iron. And so he asked Echo about the poet from Rome, about the exile and his mad servant up in the mountains. And the rush of the rain sounded like the soughing of stone pines on the Piazza del Moro as Echo casually said *yes*, of course – as if it were quite self-evident – everybody, as far as Limyra and beyond, knew about poor old Naso.

The rain had washed the strands of Cotta's hair into his face. He stood there stock-still, dripping onto the dry sandy floor under the overhanging rock, listening to Echo, who spoke now as if it had taken this password, the mention of Naso's name, to transform her monosyllabic answers into stories. Naso and his servant came down to the coast from the mountains every four or five weeks when there was no snow. The exile even visited her in the cave here, too, and brought her honey and rowanberries from the ravines of Trachila.

Dead? Naso had often stayed away from the town of iron for months on end without anyone's supposing he was dead.

Right here, on the sandy floor, he had lit his fire, one of his many fires – they burned wherever he would settle in and start up with his stories. Why, even when he sat and drank in the brandy cellar, he would kindle little fires in the plates and pots on the table, using wood chips, shavings and wool for fuel.

Poor old Naso claimed in fact that he could read both the flames and the white, warm ashes, claimed he could decipher in his fires the words, sentences and stories of a whole book that had perished in flames one dark day of his life.

People in Tomi thought he was an arsonist at first – so Echo said, there beneath her rocky roof – and stamped out and smothered his little fires and blazes and treated him so badly that he finally had to take refuge in the mountains, in Trachila.

But with time, people in the town of iron came to realise the exile was harmless, and they were glad to sit by his fires whenever he came down to the sea for the necessities of life, to listen as he read from the glow.

Whatever else the poor fellow lost in that fire, Echo said, there must have been a book about stones, a catalogue of strange minerals. Because, at least in the fires he lit under her rocky roof, he saw nothing but corals, petrified rocks and pebbles – always the same thing in every blaze, line for line, just stones.

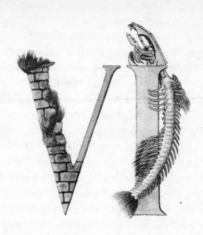

The year turned dry and hot, unlike any ever known in the region of the town of iron. For weeks the sky above Tomi was cloudless. The air became glassy. The horizon began to flicker, to melt. In the still air the breaking waves subsided, but the roar remained – it was the sound of pale green torrents that glutted themselves on the melting glacial snow of the coastal mountains and plunged down gorges and ravines, scattering at times in veils of mist, until they reached the inlets and valley floors.

The Black Sea lay glistening like a lake below the cliffs. The water turned warm in the lagoons, as if they were turquoise shoals, so warm that the mullet, accustomed to the temperatures of ice floes and snow, fled in panic from the warm tide, skipped across the surface and onto the shore, where with fins flapping they wrapped themselves in a grainy armour of sand and mother-of-pearl and suffocated. The inhabitants of the town of iron gathered up nine such swarms of frantic fish and buried them. There was too little hunger to eat them, too few hands to dry them. Even in the cool fresh air after sundown, the putrefying stench blanketed the coast, then crept up the rocky slopes at dawn, luring jackals to the sea. Evening after evening, when only the highest peaks and ridges towered red among the shadows, vultures from the wastelands above the timberline descended in flocks. Even Fama and the oldest inhabitants of the town could not recall such a spring and interpreted all the phenomena of the warming trend as omens of a new and calamitous age.

One morning Tomi was awakened by the harbour siren and the terrified cries of fishermen. The sea had lost its colour. The water in the bay was yellow, sulphurous yellow, matt and inert. A bewildered crowd gathered on the jetty, but no one dared to dip a hand in this brimstone – until Arachne appeared. She came down a narrow street with arms stretched wide, gesticulating, her hair unbound, and opened her mouth to soundless screams – and from them Echo at last deduced that the weaver had seen a sea like this once before, on the coast of Ausonia. The sulphurous yellow was only pollen borne by the wind, pollen from endless forests of stone pine.

Stone pine? they signalled to the deaf-mute, what is that?

Their bewilderment yielded to relief, indeed to a kind of merriment – but only after a sluggish current took the pollen away with it, a golden, tattered veil, and revealed once again the deeps the fishermen knew.

Cotta thought often these days about the riddle of the mulberry tree in Trachila, about the six-foot ferns of Naso's garden. Above the roofs of Tomi, in the waste-dumps of the mines, he found blue safflowers, nettles, mignonettes and lavender. Beach lilac and star clover bloomed in the chinks and cracks of the square outside the harbourmaster's office. No such plants had ever grown before in the town of iron, not even in its gardens or fields. Many of them seemed so strange and precious to the smelters that they ate the blossoms dusted with sugar or dipped in honey.

The fish plague abated and the beaches no longer smelled of rot. After a thunderstorm that raged for two days and a night, the steady wind from the sea returned, and with it the breaking waves. It was a parching, midsummer wind that in the heat of noon bore the odour of nameless spices over the ruins and slopes. It shrank and muffled the torrents.

The people of Tomi began gradually to accommodate themselves to the temperatures of this incomprehensible weather, as they had to frost and ice-storms in other days – and, in the end, the town of iron turned away from its gaudy new vegetation with the same indifference with which it had at one time regarded an impassable snowdrift or the bizarre forms of ice jams on the beach. In the tunnels and horizons of the mines, a cloudless sky was just as invisible as one hung with grey. Herbs and strawflowers might now be growing in the gravel above the adits, on the waste-dumps and walls outside, but deep within the mountains, along the sooty faces of the front galleries, it was just as cold and dark as ever. The sparks raining from a smelter's furnace did not let up, the searing heat at the open firing-doors did not cool, even if all around them the year was in full bloom. The fields remained stony, the herds small. And after the dead bodies of the last beached shoals of fish had disappeared into smoke-houses or dung-pits, the sea once again seemed as unfruitful and barren of fish as in the days of frost.

Little by little the gossip and idle chatter in Fama's shop and in the brandy cellar began to revolve around the old life again. As they complained for the hundredth time about the cares and difficulties of poverty, people seized on one juicy item of news – a pair of lovers, who by all accounts had found one another the day the projectionist left town: Cotta and Echo. Wherever the two were seen these days, they provoked gossip, from malicious to malevolent. Because it was a society of expedient marriages and tight family connections, the town of iron used gossip to punish any presumed or actual affair that threatened to escape its control.

They saw the stranger walking the mountain trails at Echo's side. They saw how he waited in broad daylight outside her dwelling, and saw, in particular, that he talked with her. Whatever it was that linked these two, it had to be more, very much more, than the things a farmer or a smelter did with the scaly woman under the cover of darkness. So then, was this Roman a relative, a friend of the exile – or simply the agent of some distant bureaucracy or other, sent to check out the state of things along this coast and using gullible Echo to do it?

Here, along the coast, the laws, the might and will of Rome got lost in the wastelands. Round here! somebody in the brandy cellar whooped, round here! he can stick his nose up the skirts of the village whore, but he won't find out what Tomi wants to hide. . . . All the same: Echo was talking with the stranger. And she never talked to anyone. What was she telling him as they walked down to the mole or passed the open gate of a smithy? About Tereus's visits at night? About how generous Phineus the brandy dealer was, how he gave Echo gifts of coral necklaces and demijohns of brandy to try to get her to grab hold of his stinking cock? Or that even Fama had carried flour and raisins to Echo's cave to ask for an hour of caresses for her Battus, hoping that might free the epileptic teenager of his twitching lust for one night at least. And Echo knew something else about Fama, too – that years before she had tried to poison her stammering child with an extract of cyclamen and daphne blossoms, so that the misbegotten creature might leave this world as painlessly, as feverishly as he had been conceived beneath the sweat-drenched bulk of a migrant miner. . . .

Everyone in Tomi had a secret to hide – if not from Rome, then from his neighbours. And Echo knew many of the town's secrets, of which perhaps one of the least important was her recollection of how, despite the law forbidding it, the smelters had associated with the exile.

Cotta sensed that Tomi had begun to watch, indeed to lie in wait for him. Phineus, the brandy dealer, was the first to try to get close to the Roman by asking antagonistic questions to find what might be expected, hoped or feared from him. But the stranger, or so the brandy dealer claimed to know after an afternoon of tippling, was as harmless as the exile up in Trachila.

Cotta was one of many. In the years of Augustus's reign, increasing numbers of Rome's subjects and citizens left the great city to escape its apparatus of power, the omnipresent surveillance, the forest of flags and the monotone bawling of patriotic slogans. Many of them were also fleeing the draft, or simply the boredom of a citizenship whose every ludicrous duty was prescribed. Somewhere on the uncivilised borders of the empire, far from the symmetry of a well-ordered life, they went looking for independence or the images of their own romantic imaginations, but above all for a life free of supervision.

Both in the jargon of the government press and in police files, travellers of this sort were called *fugitives of the state*. They gave themselves no name – the reasons for their departure from Rome were too disparate and varied for that. Many of them rotted in the wilderness or in remote outposts along the endless coasts of Augustus's empire. They slept in the open or like Echo camped in ruins and caves, believing that they had left their marble origins behind forever. They planted scrubby gardens or potato patches in little clearings, or they sold toys and glass gewgaws on train platforms or stairways. Some of them spent their days begging along the wharves of harbour towns, some withdrew into ever more remote districts as they fled bureaucrats and police patrols, disappearing at last into the wilderness, dying of exhaustion or under the battering blows of some atavistic culture, which had, of course, been overrun by the emperor's armies at some point, but had never come under their control.

As always when a great man fell, Naso's fall set Roman society, if not in tumult, at least in motion. Like concentric circles of waves on the surface of a stagnant pond, the consequences of his fall moved for a long while over the depths into which the exile had vanished. The ashes from his burning manuscripts were still drifting from the windows of the house on the Piazza del Moro, when those who despised and envied Naso began to take advantage of his misfortune and, in time, sought public approval for the hate they had concealed for so long. Then, in the second circle of waves, libraries tidied up their collections, faculties their curricula, and book dealers their display windows. . . .

Obeying the laws of physics, the waves of sympathy for the disgraced Naso grew smaller the further the circles were from the incontrovertible fact of his banishment, but eventually they reached the shore, lapping the fringes of society – malcontents, the outlawed opposition and all those who either wanted to leave Augustus's capital on their own, without first being forced to, or had done so long ago. Only then did the waves roll back in broken patterns from the fringes to the centre of power. One morning the walls of the Palace of Justice were smeared with abusive graffiti, and a bonfire of waving banners and placards blazed in the forum – above the flames a scarecrow, and around its neck a picture of a rhinoceros, the insignia of Augustus's reign.

The banished man had had no contacts with the opposition – not to moderates, not to the fugitives of the state, not to radical underground groups who struck from the labyrinth of the catacombs – nevertheless, many of his poems appeared in the flyers of the resistance, whenever the occasion required that utopia be conjured up:

In that first age of mankind,
men knew neither laws nor revenge.
Needing no soldiers or armies,
Nations lived gently, passing
Each year in untroubled ease.

To be sure, Naso's rise to fame, his popularity and wealth had been cause for constant suspicion in opposition circles – at one mass rally in Turin, the crowd, choking under clouds of tear gas, had set up a mocking, chanting chorus: *Man for All Seasons*. But over the years the fugitives of the state took the same care to safeguard his books in their leather bags and canvas pouches that aristocrats did in their vitrines.

It was only after the poet had disappeared to the shores of the Black Sea that virtually all opposition factions claimed him, mentioning and quoting him on their placards and in their flyers so frequently that for Roman officialdom his removal must have seemed unavoidable in retrospect. Any man whose plight could set a fire blazing in the forum and sully the marble of the Palace of Justice was mercifully out of the way there on the cliffs of the Black Sea. A mimeographed call-to-arms, still reeking of spirit when it was seized before distribution, went so far as to celebrate the exile as a hero of the rebellion against an almighty emperor, as a poet of freedom, democracy and so forth. . . .

But whatever enthusiastic forms the endorsement of the poet by his new, outlawed audience might take, no one in the catacombs – or wherever the enemies of the state had taken refuge – was willing or able to fight for his pardon or transfer to some place less harsh. A famous, broken victim of dictatorial cruelty could prove much more useful to the goals of the resistance than a reprieved, or worse, a happy man. Besides which, the sombre greys of the cliffs above Tomi suited a persecuted *Poet of Freedom* far better than a luxurious villa on the elegant Piazza del Moro, than fountains and gardens in the shade of century-old trees. People in the catacombs demanded little more of a poet than that he be present in his writings and not in fine salons – a myth among myths.

To be sure, in the years after Naso's disappearance, petitions and requests for his pardon by undaunted friends also arrived at the emperor's palace, but none of these appeals ever found its way into the heart of power, into the room where Augustus sat at the bay-window staring down at the rhinoceros, whose massive body showed no traces of the passage of time. Generations of flies, vermin and birds that the rhinoceros bore on its plated back – they grew older, died and renewed themselves. But the animal in the bog, who nourished all these creatures and crushed them when it rolled in the dust and mud, stayed the same over the years like a stone.

To be sure, letters also arrived in Rome from the town of iron. Crumpled, stained by the hands of their carriers, by seasonal damp, tears or sea spray, Naso's petitions would finally arrive by post in the capital months later, only to disappear for good somewhere in the corridors and suites that led to the emperor's chambers. In those dimly lit passageways the case of the poet Publius Ovidius Naso was considered settled long ago, a file among files, a problem solved, and the exile's fate seemed important only as renewed proof that every subject of Rome could court only once the attention of the emperor, the world's mightiest and most inaccessible man, and that even the greatest poet of the empire did not get a second chance.

The view from the catacombs was the same as that from the chancelleries of state. Once he was banned from Rome, Naso existed in limbo between life and death, in a state whose every token of existence was like a memorial statue, frozen in motion at the moment the emperor's words of banishment had reached it. And so, to his enemies the poet was a petrified symbol of the justice of Roman law, a system concerned solely for the welfare of the state and therefore blind to the glitter of celebrity. But to his supporters he was the innocent victim of power. Where for one party the memory of Naso was kept alive as a warning against the stupidity and futility of any resistance to the emperor's rule, for the other it served as a revolutionary icon to be held high, an exemplary life that demonstrated how just and necessary such resistance was.

Under the blows of politics, Naso's fate shattered into many myths, but however many interpretations of his exile there were, they all remained chips in the propaganda games played by those struggling for power, each useful to a different party in different ways, needing therefore neither to be proved nor reconciled in some fashion with the facts of exile and of Naso's real life.

The poet's friends – including his wife Cyane, a beautiful woman from one of the important families of Sicily, who had grown unsociable and mistrustful – had nothing with which to counter this propaganda except their grief, private protest, silent anger and a vision of Naso's eventual pardon and triumphant return to Rome. They too received letters from Tomi at very sporadic intervals. Enclosed with these testimonies to despair, utter poverty and a love that had grown boundless in its abandonment, the recipients often found poems and epic fragments, scraps that they hoped might be fitted together piece by piece to restore the charred manuscript and allow the exile to return home in his *Metamorphoses* at least. But the letters grew sparer from year to year. Their contents remained no more than glittering shards from a world of tears and dreams.

Only a few of the poet's friends had ever made the hopeless attempt of asking official permission to journey to the end of the world, to visit the town of iron. Like all attempts to surmount the insurmountable barrier erected long ago to divide Naso from Rome and his world, it always ended in the same old song and dance. No passport. No travel permission. No comfort. A person under banishment forfeits all claims to companionship. He alone is to bear the burden of solitude, just as he alone bears the responsibility of his crimes against the state. Should a relative fail to take full advantage of a special dispensation by the emperor and choose not to accompany the delinquent from the first day of exile, he or she permanently surrenders all rights of familial proximity. Visits, subsequent meetings, are forbidden the exile and all other parties. In the case in question, the Roman citizen Publius Ovidius Naso left the capital alone and absent all attendance, therewith effecting *in persona* all concomitant provisions of the law. . . . *In re travel request: decision is therefore to be rendered as per regulation.* . . .

On the day of his departure from Rome, Naso, hoping for an early pardon, had prevented Cyane from accompanying him to the Black Sea. It may also have comforted him to know that his house and fortune, which had escaped confiscation as a result of a magnanimous gesture on the part of the courts – or perhaps through intervention by some unknown party – would be under the care and management of his wife. But by the second year of his exile, Cyane knew that she could not hold onto the villa on the Piazza del Moro. It was and remained Naso's home and its very substance seemed inseparably bound to Naso's presence – the marble floors to his footsteps, the white walls to his shadow, even the jets of the fountains, the tiger- and water-lilies of the gardens to his attentive care.

The estate fell into ruin. The fountains sank back into their basins. The surface of the ponds was covered with pine needles and leaves. A chill seemed to come from the blackened chamber that officials had sealed with lead and then forgotten, preserving within it the ashes of the book-burning. The chill spread from the balconied room and gradually filled all the others too. Cyane could not sleep. The nights were misery for her. But the longer the hours of her sleeplessness, the longer the weeks and months of waiting for a sign from Naso, the more swiftly time passed across the lifeless remains of his property and destroyed them. The delicate glass in the cupboards shattered for no apparent reason. Books began to mould, and the wooden blinds at the windows rotted. The household servants, no matter what pains they took, could not cope with the decay.

In December of his second year of exile, Cyane fled from the relentless deterioration to the muffled plush velvet of dark apartments on the Via Anastasio. In her letters to the Black Sea, she began to lie. She had to be careful not to stain the paper with her tears as she pretended still to be writing from the garden on the Piazza del Moro, reporting to the exile about life in a house whose windows had long since been nailed shut. After months of hopeless waiting, a letter from Tomi finally arrived. Memnon, the Ethiopian gardener and the last resident of the abandoned estate, took receipt of it and ran breathless to the Via Anastasio. But in it, Cyane read not one question about conditions in Rome or the state of affairs on the Piazza del Moro.

Perhaps Naso surmised that the house had been lost and tried to comfort himself with Cyane's compassionate lies, perhaps, too, any memory was unbearable for him – in his letters at any rate, not a word was mentioned about the happy years. He asked no questions, and answered none, but only described his forlorn world, the cold mountains and the barbarians of the town of iron. In the months it took for letters to travel between Tomi and Rome, sentences aged more quickly than in other Roman letters, many lost their meaning altogether, so that finally Cyane, too, wrote more and more in empty generalities, until the exile and his wife exchanged only long, sad monologues, always with the same phrases of reassurance, hope or despair, and neither knew any more whether a letter actually arrived or was still lost somewhere between the town of iron and the eternal city.

In the seventh year of exile the onward march of speechlessness was checked and yielded to great expectations: during that oppressively hot summer, as fields burned and black cracks burst open in the earth, Octavianus Gaius Julius Caesar Augustus, Emperor and Hero of the World, died of consumption. Perhaps the edict of banishment – or so the hope was nourished and discussed in many variations on the Via Anastasio – would perish with the emperor.

Mourning was imposed on Rome. Any sound not drowned in the whispers of the wake or the chorals murmured in cathedrals and temples was considered a violation of the decree of silence and quelled with force. Not a hammer blow could be struck, not a machine set in motion. Traffic came to a halt in the streets. Every day the Venetian guard and patrolling police combed the city, bound and gagged drunks and street vendors, and beat them unconscious. Barking dogs were clubbed to death. The wind lay still. The law of silence was breached only in the sky above the roofs and in the treetops – mourning Rome was filled with the voices of its millions of birds.

One morning, black funeral barges, unmanned and with black sails, black rigging and black masts, drifted in flames down the Tiber. When the sun had reached its zenith, the corpse of the emperor burned as well, atop a pyre of precious woods. Rome sank to its knees even before his ashes. Forty days after his death the news was announced by megaphone to the silent empire. It echoed above the walls of the capital: the senate had elevated Augustus to a god.

By the time the town of iron heard of this transformation many weeks later, an army of convicts was writhing at hard labour, excavating new temples and scrambling on their scaffolds. By then, all hope was lost on the Via Anastasio. For a good while a new dictator had been staring from the bay-window of his palace room down into the rhinoceros's bog. He was Tiberius Claudius Nero, the god's stepson. He was so good at preserving his inheritance intact that he revoked none of the old laws, lifted not a single decree of banishment, and so zealously emulated the god in every question and decision of power that ultimately he assumed his name as well and had himself adored as Julius Caesar Augustus.

The succession left the town of iron as unaffected as it had the fate of the poet. Under the new ruler, too, a man under banishment was as lost as a dead man. Despite all the continued reassurances and comforting phrases that Cyane sent to the Black Sea – from Tomi there were no letters, there was no news for three years. It was as if the hush of mourning that had pressed down upon the capital in the days of the emperor's cremation had silenced the shores of the town of iron now, too.

And so in the ninth year of the poet's exile and in the third of Tiberius's dictatorship, when the rumour of Naso's death first reached the great city, it was received both at police headquarters and in the offices of the bureaucracy as no more than superfluous proof of a fact long established. During the years of uncertainty, any rumour to that effect was of course only one among many, but this one was the first to be spread that could cite a will written in the poet's own hand. An amber merchant, who called himself Ascalaphus and claimed to have been in Tomi, brought this last testament to the Via Anastasio one mild, rainy winter afternoon. It was a tinted pastel postcard of a cloud-covered mountain range viewed from the sea. Beneath enormous mounds of tailings could be seen the white ridge of breakers and houses strewn among the waste-heaps: Tomi, the town of iron. The photo was pockmarked with mildew, and on the back, written in Naso's hand – were those weary scribbles really his? – it read:

> Cyane, dearest,
> I bid you recall the serenity of words
> with which we have closed so many letters,
> have comforted each other at so many partings . . .
> I set them once more here at the end;
> it is of all wishes the only
> one I have: Fare well.

As so often when death recalls a forgotten man to public memory, this time, too, something happened that Naso's enemies could not prevent and that his spokesmen had been unable to accomplish in recent years: the exile's fate became a controversial topic in Rome once again. The old questions were asked again in public, questions about the poet's offences and merits, about the censor's hostility to art and the arbitrary power of the courts. . . .

Wherever public outrage was heard, for whatever reason, someone always referred to Naso's unseemly end on the shores of the Black Sea. And although no one could confirm the fact of the poet's death – even the amber merchant had seen neither corpse nor dying man, but had only received the news along with the rest of Tomi's mail from the hands of a woman who ran a grocery, he could not recall her name – although this grimy picture-postcard of the town of iron and a few scribbled lines remained the only evidence of Naso's death, the newspapers in the major cities published commemorations and obituaries and, in time, even cautious tributes to his major work, still under lock and key.

Officialdom was too late in recognising that undying fame now threatened the exile. They did not seize any of this printed matter until Naso had already been transformed into a martyr and his forbidden or burned books had become revelations for a broad segment of the public. Naso may have gone the way of his *Metamorphoses*, have long since been turned to ashes or lie buried under the gravel of a barbarian land, but for the officials (who, so rumour had it, had been considering a quiet pardon these last few years) the poet's scandalous death had made him a totally unpredictable – and therefore, for the first time in the history of his rise and fall – dangerous quantity.

Naso had escaped every control for good and all. Naso was unassailable, invulnerable. And anyone could make use of his memory as he or she pleased without fear of ever being contradicted by a note passed from the prison of his exile, by his return or pardon. And there would be hell to pay if still more lines or stanzas were to be found in the literary estate that could be yowled as hymns or battle songs or used as slogans on the banners of the catacomb dwellers. . . .

In the most vigilant heads of many-headed officialdom, all the surmises and speculations slowly hardened into the fear that the poet's death out there at the end of the world could turn every sentence, every posthumous word into the signal for revolution. A separatist movement in Sicily had already raised Naso up as their symbolic leader and called for a silent march through Palermo, which had been forbidden, but to no avail, and had led to a bloody street-battle with the police and military. For three days, barricades, vehicles and shops burned in the streets of Palermo. More than two hundred separatists were arrested – four of whom met their deaths behind the opaque windows of a police barracks. Flags waved at half-mast before the national monuments of Sicily. In Rome, officials took precautionary measures.

Three weeks after the amber merchant had delivered Naso's will, a commando unit of police stormed the dilapidated house on the Piazza del Moro shortly before dawn. They shoved the stammering, drowsy gardener into a tool shed and locked him inside, then rushed the second storey as if moving in against snipers, broke open the lead seal on the door to Naso's balconied room and went to work on the nine-year-old ashes of his manuscripts.

Bundles of charred paper, which crumbled in their hands from the damp absorbed over nine winters, were stuffed into numbered plastic bags. The ashes of manuscripts, black greasy globs, were swept up with whisk brooms and dustpans. The burning books, hidden now under thick dust, had left behind a hard-baked crust. Knives were used to scrape it from the shelves and the hearth that had once been Naso's desk. Nothing – not the most insignificant scrap from which a word or a single letter could have been read – escaped the clean-up. When the commando unit departed from the villa an hour later, they left behind an unharmed Ethiopian gardener, but the site of the old fire lay in total ruin.

But then, within a few days after this raid – about which the intimidated Ethiopian said not a word, not even to Cyane when he visited her on the Via Anastasio – the same heads that had just ordered the clean-up and impounding of paper appeared to recognise at last that nothing was going to stop Naso's apotheosis now. And so officialdom came to its senses. If, in fact, anyone could lay claim to the poet for his purposes, be it a terrorist from the catacombs or some Sicilian peasant and arsonist, why shouldn't true patriots and citizens, law-abiding Rome itself, do the same?

And once they had claimed him, might not the catacomb dwellers hesitate in the future to honour this Naso as a martyr, particularly if a monument were erected to him at the behest and in the name of the emperor? A monument! And although, regrettably, he had not lived to experience his pardon by the forbearing, merciful and divine Julius Caesar Augustus, the banished man was after all a *Great Son of Rome* – as he was now called in a public proclamation from the palace, an unhappy son, to be sure, a difficult son, misunderstood for many years, to be sure, but happily come home in the end to the favour of his emperor. . . .

One hot day in early summer, the ambassadors of officialdom appeared once more on the Piazza del Moro, but they paid no attention at all to the gardener, who was so terrified that he panicked and sought refuge in the reeds of a pond. The squad did not bother the Ethiopian with a single question, did not even enter the house, from whose shattered and boarded-up windows elder saplings and grass now grew. No, instead they merely propped a ladder against the stony wreaths of seashells bordering the front door, bored holes in the façade and bolted a plaque of red marble onto Naso's house, a memorial plaque, which bore his name chiselled in gold, the years of his birth and death, and beneath these numerals one large-lettered sentence from his banned masterpiece:

Each place has its own destiny

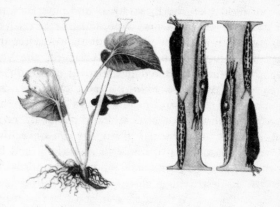

Cotta was one of many. Along with two hundred thousand other Romans in the Stadium of the Seven Refuges, he had admired Naso – a distant figure in the night, banished by spotlights to an oval framed in torches blazing like gems, inaccessible inside that raging expanse strewn with lights.

As one among many, Cotta had applauded the poet's speech about the plague on Aegina, and, later, had felt the same dismay at Naso's banishment as all the others who did not love the emperor. And they were many, too. For a long time, he had thought of himself as bound to their number, at least by a feeling of triumph whenever some act of derring-do by a disobedient or rebellious citizen undermined the emperor's omnipotence – when, for instance, a fugitive of the state outfoxed the border guards, slipped beyond their reach, and made fools of the sharpshooters up in the watchtowers, with all their packs of dogs and binoculars.

Together with many secret enemies of the state, Cotta also experienced silent, unexpressed satisfaction when an outlaw from the catacombs took a shot at some bureaucratic bigwig, a senator or general, maiming or killing him and instilling the fear of assassination or horrible death in every ally and beneficiary of Augustian dictatorship. But neither while he was a pupil at San Lorenzo nor during his years at a university (famous as the *Accademia Dante*), did Cotta himself ever descend into the catacomb labyrinth that reeked of myrrh, cold wax and putrefaction – the holes that led down into that world were hidden in the cellars of the slums, in sewer tunnels or sooty suburban backyards and coalhouses. Whenever an entrance was betrayed, the Venetian guard began its raid by setting molten fires of slow-creeping phosphorus, which could not be extinguished as they ate their way into the darkness.

But there was perhaps one feeling that differentiated Cotta from the rest of the large, anonymous and fickle readership of the poet Publius Ovidius Naso. To his horror, he saw the poet's fall not merely as the tragedy of a celebrated man, but even more clearly as proof of an all-destroying, all-transforming impermanence. Whatever is, will not last – the adolescent shock at this realisation subsided, but even as it did, Cotta reimmersed himself in the circle of the many people who counted themselves as Naso's admirers, indeed as his acquaintances, even if the first time they had ever been permitted to enter his house on the Piazza del Moro was on the day the poet took his farewell from Rome.

During the years of banishment, many in this circle would also occasionally drop by the Via Anastasio to sign a petition for the poet's pardon displayed in the entryway or simply to listen to Cyane give a public reading of a paragraph addressed to all of Rome from one of the exile's increasingly infrequent letters. At one of these gatherings, which were tolerated but kept under official watch, Cotta also learned about an amber merchant's courier service and Naso's last message. But Cotta was never really close, never closer than others, either to the poet or to his wife, who was homesick for Sicily and tormented by Rome.

The dismaying rumours about the poet's death set the town talking. And, ultimately, the talk set in motion a transformation. It pulled Cotta out of the faceless crowd, out of a docile society that submitted to the surveillance of even its bedrooms. It led him into the restless life of a fugitive of the state and brought him closer than ever before to the fate of the exile. Because – following the general outrage at Naso's death and the many unsuccessful attempts to refute or confirm the news, following the condolences, the glorification and the first marble tokens of rehabilitation – the talk of the capital's salons was that officialdom was preparing an expedition to Tomi to transport the body. Naso's bones, his ashes or whatever remains there were, so it was said, were to be salvaged by a committee and brought to the capital, to be placed in a sarcophagus and to outlast the ages inside a mausoleum.

But while the rumours in Rome moved on from this to that and the guessing game began as to whom officialdom would coerce for the trip to the town of iron, while a sculptor pounded with equal precision and apathy to rough out features for a bust of the poet (though the red marble plaque on Naso's house remained the only certifiable evidence that he had been rehabilitated), Cotta – furnished with the passport and papers of a sailor from Trieste who had died of gangrene – was already into his second week of enduring spring storms on the Mediterranean Sea aboard the *Trivia*.

For a long time he refused to permit himself to flee below deck. He clung to the railing and tried to console himself by picturing the triumph that would await him in Rome – if in fact he succeeded in returning from the town of iron, well before some official committee, with the indisputable truth about the poet's life and death. Who knew, perhaps even with a new version of the *Metamorphoses*, or a copy smuggled into exile. . . . He was a fugitive of the state, and an achievement like this could turn out to be just as important for the opposition and the underground as for the advisers in the emperor's antechambers, and he, *Cotta*, would demand acclaim for his rediscovery of a great poet's work – from whichever party he might choose. But the violent winds did not abate, despite this consolation.

With each breaker that roared over the decks of the *Trivia*, the picture of his future triumph grew paler and hazier, until at last Cotta came to regard not just his own trip to Tomi, but indeed any voluntary trip to the Black Sea as mad, absurd. Only as the torments of the storm continued, did Cotta gradually come to realise – despite his disgust at the stench of seasickness and amid fear for his life – that he had undertaken this trip, as he had everything else in his life so far, out of boredom.

How much more difficult it became, then, to brave the angry waters and imagine, if only fleetingly, the glutted affluence, the ease and security of Roman life, the lavish wealth and solicitude of his family, which the generations had made indolent and garrulous. . . . On board a schooner steering for the town of iron even the bureaucratic chicanery he had endured began, it seemed, to weigh more lightly, and finally every reason for leaving behind the splendour of Rome shrank to insignificance.

As the last nooks of the *Trivia* filled with terror and stench, as the schooner pitched and heaved past the islands of Greece, hidden by curtains of rain and encircling waves, sailing past desolate coastlines empty of human life, as Cotta endured the swells and troughs in his dark cabin, he cursed his decision and, finally, Naso too. But since a passenger aboard the *Trivia* had forfeited all choice, and since the ship itself offered the only refuge from the stony sawteeth of the reefs and the brute force of the waves, and since the helmsman swore that in winds like these it was better to fly before them full-sail than to heave to or take a bearing for one of the silt-filled harbours of the Aegean, Cotta resigned himself to his own decision and began to trust his fantasies: he would bring the truth about the poet back to Rome, perhaps even his lost masterpiece – and he still believed it when after seventeen days he finally disembarked and staggered along the jetty to the town of iron.

Although Cotta had climbed the stony slopes of the coast and up into the mountains searching for these dreams, at last discovering Naso's final refuge among the ruins of Trachila, he felt that not until now was he actually drawing nearer to the exile, step by step at Echo's side, this woman cursed with scaly skin, who became his lover on that first night after the disappearance of the projectionist. The smutty jokes whispered about the couple the very next morning were salted, as all gossip is, with malice, but with truth as well.

On the day of Cyparis's departure, there beneath the protecting rocky overhang at the entrance to her cave, to the soothing rush of rain drenching the thin, stony soil of the terraced fields, Echo had unfolded for Cotta her memories of the exile until dusk became night – her memories of glowing fires and the tales of life's injustice that Naso had read from the flames. She talked on and on, until at last she fell into a long, weary silence, and Cotta took her like a suitor turned coarse and breathless with desire.

There was that stillness at the end of her tales, his utter attentiveness to everything the woman reported, and would yet report, about Naso; there was the oncoming night, which like a dying fire turned every face into a shadow, every body into a simple outline and every human life into loneliness. And Cotta was suddenly seized with such a longing for her body, such a craving for her embrace, her warmth, her mouth, that he abandoned himself to the belief that this woman would open her arms to him as readily as she had her memories, and he pulled Echo, rigid with fright, to him and kissed her motionless mouth.

Stammering sweet words and apologies, he pushed her into the darkness of the ruins, led her, chained in his embrace, to the bed shoved up against the naked rock, sank with her onto coarse, cold linen, tore at her clothes while twisting out of his own, and did not let her go. Echo endured his kisses, his hands, without resistance, without a word, without a sound. Silently she clutched the irrational man as he forced her under his body, sank her nails into him as if he were a pouncing animal whose blind and furious motions she hoped somehow to restrict. No longer listening to his gasps at her ear, she closed her eyes and heard only the roar of the rain and, hidden deep within it, the gobbling of a turkey from her neighbour's hen house. She lost herself in that distant, silly bird's voice and, even when she returned from the distance to herself, realised that Cotta was no different from a herdsman or a smelter from the town of iron, from any of the other lovers who fled to her from a workaday world to run amok under the cover of night. Not until then – as the numbing effect of the rain and the gobbling turkey receded and she felt the clawing pain of disappointment that this Roman, too, was only one of many and as rough as most of them – did she try to shove him away. She screamed.

Whenever Cotta thought back to those moments of irrationality, he froze with shame. What thrust him out of madness and back into the reality of that night, turning his desire into deepest humiliation, was not Echo's scream or the violence with which she warded him off, but rather a sudden sense of disgust. For in his attempt to stifle Echo's screams and desperate resistance with tenderness, his hand glided down to the hidden scaly patch on her back, a large area of ravaged skin, so desiccated and cold that he instantly thought of a lizard. The disgust hit him like a shock that shattered his lust, congealed every motion.

At that moment he let go of her. Hidden from one another in the blackness, they both sat up and groped cautiously for their clothes, each trying not to touch the other. Echo kept her eyes closed, and for a long while Cotta did not risk a glance into the darkness into which she had sunk back. She wept.

Cotta spent the night with his victim. Invisible, he crouched in the darkness beside the invisible woman, until his joints ached and finally went numb, and he tried to console her and himself. He spoke to Echo in urgent, insistent words of devotion, as if they could transform her back into that beautiful woman whose hand he had grasped in the dusty cloud that afternoon. He complained of his loneliness in the town of iron, of his disquieting dreams in the attic room and again and again of how blind he had been to make such a disastrous mistake about Echo's feelings. During this doleful plea for understanding and forgiveness he thought at times he could see Echo's face hidden in the blackness of the night, an easing of its distraught expression. The fact was, however, that as Echo's sobbing subsided, fading to silence, the last token of her presence was extinguished as well. He kept on speaking to her, but was staring only into the hush of darkness.

Did she want him to be silent? To disappear? Echo gave him no answer. The rain roared on with unabating violence until night ended. As morning dawned, Cotta saw that his victim had fallen asleep. The peaceful sight of Echo calmed him. Her falling asleep beside him meant, perhaps, that she had forgiven him. When he got up his stiff joints were like shattering clay, he moaned in pain. Echo slept. He staggered and limped out of the cave into the open and into the steaming, undulating grey coastline. The rain let up. A hot wind wrapped the mountains in clouds. Dejected and weary, Cotta reached the ropemaker's house, and as he climbed the steep stairs to his garret, Lycaon opened the door of his workshop and waved to him but did not speak. The odour of meat and oakum seeped through the open door.

In the days after this first and last night of love, during a period in which Cotta and Echo no longer touched each other, hardly dared even a look at each other, what rumour had long since anticipated in Fama's shop had at last come to pass – the two became a couple. People saw them together in the mountains, wandering the mule tracks. Echo permitted Cotta to accompany her.

When, for the first time after that horrible night together, he met her again in the overgrown lane outside her ruins and began to walk along beside her, she endured his presence but said nothing, provided no answers as they walked for hours and she cut ferns and wormwood shoots and stuffed them in a linen sack. But when he came back the next day, she returned his greeting and spoke haltingly, tersely about the plants she was gathering on the slopes of a bay. On the third and fourth day she began at last to tell him again about Naso's fires and stories. But even after such gestures of reconciliation Cotta was still denied access to the ruins, even to the sandy threshold under the overhanging rock. Whatever memories Echo might share as they walked along, she said not a word about their night together and would not permit Cotta to speak of it again either.

During this period, the Roman watched as the scaly patch crept across Echo's face and then disappeared from her neck. At night she continued to receive her occasional secret visitors and let their gifts rot in some cranny of her cave or threw them to the pigs and turkeys. She took hulking mountain men to her bed, put up with smelters stupefied by schnapps – once even with Tereus. One lover somewhere up in the mountains, so it seemed, was no longer enough for the butcher.

Echo surrendered herself to him and to each of them with stolidity, as if she, a defenceless stranger on this coast, were paying the irreducible price for living in the shadow and safety of the town of iron. Cotta, however, was the only man with whom she would also show herself by the light of day – each hotter and dustier than the one before – the only man whom she would never again embrace or touch, but who nevertheless was at her side almost daily. As the two separated at Echo's ruins after an arduous trek across beaches and slopes, there were evenings when, hidden behind a blackthorn bush or the remnant of a wall, a shepherd or pig farmer already stood waiting for her and for nightfall.

None of these lovers, who stank of soot and wet straw, understood that the Roman and the scaly-skinned woman were forever separated by the humiliating shame and disgust of a single night, and were bound together only by words, by memories of Naso. They began to consider Cotta one of them, greeted him with a grin and thought of him as a pal – the fellow wanted the same thing they all did from the wench in the cave. Not saying a word, Echo would then leave him beind. Accepting from an admirer's hands a wicker bottle, some plaited wool or a chicken with its beak tied shut, she disappeared with him into the shadows of the rocks and walls.

When Cotta would return to his room on such evenings, the ropemaker's house was always unlit and deep in silence. Sometimes he would sit for hours in a tottery wicker chair and, by the light of his kerosene lamp, stare at the wall hangings that hid crumbling plaster and mildew stains, would lose himself in the delicately woven pictures of black-green jungles where flamingos and moorhens took wing, lose himself in thunderclouds and the crowns of plane trees lining a white road – the road led into the night. Each forest outline, each pond, the course of each river in these tapestries had glided through the hands of Arachne the weaver, the deaf-mute, for whom, so Echo said, her loom was a window trellised with threads and looking onto a garishly bright and soundless world.

The walks at Echo's side were strenuous, often leading deep into the wilderness. The two would climb ravines and high gorges, Cotta barely able to follow. Ten, sometimes fifty steps behind Echo, he fought for air and was seldom able to speak in anything but gasped phrases and breathless questions. Echo found a way through boulders and underbrush, moving with apparent ease up even the steepest slopes. At times she seemed to him a disembodied mirage skittering up ahead, leading him astray down impassable trails, but then without looking back, she would call the name of a plant to him over her shoulder and he felt reassured, though he had heard almost none of the names before.

Even during the hardest going, Echo spoke – as if talking to herself and without ever looking at him – about the book the exile had read to her from the flames and that she secretly called a *Book of Stones*. Sitting beside his fires in the town of iron, Naso himself had never given his stories a name. They were stories in which ships flew along transatlantic routes, their sails snow-white clouds beneath a clear blue sky, then suddenly turned to stone and sank.

On another walk, Echo told about a rejected lover, who in his despair had hanged himself from the lintel of a door and, still twitching in his death throes, banged his knees one last time against the door that had been locked to him for so long and only now finally gave way to his knock, opened by a shy, horrified woman, who froze at the sight of the man dangling there – and was still standing on the threshold, her own monument, long after the dust of the strangled man's grave mound had blown away, the house fallen to ruin, the mighty, rustling trees of the garden rotted to mould.

Echo told of mourners so pained by mortality, of people so enraged by hate, that they turned to stone, to indestructible images of the final and perhaps only genuine emotion of their lives. . . . Even for the animals in these tales, petrifaction was the only way out of the chaos of life. There was a whippet, for example, chasing close behind a fox during a hunt, the dog mad with primal wolfish lust, the fox in fear of its life. The whippet was ready for the final pounce on its prey, it leapt – both hunter and hunted shooting through the air for one brief moment, perfect models of jaws snapping tight and of panicked flight. And whippet and fox suddenly fell to the ground – bulky stones, two grey erratics, remnants of an eternal dead-heat. . . .

Stones! Echo shouted back over her shoulder and went on climbing a path hewn in the rock, stones, always just stones. The exile ended every tale with a petrifaction, and sometimes – hours after he had left her cave and his fire had gone out – she thought she could make out in the rough boulder above the hearth the faces of those unhappy people whose fates he read from the flames during his visits. Stone noses, stone cheeks, brows and lips, sad eyes of stone above the pots and glowing embers. Naso told his tales so terrifyingly, so wonderfully. He interpreted them for her from the rocks, even from the gravel of dry creek beds. He saw an epoch in every layer of sediment, a life in every pebble.

Sometimes as she listened it seemed as if the serenity and imperishability of a basalt column or petrified face gave him the consolation he needed to endure his own wretched, fugitive existence in the ruins of Trachila. What material – Naso had asked a drunken party gathered in Phineus's brandy cellar on the night of the most recent harvest festival – what material was better suited than stone to carry within it at least a hint of incorruptible dignity, of permanence, yes of eternity. Stone – removed from the dizzying shifts of time, freed from all weakness and all life? And what if the gnawing and scraping of millennia, the destructive erosion of weather or the forge of the earth's core can make a ruin of a cliff, melting, pulverising, and building it anew as if it were some form from the organic world? The most ordinary pebble will survive infinitely longer than every realm and every conqueror, it will lie peacefully in the shadow of a crevice or in the soft clay floor of a cave long after all the palaces of an empire are in ruins, their dynasties rotted and the shimmering mosaic floors of a throne room buried under tons of soil so arid that not even thistles and wild oats will grow above the sunken splendour. After all, how much more comforting and fitting is the ultimate destiny of petrifaction than the nauseating, putrid process of organic decay with its lace curtains of worms and maggots, Naso said. Compared to that abomination, transmutation into stone seems nothing short of redemption, a grey path into the paradise of rocky slopes, gorges and deserts. The flashy splendour of life passing like a meteor is nothing, the dignity and permanence of stones is all. . . .

Naso, Echo shouted back over her shoulder, spoke and drank with abandon in the brandy cellar that night. And back then the smelters had not hesitated to flout publicly the law that forbids associating with exiles. They had laughed a lot at the poet babbling his wisdom and opinions in his cups.

Among the countless rockbound spots that Echo and Cotta visited on their outings together, there was one where they seemed to end up again and again. They might arrive at it from any number of directions – wending wearily home, heading to some pale blue neck of land in the distance or simply going there for a silent hour of rest and then returning. Sometimes it seemed to Cotta as if this spot, barely an hour's walk from the harbour of the town of iron, was the secret middle point of the paths he took with Echo, a star from which they all proceeded or to which they led. It was a wide bay, its border a small strip of mussels, plaited kelp and black sand, where long lines of thundering breakers rolled in from the sea. Only shouts could be understood there, every other word was swallowed in the roar of the water or the wind.

The bay lay in the shadow of a cliff that rose straight up, six hundred, a thousand feet, enclosing the beach like the hollow of a monstrous hand. Looking up from the depths of the beach to the rim of the wall, Cotta had to hold his head so far back that the sight of the rim running endlessly high above – and of clouds sailing beyond that – made him dizzy. The eerie thing about this cliff, however, was not its alarming size, it was the jutting cornices, balconies and balustrades of ancient rock that covered its entire expanse, turning it into an auditorium, its tiers overgrown with hanging shrubs and clumps of grass. The first time Cotta stepped into the shadow of this cliff he suddenly felt himself transported back to the monumental opera house – a darkened world of plush velvet and ebony and parmazo marble – that the emperor had built as a gift to the people of Rome for the gala anniversary of some battle or other.

In the cold years now past the people of the town of iron had come only rarely to this place of tumult, where icebergs were left stranded in the spring and the leached, scattered remains of a ship were sometimes found in the weeks after great storms. For a long time Arachne the weaver was the only resident of Tomi who came here regularly. Echo recalled that she had had to accompany Arachne to the bay even on days in January, when the old woman would sit wrapped in pelts on one of the lower balconies and stare at the flow of the glistening pattern that a cold sun would leave on the surface of the sea, a play of light she would later try to weave into her tapestries with white silk and silver threads from Cythera.

As the climate in the region of the town of iron grew warmer with each sunrise and plants never seen before began to emerge from the earth, it was not only the deaf-mute and an occasional gatherer of flotsam who came to the Bay of Balustrades, but more often now, the blacksmiths, miners and smelters with their wives and children as well. On the few days they did not have to work, they took over the stone balconies, enjoyed the roar of the surf (which relieved them of words and conversation), slept away the afternoon heat under awnings or got drunk on sulphurous wine from goatskin bags they had brought along. With each rise of one degree in the temperature of the air above the wilderness surrounding Tomi, the number of sleepers and idlers in the bay seemed to rise as well – for these stony platforms and balustrades were among the few places in the vicinity of the town of iron where the coastline, with its barrier of jagged cliffs falling abruptly to the shore, provided enough of a foothold for a few restful hours under the sky that opened above the sea.

And so, on their walks along the black beach, Cotta gradually became used to seeing awnings fluttering high up on the cliff and wind-tousled heads that appeared at the railings of the balconies, calmly watching the couple strolling in the depths below. Those two tiny figures down there walking along the beach, so close to the water that they sometimes barely managed to dodge the waves, were no longer a suspicious or annoying sight in Tomi. As the weeks grew warmer, the smelters came to regard the Roman and his companion with much the same grey indifference they felt for any man, any woman on this indifferent coast.

It was on a white, hazy afternoon in the Bay of Balustrades that Echo revealed the one tale Naso had told that she remembered as ending not with a petrifaction, but with the transformation of pebbles into breathing creatures, into human beings. It was to be the last tale from the *Book of Stones* Cotta would hear from Echo. She had difficulty that day shouting above the thunder of the breakers. Laying her hand on her companion's shoulder, she was closer to him than she had been since that fatal night, yet Cotta hardly believed his ears as she shouted to him that he would now hear the story of the imminent end of the world, a revelation of the future. . . .

In her sudden eagerness and abandonment, Echo appeared so changed at that moment that Cotta came to a stop and looked at her in puzzlement for the first time in many days. They were both standing ankle-deep in the water of a receding wave. The end! Echo shouted, the end of wolfish humankind. Naso had perceived the catastrophic future better than anyone else, and perhaps his prophecy had been the real reason for his banishment from Rome. What resident of the greatest and most splendid city in the world, of all places, would want to be reminded, with the passion that Naso brought to his prediction, that all greatness and splendour will end?

Cotta felt the waves washing the black, fine-grained sand into his shoes, felt the water licking its way over his shoes up onto the beach and sliding back into the sea, erasing each footprint from the path behind them. Yet he did not budge, but stood there as if spellbound by Echo's hand, bent down to her, listening to the destruction of the world.

It was a vision he had never heard about in Naso's speeches and lectures in Rome. In a strange voice filled with almost fanatic energy, Echo announced a cloudburst that would last a hundred years, that would wash the earth clean, and described the coming flood for him as precisely as if it were a catastrophe from the past.

Even in the first year of the rain, every river ground away at its bed, erasing it like a footprint from the sand. Every sea buried its shore beneath it, transforming promenades and parks into impassable morass. Dams burst or lost all purpose under the rising waters, and torrents gushed from mountains and valleys onto the plains and towards seas that lay under the impenetrable cover of clouds.

Whatever could move, did, saving itself on ships and rafts, and aboard these and even sorrier refuges drifted above the cities and forests long submerged. And still the waters rose, sluggish and insatiable, gathering up anything not rooted or floating, closing over everything that did not rise with them.

Gradually the currents united into a single flood that reached the ocean, drove it high above its shores and pushed every coastline heavenward over the swell of the continents. Only the glacier-covered peaks towered like fissured islands above the water now. But the rain gnawed away the ice, too.

As years and decades passed, the ships and rafts decayed, rotted on the open sea, split and sank. At the end, what or whoever had hands or claws swam and battled to cling to the pulpy, waterlogged debris. The water around every stick of driftwood seethed with arms, hands and paws. Then the birds, vainly searching for somewhere to rest, fell exhausted into the waves and sank in flocks down onto the fields and towns of the ocean floor. Dolphins glided down the barren avenues, through rows of columns and arcades. Sea anemones grew on the gables, coral on the chimneys. Flounders camouflaged themselves in the dust of the streets. As if celebrating the return of the birds that sank flock upon flock into the deep, flags of algae and kelp waved atop the houses.

How silent it was down there! Echo shouted, how unimaginably soundless. Cotta saw the flourish of awnings along the stone balustrades of the bay, saw the silver green flag in the deep.

And now, when the last form of earthbound life had apparently fallen back into the sea, the roar of the rain finally, gradually abated, passed away, and the blue sheen of the sky broke through a gaping rent in the clouds for the first time in a hundred years. The sea grew smooth. But the calm was no deliverance, only the cruel finale: it was the dead, green silence of the ocean floor risen to lie heavy and glassy upon the waters.

At last, under a corrosive wind and the warmth of a long-forgotten sun, the flood receded, sank slowly, very slowly to reveal its work to the heavens and the reborn stars – a lifeless bog of a world. The flood fell, and the fish met the fate of the drowned. Those that dawdled behind and failed to save themselves in the receding waters, in a rivulet, a current, in the depths, were left in tepid swamps and ponds, lay flailing their fins in some parched upland valley, in a gully, in a ravine, fanning the suffocating air with their gills.

When the exile finished reading the world's doom from the fire, Echo shouted, she certainly did not hide from him her dismay and sadness. She sat there before the glowing embers of the fire, freezing, staring at Naso and waiting for some comforting conclusion to his prophecy. So perhaps it turned out the way it did simply because, as the sole witness to his vision, she had wanted to hear this ending or one like it, or perhaps it was indeed a scene from the future: a raft that the exile set drifting through the receding flood after the end of the world.

It was only a few empty wine barrels chained together, a stable door lashed on top. Two castaways lay on the planks in a tight embrace, a man and a woman, who had been destined to witness the world perish *and* re-emerge from the bog. At the mercy of the sluggish eddies washing the flank of a mountain, they glided ever downward on board their raft.

Naso called the man Deucalion and the woman, Pyrrha, and he said no one except these two would survive the flood.

Creeping back into its framework of coastlines, the ocean stranded these last human beings on a steep stony slope. For a long time the couple on the raft did not dare leave the safety of their planks and barrels and only gazed about in horror. How grey and dead and scattered lay the world's residue here where they had found rescue – piles of fish and birds; corpses layered in the branches of barkless trees, hanging there like contorted acrobats; cows with ballooned bellies beside the cadavers of lions and wolves, their flanks burst open; chickens and sheep on top. It was as if all the trash of the world had been emptied out over a silted desert littered with cadavers and corpses: flagpoles, antenna trees corroded by rust and salt, flying buttresses trimmed with stone roses, beds and choir stalls, the paddle wheels of turbines, arched street lamps and a bronze horse bearing the torso of a general. . . . Or had it all been no sooner washed away and sunk than to sprout in an extravagant new growth? No, nothing grew now. It all stuck straight up and stared a shattered stare into a now cloudless sky.

No one, Echo shouted, can imagine the loneliness of these two people amid the desolation, who, as they gaze out at this garbage dump, the sun circling overhead, come to realise that they are the survivors, the last and only mourners at the grave of humankind. And how very much, Echo shouted, must a loving couple like Deucalion and Pyrrha wish that they, too, could lie contorted or buried among cows, lions and rubbish like all the other victims. The loneliness of survivors, Echo shouted, is surely the worst punishment of all.

Deucalion and Pyrrha. The last human beings. There they crouched freezing on their raft, incapable of a gesture of pain, incapable of acting, speechless. The first day after running aground they spent hours tugging and plucking to groom each other's clothes and hair, then lay back down, whimpering, embracing, sat up sometimes as if terrified by some new tidal wave, then fell back into passivity.

Not until the grey of dusk did Pyrrha reach over the edge of the raft to touch solid earth, as if to test whether the ground would be able to bear her first step or secretly to convince herself that this desert wasn't really only a mirage and every mountain only a mountainous wave. And so she reached into the morass and found she was grasping a stone, a polished pebble, which she picked up and smelled the way an animal smells its prey, closed it in her fist, rolled it between her palms, but all the same, seemed to have forgotten it when at last she tossed it carelessly back into one of the ponds. Then she lay down on the raft, her face turned to the still pale stars, her distracted expression that of a lunatic, and she let her hand drift down again and again into the silt, grasped a second pebble and a third, picked up stone after stone and tossed them all back into the water, into the slime, steadily, automatically, so that the stones' plopping into the liquid and mush began to sound like the ticking of a clock. The ponds and puddles before her were rippled with waves like washboards.

Deucalion, who had given in to his exhaustion and fallen asleep, did not start up in alarm until Pyrrha had thrown a hundred or more stones, but was suddenly wide awake when he saw how one of them, a fist-sized rock that had just been tossed on a bed of muck, did not stay dead and immobile, but lifted itself halfway up out of the water, driven by some invisible power, rolled across the soft ground, wallowed in it, *moved*, followed a meandering path, expanded like a snowball rolling down a slope. The muddy crust of its hide sprouted bristles, boils, tentacles, which became fidgety little legs, arms, hands that grasped the empty air – and grew.

Noticing the dread in Deucalion's eyes, Pyrrha followed them and stared now, too, at the spectacle in the pond, stifling a scream with her muddy hand as she realised that bit by bit the stone was assuming human form – a woman bent in a crouch, but now slowly straightening up. In the hope that by throwing stones she could drive this spectre back underwater, frighten it off or smash it to pieces, Pyrrha now reached with both hands into the mire and in her terror threw pebbles, coarse sand and gravel at the sprouting woman, and Deucalion, as panic-stricken as his lover, did the same. The ponds turned frothy under the pelting barrage.

But the ghost did not retreat, nor shatter, nor dissolve, but instead it grew until it was the same size as the last two human beings. And then the terror grew worse. For as the pebbles and stones, thrown by the handful in long low arcs, hit the water or slid down from the woman's naked body and sank, they all sloughed off their inert rigidity, they all rolled and wallowed through the muck and grew under mantles of silt and clay, bursting at last like shells in a clutch of eggs.

And human beings rose up out of the morass, a host from every pond. The pebbles Pyrrha had flung became women, and Deucalion's gravel, men. A vast army of mute, staggering, naked forms sprang up and gazed down on the last humans born of humans, who sank back whimpering onto their raft, hid their faces in their hands to avoid the burden of those vacant eyes. And still the water seethed and bubbled, the thronging ranks grew denser.

Out of a hail of stones, Echo shouted, the new human race will be born after the all-destroying flood to come – Naso read this future to her from the fire one winter day. Out of every pebble, a monster! Echo shouted. The exile's prophecy to the world: humans of stone. And these creatures creeping from the slime of a race that had perished of its own wolfish rapacity, stupidity and thirst for power, Naso called them the true, the genuine human race, a brood of mineral-like hardness, with hearts of basalt, eyes of jade, without feelings, without a language of love, but likewise without any stirrings of hate, sympathy or grief, as implacable, as deaf and durable as the rocks of this coast.

When Echo at last fell silent she fought for air as if wearied by physical exertion. High up on the stone balustrades of the bay the smelters sat or lay under their awnings – in their midst, the deaf-mute weaver, staring at the bas-relief of the cresting waves – untouched by Echo's tale, not bothering to send a second glance at the two figures wreathed in the spray of the surf below them. Then Echo's hand slid from Cotta's shoulder, slid gingerly down his arm. Only now did he again notice the mark of her illness, and was as frightened by it as on the first day. He saw the back of her hand covered with grey scales, flakes of dead skin, he saw how her hand seemed to be of slate sparkling with mica, or of grey feldspar, of chalk and coarse-grained sand, a delicate sculpture of brittle aggregate stone.

The two wandered back from the Bay of Balustrades in silence that day, returned to the town of iron lying in a white haze. Cotta walked along thinking of Naso's readings in Rome and tried to recall a vision of the end of the world comparable to Echo's story, but to no avail. In his mind, he could indeed hear Naso reading and speaking – but not one word about a flood.

Echo walked beside him, so wearily it seemed that she had not only put all the power of her voice into her shouted account of the exile's prophecies, but all the power of her memory as well, walked so wearily it seemed that in transmitting this apocalypse she had played out her predestined role to its final word and was now sinking back into speechlessness.

That afternoon they parted on the mole with a careless, hasty gesture. Cotta sat there for hours on the stone blocks with their petrified forms. Lost in thought, he stroked the shells and tentacles of primeval snails, sea worms and crabs, and surrendered himself to his homesickness for Rome – since his departure it overcame him at times for no particular reason and, once its swift series of memories had glided past, left him just as abruptly. He counted the segments on the backplate of a sea louse eternally bound to the stone and thought of the white, polished smoothness of Carrara marble, could feel the day's heat stored within the stone blocks, and longed for the indolent comfort of idle hours on a veranda, for sofas and pillowed wicker chairs, heard the boats moored to the jetty bumping against one another, scraping and scratching – and the sound was like the wire brooms and brushes the convicts from Trinità dei Monti used to clean the great stadium or a vaudeville theatre after some gala evening.

It was dark when he finally got up. His nostalgia had spent itself in images that grew paler and paler, finally leading him back again to the place to which time and the confines of the Roman Empire had relegated him – to this deserted mole in a harbour at the end of the world, to a place of banishment, but also of unfaltering resolution. The *Metamorphoses* – burned, squandered on smelters and swineherds and never written down a second time – nevertheless, he, Cotta, would take possession of the work and lay it once more in the hands of Rome. From Echo's memories or from the recollections of other guests at Naso's fires he would collect the exile's stories, even if he never found their author in the wilderness of Trachila. A book of stones, Echo had said. And so, once Cotta was back in his garret at the ropemaker's, he wrote *The Book of Stones* across the top of his notes, his record of the end of the world.

While he sat bent over his chronicle until late into the night, a storm moved in from the sea, wedging itself in the ravines and nearby upland valleys, and then struck the town of iron with such fury that Cotta suddenly felt he had been transported into Echo's story of the flood. As he was closing a shutter banging in the wind, he looked down into the street and saw how the moss, slates and reeds of the roofs were being torn away by the gusts and flung into the brook raging through the town. Trash, splintered wood, fencing and uprooted shrubs danced down the brook, which had grown so white and powerful within a few minutes that it began to rip at the trestles of the wooden bridges and at the foundation of a row of houses built on its rocky banks.

But Cotta waited in vain at his window for the tumult of catastrophe, for shadowy figures running and gesticulating wildly, for their screams. The houses remained dark. No one in Tomi appeared to notice the storm. When a gate or grating sprang open in the wind, it was not closed again. A battered windwheel was left where it had fallen onto a porch roof. No one tried to stop a runaway mule dragging its hitching post behind it, and a pen full of piglets was swept away down the brook. The havoc took its course, met no resistance. The town of iron slept as on a mild summer night.

Cotta stood at the window of his room waiting for the next thunderclap, paralysed, blinded by the thicket of lightning bolts, heard the beams and rafters groan with the storm and was incapable even of waking the ropemaker – asleep in a corner of his workshop at the far end of the labyrinth that led downstairs, through hallways and storage rooms. Or was he awake?

But then the storm calmed as suddenly as it had broken, took the hurdle of the coastal mountain chain and drifted off with all its towers of clouds and fulgent lights like a burning fleet of ships. Then the roar of the brook lessened, too, withdrew into the distance, then the echo of the cloudburst could be heard only in the water of the gutters, and the back yards were silent again except for the dripping treetops. Exhausted by the terrors of the storm and his chronicle of doomsday, Cotta fell asleep over his notes that night.

The next morning was rich with the scent of dewy flowers and freshly felled timber. It bathed the coastal cliffs in such a hard, golden light that as he drowsily opened his window, Cotta was ready to regard last night's thunderstorm as a dream – and saw the residents of the town of iron busy removing the traces of wreckage from the streets, courtyards and gardens. Tomi resounded with the pounding of hammers, the pull of saw blades through obstructing tree trunks and the scratching of shovels on the pavement. With a curse, the smelters accepted the devastation.

The ropemaker's house had been left untouched. Lycaon was not interested in the condition of other houses. He stood in his workshop, bending over a yarn winch and seemed so immersed in his work that Cotta had to repeat his questions several times before he got an answer.

The storm last night?

The ropemaker hadn't noticed any storm, had been sleeping right by an open window and hadn't felt a breeze.

Uprooted trees?

Rotten trees fall down sometimes, even on the calmest night.

And the debris in the streets?

With all these deserted houses and ruins, there was always something crumbling and breaking off somewhere or other. He had slept the night through. Had work to do today. And turned back to his winch.

Strangely upset and confused by Lycaon's gruffness, Cotta set out that morning for Echo's ruins. But whoever he asked about the storm – Thies the German, who was boarding up a break in a wall, or the brandy dealer, who was kneeling among the broken staves of a vat of mash that had tumbled down the steps to his cellar vaults and cursing as he ladled the green malt back into buckets – no one admitted to having heard the boom of thunder or to have seen so much as a flash of heat lightning. Despite the general devastation, all the damage was passed over as an everyday accident, caused perhaps by a sudden gust or an animal. Violent winds? A cloudburst? The Roman must have had a bad dream.

Cotta received no answer when he stood in the rubbish outside Echo's ruins and called her name. The cave – this was the first time he had entered it since that fateful night – looked as if it had been the scene of a struggle. A china cabinet had been knocked over and smashed. In it Echo kept delicate vases, goblets from Murano, painted carafes and glass balls strewn with quartz, items she had collected as a lover of filigree work and blown glass. Multi-coloured fragments and splinters lay scattered over the hard clay floor and reflected the slanting morning light in emerald, silver and ruby flashes. Into this dazzle, four turkeys had fled from the neighbour's farm after their wirecage had burst open under a rock slide, and were now perched on Echo's bed, table and cold stove. Frightened by Cotta, they made for the outside, strutting over the topsoil of glittering fragments to the tune of a soft, melodic tinkle. Echo had vanished.

All morning long Cotta scoured the streets, filled now with acrid smoke. Large fires had been lit in several squares to burn debris and broken wood. But the people at these smoky hearths simply shrugged when Cotta inquired about the missing woman. Those gathered around Phineus the brandy dealer laughed when he took his false teeth out of his mouth, clattering them like a puppeteer and informing the baffled man that even along the Black Sea a floozie couldn't live off just one Roman and had to go to see a swineherd in the bushes once in a while.

Cotta left the town behind him and retraced many of the paths he and Echo had walked together. The crags and slopes, the whole coastal range seemed deserted that day, and on all sides presented possible backdrops for a vanishing act: chasms, ravines and potholes to fall into, mounds of scree to be buried under, and raging torrents in which to be washed away down subterranean rivers. It was late afternoon when Cotta crossed the black sand of the Bay of Balustrades, then scrambled ever higher up the oriels and balconies – and not until he was already on the back side of the rocky ridge did he realise that he was on the path to Trachila. Only yesterday he had heard about the end of the world there, far below on that dark crescent hugged by breakers, and shortly after his arrival he had seen there a procession of ashen-faced people marching beneath banners and canopies. The beach and rocks were deserted now.

In the columns of warm air ascending from the sea, buzzards glided in corkscrew flight up to where Cotta stood. Echo could not have taken this path up into the mountains – in many places it was washed with soft sand and rivulets of loose earth, but bore no footprints.

How familiar this desolation had become. The fields of snow that had made his first trip to Trachila so strenuous had all been eaten away by the sun now. The slopes lay beneath blossoms. Broom, squill, myrtle and saxifrage shimmered in the gravel like the iridescent shards in Echo's cave. Distorted to an ellipse, the sun was sinking in the hazy barricade above the horizon. As Cotta turned to go back, darkness was creeping from the ravines and with the darkness, fear – the fear that had driven him from Trachila in the days of carnival and now kept him from it, his last destination.

For a moment he thought he saw, high up in the cliffs, the fluttering rags woven into the cairns. During the descent he tried to find refuge in his own voice, called Echo's name over and over as he climbed down to the sea. But as often as he called out her name – from the abysses, the overhanging rocks and vertical walls, where moonlight was refracted now in crystal and scaly mica, only the echo of his own voice came back to him.

Echo did not return. A second day passed with no sign of her, a third. All week Cotta looked in vain for the missing woman. The town of iron lay torpid in the heat of the season and seemed unaware that one of its women had vanished. Phineus the brandy dealer didn't care about some runaway woman. Yesterday a servant, today the village whore and tomorrow up and gone, he mumbled in his cellar, which still reeked of mash from the night of the storm. But maybe that scaly female was setting a good example, probably was the best way to get in and out of a place like Tomi – no greetings, no traces.

Echo's cave was plundered. In the course of a single night all her suitors' gifts disappeared – the rusty bars of iron, pots full of rancid butter, the plaited wool and fleeces. . . . And whatever household goods survived the plundering intact were smashed to bits by a man gone berserk. Marsyas was a charcoal burner who descended to the coast from his smoky valley and kiln three or four times a year. He had got drunk with Phineus and then waited in vain all night for the only woman who hadn't fled from him. He shouted for her in the empty darkness of the cave and, seeing that his expectations were not to be realised, flew into such a rage that he kicked and smashed to pieces anything not already kicked and smashed to pieces.

He kicked so hard at the rock walls that he fell to the floor. He crept over the strewn shards, lacerating his hands and face, then crouched in the darkness, whining and bloody. But once he had caught his breath and calmed down, he picked up two empty schnapps bottles and blew on them as if they were panpipes. It sounded like a ship emerging out of the mountain. This night-music and the howling chant that Marsyas intoned between foghorn blasts robbed the neighbours of their sleep. By the time Tereus the butcher flung open the gate of his courtyard at dawn and, panting and cursing, headed up the street to silence the drunk, Echo's cave no longer resembled a human habitation. Tereus was no further than the entrance when the stench of shit hit him. Marsyas was lying in his own faeces, his face crusted with blood, two bottles, their necks shiny with spit, pressed to his chin. The floor was splattered black with his blood – rubbish all around him.

Tereus grabbed the helpless man, then kicked, punched, dragged him by his feet out to a watering trough, picked him up and threw him into the murky water. Without once looking around, he strode back down the street. Procne – wringing her hands and murmuring unintelligible, soothing words – came out to meet her husband. He pushed her aside and banged the gate behind him.

Marsyas had the butcher's fat wife to thank that he did not drown in a stone trough that morning. Sobbing with shame at her husband's violence, she tugged the unconscious charcoal burner out of the water, patted his face with her red, swollen hands. Once he opened his eyes, she made a bed for him on the cobblestones, spreading over him the blanket she had draped around her shoulders – he had sunk back into sleep by now – and shoved his boots under his head. And there she left him. And there Marsyas lay in a drunken stupor, in a tangle of heavy dreams until afternoon. He thrashed about on the mossy stones, snoring and groaning, his mouth wide open. He did not awaken as the morning sun beat down nor when the children played nasty tricks, tying two rotting fish to his feet and decorating him with goose feathers, thistles and mud pies. Dogs sniffed at him, then ate the fish. Miners shouted their hallos into his dreams and kicked him. The charcoal burner slept. Cotta, too, walked past the sleeping man that morning, barely taking time to notice him. But for a brief moment he had the feeling that this man, lying humiliated in his own filth, was the only person up and down the coast of Tomi who felt any sadness at Echo's disappearance.

Cotta hurried past the trough and on toward Fama's shop. From the window of his garret he had seen a man leading a mule up the steps of the path from the harbour – a frantic old man, scolding and cursing his mule, though sparing the rod as he tugged it behind him. Empty, chinking bottles, empty sacks and willow baskets were tied to the mule's pack frame. Even from his window, Cotta thought he knew this mule driver, but in his attempt to make certain, he almost took a tumble down the ropemaker's steps as he ran out onto the street after the man. It was quite possible he would only bump into another one of those haggard, coarse shepherds who were passing through the town of iron these days, now that heat had scorched the grass of their meadows and forced herd after herd into the shade of the valley floors.

Cotta finally caught up with the new arrival at the door to Fama's shop – with its crates full of leathery apples, its displays of head lettuce, beets and dried horse chestnuts. He had not been mistaken. The mule driver was Naso's servant.

Pythagoras stood bent over a keg of sea-salt, letting the crystals trickle through his fingers. He pulled up in alarm when Cotta addressed him and stuck out a hand. The servant stared at him, then gave a relieved smile and turned back to the salt keg. Pythagoras did not recognise his guest. A visit at carnival time? Stone columns in the garden? Slugs? Yes, yes, Pythagoras nodded – the stones, the slugs. He had a clear recollection of his hopeless battle with that plague of slugs, of their dying in the vinegar, of the moon, of everything . . . except his visitor that night. He had not seen a stranger in Trachila for years now.

Behind the old man's back, Fama signalled to the speechless Roman – no point in talking to him. He remembers everything and nothing. The old man appeared to be a trusted customer. As if filling this order from Trachila at regular intervals was a matter of course and she had long since learned it by heart, Fama brought packages and bundles wrapped in newspaper from the depths of her shop, piling them all on a display table outside the door, and her son, who was currying and smelling the mule's neck, excitedly bawled out a name each time he thought he guessed the contents of a package: soap! tea! codfish! candles! . . .

Pythagoras filled his baskets, sacks and bottles, tying supplies to the pack frame until the mule grew restive under the burden. The epileptic tried to calm the animal by laying his hands over its eyes, but the lids started twitching under his palms, making him laugh so hard that Fama slapped his mouth with a rag and told him to hush.

Not yet recovered from his bewilderment at the servant's taking him for a stranger, Cotta went on talking to the old man as he packed. He tried to jog his memory with descriptions of his night in Trachila, with insistent questions. Had Naso returned from his trip into the mountains? Had Naso accompanied his servant to the town of iron?

The servant replied politely, bowing several times to the Roman, but not a word he said betrayed that he knew the man to whom he was speaking. No, his master had not yet returned from his journey into the mountains. He had had to survive the last weeks of winter alone, survive the spring avalanches alone, and a rough time it was, until two days ago he finally succeeded in negotiating the miry path to the coast. He had fought his way down into town over walls of debris and across slopes cut in two by mudslides, just so he wouldn't have to greet his master with an empty cupboard on the day of his return. Wine, sweetmeats – it was all in those baskets, ready for the day. . . .

The old man turned talkative, showing the Roman his hands, bruised from digging and scrabbling in the mudslides, spoke about the wind harps he had tied in trees to mark the path for the exile, wind harps all the way up into the narrowest valleys. And as he spoke Cotta gradually began to understand the leery silence and uneasiness that the mere mention of Naso evoked in many homes in the town of iron. Every locality to which the authorities assigned an exile – so Rome's law decreed – would be held liable both for keeping him alive and preventing his flight. The law made guards of the inhabitants of a city chosen as a place of exile. Conversations and any intimacy with said enemy of the state were forbidden, denunciations a matter of honour, vigilance a duty. Should a city neglect or fail in its guard duties, all privileges, tax abatements and trade concessions would be forfeited.

Tomi had surely realised long ago that the exile was not simply on a hike in the mountains, but had disappeared. Tomi had permitted someone to evade the will of the emperor. Tomi had fulfilled its duty by forcing the poet into the mountain-encircled remoteness of Trachila, by placing at his side a madman who unwittingly assumed responsibility for the whole town. And driven to this last refuge, Naso had perhaps fathered the rumour of his death, so that he could camouflage the worst crime an exile might commit – flight.

Cotta recalled a slogan on banners protesting the cruelty of Roman justice: The road back from exile is the road to death. Whoever fled from exile would sooner or later fall beneath the shots of a firing squad, whoever hung on, died of loneliness. For unlike a fugitive of the state, who was struck from the files – and so from the memory – of the authorities after five years, a banished man remained under their purview for as long as he lived.

No land would have been vast enough, no sea broad enough and no mountain range desolate enough to protect a runaway exile from the wrath and justice of Rome. The perseverance shown by the emperor's law enforcement agencies in carrying out a sentence was not to be dampened by vastness, breadth and desolation. No matter what wilderness a fugitive might seek out as a hiding place – at some point every eye, every ear in the neighbourhood began to be transformed into the eyes and ears of Rome.

If this was true for some nameless enemy of the state, whose picture was posted at border stations, harbourmaster offices and turnpike tollbooths, how much greater was the threat for a famous culprit, a man whose portrait had appeared on billboards lining major highways and in every newspaper, whose features mint-masters had stamped into dyes, sculptors into stone – and, to top it all, who was also a man with such an unmistakable, unforgettable nose!

A fugitive with a face like that could not hide for any length of time in city throngs or in sparsely populated districts, where every stranger provoked insatiable curiosity – not unless they had stopped looking for him in this world because he had been given up for dead. . . .

Apparently guessing Cotta's thoughts, Fama began to argue the point. While Pythagoras tied a tarpaulin down over his mule's load and Battus crouched behind a vat of sauerkraut and blubbered at being punished, the shopkeeper pulled the Roman aside. Everyone in Tomi knew that the exile sometimes went off into the mountains alone for weeks at a time. He spent the nights in barns, ate every bit of the supplies amber-hunters left up there in caches, collected moss, fossils and clouded emeralds you could find in the gravel of brook beds. Sometimes he paid his bill at Phineus's with the stuff he found or traded it here in her shop for tools and groceries. Battus had a collection of stones and minerals arranged on the shelves in the back room, including two nice opals from Trachila.

Escape? Nonsense. Where was he supposed to escape to from Trachila? There was no way over the mountains. And if someone kept on climbing all the same, he would only find a new abyss behind every ridge, a valley, the next mountain to ascend, each peak higher than the one before and finally sheer walls so high the top was indistinguishable from the velvet blue of the sky. . . . No running away, no vanishing act. Only two ways led out of the town of iron into the world: the coast road or the sea.

Cotta accompanied the servant high up the slopes that morning. Tereus had set two starved shaggy dogs on the trail of a wolf, but they had lost the scent in the shimmering heat and now trotted along in the wake of the swaying mule pack with its odour of lard and cheese, until Cotta drove them off with stones. The dogs didn't bother Pythagoras. Pleased to have found such a persevering listener, he strode on. Cotta asked no more questions, but he learned that Naso had often visited the Bay of Balustrades lying deep below them now, had spent long afternoons there huddled beside Arachne the weaver, while his servant waited for him, out of the wind under a jagged rock, and froze. Those flamingos, the groves of palm trees, the servant said, everything to be seen on the deaf-mute's tapestries – she had read it all from the lips of his master.

During the slow climb from the town to the timber-line, where he parted from Pythagoras, Cotta interrupted the old man only once. Had he ever heard Naso tell about the end of the world, about a raging, foaming sea, about how humankind perished in waves and mire and was born again from stones?

End of the world? Pythagoras stopped so unexpectedly that his mule bumped his shoulder with its muzzle. He bent down for a piece of gravel and flung it into the depths. No, there had been no talk of drowning. Down there, on the shore, in Tomi! you could see the end of the world more plainly than in any horror show somebody might dream or imagine. In those ruins, those smoky, tumbledown streets and fallow fields, in the sooty faces of its inhabitants and the dirty holes they lived in, in every nook and grunt of Tomi, the future was already audible, visible, tangible. Why the phantasms? Look in any sewage pond in the town of iron, the future was already mirrored there – every cesspool, a window onto a world laid waste by time.

Cotta stayed behind once they reached the grey barricade of a rockslide that had buried the path to Trachila beneath it. Pythagoras appeared hardly to notice his departure. Without pausing, he scaled the barricade, tugging his stumbling mule behind him, and disappeared into the stony rubble and uprooted stumps lifting their soily claws above the scree.

An exhausted Cotta rested beside this wasteland. Here, halfway between Tomi and the ruins of Trachila, he sensed such an indifference to everything that had once moved him and led him from Rome into these mountains that he felt as if he was already becoming like the stone on which he leaned – grey, impassive, mute, vulnerable only to the forces of erosion and time. His hair grew and mingled with the moss, the nails of his hands and feet turned to slate, his eyes to chalk. Beneath the colossal mass of these mountains nothing that was not itself of rock possessed solidity or meaning. The ravines knew nothing of Naso, of all the generations before and after him. They yawned impassively at the clouds, whose shadows glided impassively over the mountain slopes. Rome was so distant it was as if it had never been, and *Metamorphoses* – an alien, empty word, yielding only an uttered noise, with no more meaning or melody than the sound of a bird taking wing or a mule's hoof striking the rock.

The cry of a jackdaw called him out of his stony bemusement. Cotta looked about him in confusion. Had he not been dreaming just now about standing in the flash of white heat coming from the open firing door of a furnace? Dreaming that he, a Roman fugitive of state, had become a smelter?

But once he stood up and left his resting spot, he forgot the heat and the dream. He only knew that at that moment he had never felt more like one of the inhabitants of the town of iron. He was pursuing an ambition that had died long ago, pursuing it as stolidly as Tomi's citizens went about their work at the furnaces, in the mine shafts or in the cracked earth of their low-walled fields. He plummeted toward his fate like a stone that no longer holds the warmth and life of the hand that picked it up and hurled it. As a stone obeys the law of gravity, so he obeyed the magnetic power of Naso's misfortune. The poet's fall had cast him out of his secure world in Rome, and now he was falling with the exile. He was tired. He no longer yearned for prestige, for applause. He did what he did. Leaving his resting place high above the sea and far below the ruins of Trachila, he descended into the town of iron. Dusk was already falling when he reached the first houses.

That night he was plagued by insomnia. He sat in his room staring at the walls, at the wall-hangings. Had he lived here among woven rivers, jungles, bays and verdant plains since the day of his arrival, without ever once recognising a landscape from the exile's imagination? Slept among these reedy banks, flocks of flamingos and shimmering watercourses of silk, wool and silver gossamer, and awakened without a thought that the tapestries on the walls of his room resembled the scenery of the *Metamorphoses*?

In the heat of the following day, a generation of cicadas in the straw of the terraced fields set up such a shrill chirping that the smelters' dogs turned savage at the unaccustomed racket, barked and howled until they were beaten back into cellars or muzzled. Cotta did not leave the ropemaker's on that blazing hot day. He sat in his wicker chair and followed the tapestry rivers in their meandering courses. The meadows along their banks, the jungles and steppes were filled with myriads of animals – hunting, grazing, fleeing or sleeping – but not one human being.

A paradise? The ropemaker had long ago forgotten whatever there was to see on the tapestries in his attic. They covered the walls, kept out winter cold, kept in warmth, and hid the cracks that frost had opened in the masonry. Whatever idyllic scenes the pattern of threads contained were of no significance to the ropemaker. The hangings were the weaver's payment for the right to live in a house he owned and was letting fall into ruin.

Arachne's house stood on a cliff at the northern edge of town, under the shadow of a lighthouse made of huge blocks of white stone. Its signal fire had gone out decades ago, and the entrance long since lay buried under the rubble of floors and stairways that had collapsed inside. The cracked stone walls of the weaver's house were propped against the lighthouse. The roof sagged badly – several sections had broken off and been hastily patched – and was overgrown with cushions of moss that had withered in the heat of this summer. Every morning the house vanished in a cloud of gulls that shrieked and battled for the garbage the deaf-mute threw to them from a window at the same time every day.

Rust-corroded iron shutters banged in the wind, a latticed gate unlatched with a screech and closed again – the deaf-mute woman knew nothing about the noise her house made. For her the arpeggios of decay were no more audible than Cotta's knocks at her door. He clanked the iron ring against its mounting again and again, until at last he recalled the weaver's disability and, offering no other signal, entered the unlocked house.

He found the old woman in a sunny, whitewashed room. She was bent over the unwoven warp threads of her loom, and with hands gnarled by gout she reached in among the threads as if they were harp strings, moving her lips and lifting her gaze now and then over the breastbeam and shafts of her loom to the sea below her open windows, to the ruffs of spray along the coast, to the line of surf as it lost itself soundlessly and white in the distant sheen. The thumping, rolling waves at her windows could easily have been the Aegean or the Adriatic. That restless deep blue out there matched the colour of the lagoons that Arachne wove into her tapestries, matched the colour of the waves that broke on the beautiful coasts near Rome.

A salty gust of wind perfumed with hibiscus and rosemary swept through the old woman's parlour, blowing the hair from her brow and slamming the door shut behind Cotta. A rufous cat, which had lain sleeping at Arachne's feet on a pile of paper patterns and yellowed magazines, was at the window with a bound and scurried out. The Roman's shadow fell on the weaver. With a start, she turned her gaze from the coast, looked with astonishment into her visitor's eyes, and read from them the embarrassment of an intruder caught in the act – and from his lips an apology, a greeting, a question. Would the weaver show him her tapestries?

How stooped and fragile Arachne had become, how thin her arms were. Cotta had not seen her since the morning when she had explained to the troubled crowd gathered at the jetty that the sulphurous yellow in the bay was the pollen of pine forests. With Echo's departure Arachne had lost the only voice she had ever had, and since then, there was no one left in the town of iron who could read her finger alphabet. People understood well enough if she came to Fama's store for salt or to Phineus's cellar demanding a bottle of alcohol to preserve walnuts in – but what the weaver was thinking, what she was feeling, that could be understood only in her tapestries now. Their colourful splendour and vitality awakened in many of Tomi's inhabitants a secret longing for foreign lands, because the beauty of these hangings, which could be had in exchange for a sheep, a couple of chickens or some wrought-iron kitchenware, was not to be compared with any garden or blossoming hillside of these shores.

The fact that no one ever came simply to look at tapestries made Arachne so suspicious that she was close to showing Cotta the door, when she suddenly remembered his face – the fellow came from Rome. He had arrived on the same boat that had brought the parcel of magazines from Milan for which she had waited eight long months. He had asked about the exile that day. From Rome! And so the weaver stood up and offered Cotta a chair. Hers was the only home in the town of iron where the Roman was not simply tolerated, but truly welcome.

With scurrying finger signals Arachne wrote in the air for her visitor about her longing for the marvels of the capital, for its grand avenues and palaces, which she knew only from her magazines and a foxed album of the city's sights that a sailor from the *Trivia* had given her years before. Cotta understood none of it, but thought he sensed what the old woman wanted to hear from him, and so spoke of Naso's fame, of his own journey to the Black Sea and praised the lovely view from her window. Arachne read his lips, storing in her memory whatever seemed part of Roman splendour and forgetting the rest, even as Cotta spoke of it.

She then eagerly led the Roman into a stuffy room kept totally dark by closed shutters. When she threw them open, the gulls outside set up an ear-shattering squall in expectation of being fed. The shadows of birds' wings shifted over the stone floor and all the junk with which the room was crammed full. Blinded by the sudden invasion of light, Cotta at first saw only furniture covered with sheets and blankets, rudders propped against one wall, empty wicker bottles, a tattered paravent – and only then, stacked in among boxes, chests and piles of paper, the rolled-up tapestries, some no wider than a hand towel, others so long they had had to be folded over, certainly too large ever to fit any wall in the town of iron. Most of them seemed to be rotting, saturated with the damp of unplastered walls and stained white with mildew.

There must have been thirty, forty or even more such rolls that Arachne carelessly stored here like so much decaying lumber. Echo alone would have been capable of understanding her explanation for this and of translating for the Roman how a tapestry was of value to the deaf-mute woman only as long as it was still growing, stretched on the frame of her loom's beams and shafts. Once completed, whatever landed in this mouldy room would be pulled out again only when a smelter or farmer wanting to decorate his sooty walls with a beautiful landscape gave her a sheep in trade, whereupon Arachne would simply cut the ropes binding its legs and let it run wild on the stony terraces of the cliffs.

While the weaver unrolled bolt after bolt of her work, while the dirty floor of the room and all the junk vanished under a slowly growing layer of paradisial worlds, Cotta began to understand that what was significant about these panoramas was not the earth or the sea, but the sky – on all the tapestries, the sky, empty, blue, puffed with clouds or hung with storms, but always *alive* – the sky, patterned by birds in flight and subdivided by their flocks.

Even on dry land or in the sea, everything that lived, crept, swam there, pursuing or fleeing, seemed to long for the grace of flight. High above the herds and packs, the many designs made by birds in flight were a token of liberation from every weight. If the sea was tossed by a storm, its lanes churned unnavigable, its coastline broken by ravines or overwhelmed by a springtide, then pink gulls, storm petrels and black terns swept above the whitecaps and reefs as if the force of the flood only heightened their own lust for lightness. Above black-green, trackless forests gyrfalcons and kites spiralled, shot out over ridges and crags – absurd barriers. And if a beast of prey was tearing its catch to pieces in a thorny thicket, larks hovered singing above the earth. No matter what abysses opened up below, the birds always soared above every obstruction and pitfall. Serene, weightless, they gave themselves over to whirlwinds, only suddenly to fling themselves out of such apparent subjugation and back onto the wind, plunging into the depths and ascending again, as if their flight were but an infinitely varied expression of their scorn for all things that must walk earthbound and erect.

In one of the last pictures that Arachne unrolled for him, however, Cotta discovered some hesitancy about the grandeur of flight – the depiction of a fall, a strange, almost menacing counterpart to the paradisial ecstasy of the flocks. It was a picture of a vast emptiness, woven in tones of blue, white and silver threads, a view onto a sea lying peacefully in the sun, a bright summer sky dotted with clouds, a gull or two above the gentle swells, but no coastline, no island, no ship.

In the far distance, just below the razor-edge of the horizon, Cotta saw two grey wings, their span as wide as a condor's, lifted straight up, helpless, disappearing into the water like the arms of a drowning man – but he saw no beak, no head. The jets of spray from the impact rose like white lances above the wings, and from overhead lost feathers, down, and delicate quills came drifting and tumbling, permitting a slower descent to the sea than the heavy body that had borne such pinions. There in the distance some great feathered thing had plunged into the waves, while dispassionate gulls hovered in the updraught, and the water, tapped by the hammer of a light breeze, reflected the sunlight back to the heavens.

Icarus – the name of the fallen creature sinking beneath the lustre – was one of the deaf-mute's many finger signs that Cotta saw as they flew up out of her hands, but did not understand.

Arachne did everything she could for her Roman guest and nodded to all the questions she read from his lips. Who had described for her these jungles and groves of palm trees, told her about species of birds that had never been seen along the shore of the town of iron? Had Pythagoras been telling the truth, had the weaver in fact spent afternoons at Naso's side on the balcony of stone? And the old woman did not once shake her head no, until Cotta asked her if the exile had ever talked to her about something other than the world of birds and the grace of flight, about crystals perhaps, about fossils and ores.

Never?

Never.

Suddenly the old woman had an urgent need to show the Roman proof of her hospitality. Without bothering any further with the tapestries, she gently shoved him out of the room, bolted the iron shutters again and sat him down in her parlour to walnut liqueur and pastries.

Confused and tipsy from the liqueur, Cotta left the house on the cliff, which had vanished in a cloud of gulls when he turned for one last look. Had Naso opened a different window into the realm of his imagination for each of his listeners, told each one only the stories that he or she had wanted to hear or was capable of hearing? Echo had testified to a Book of Stones, Arachne to a Book of Birds. The question he was now asking himself, Cotta wrote to Cyane in a deferential letter that would never reach the Via Anastasio, was whether the *Metamorphoses* had not been conceived from the very beginning as a great history of nature, ascending from the stones to the clouds.

August came – a glowing hot summer whose only adornment was the emperor's name. Under the sun of this month everything burned that was not as tough as cactus, thistle or tamarisk. In the noon hours the noise of the cicadas was so unbearable that the women of the town of iron stopped their children's ears with consecrated wax to protect them from the evil music they believed they heard in the chirping. Shimmering lizards came creeping out of the cracks in walls and rocks and licked the flies from the hot stones of the town. Snakes sunned themselves on the slate roofs.

While Thies the German was looking for aromatic plants for his tinctures, he discovered spiders the size of a man's fist in the ruins of a narrow street that had been uninhabited for decades. Their webs were so strong that not only cicadas perished in them, but weaverbirds as well, even fledgling yellowhammers.

The people of Tomi had never seen such vermin before, but their dismay did not last long. Wearied by the rapid changes in weather and the heat, they began to accustom themselves to these new plagues, just as they had to the prodigal vegetation and thunderstorms of their new climate. Only Tereus flew into a rage.

One day he crept on all fours, poker in hand, out onto the roof of his slaughterhouse to butcher the snakes, and a yowling pack of kids and the guests from Phineus's brandy cellar gathered in the neighbour's garden – his audience, who urged him on as they watched him up there and later followed at a careful distance when he ran through the spider-infested ruins with his poker and a torch, ripping down some of the webs heavy with cicadas and rotted birds and roasting the spiders on the flame. To the catcalls and applause of the mob, one of the brandy dealer's helpers dipped a finger in the dark viscous secretion burbling out of the spiders' bellies and used it to paint symbols on his cheeks and forehead.

There seemed to be nothing these days to which the town of iron, after a moment of horror or astonishment, could not accustom itself. Barely an hour would pass, and the town seemed to have grown indifferent to yet another phenomenon, however strange. But one event, which Tomi impatiently awaited and which meant more to both smelters and swineherds than all the enigmatic novelties of nature, failed to occur. They could set up as close a watch as they liked – no cloud of dust rose above the winding road along the coast. Cyparis the projectionist, who had come in August for so many years now, never appeared.

Their longing for the Lilliputian's shows was so great that one morning they found the slaughterhouse walls had been painted, covered with clumsy stick figures done in charcoal and coloured chalk – the scribbled memories of the dwarf's last films: flaming helmet plumes, horses' maines, sails, banners, lances.

Tereus hung a wreath of sausages around the neck of the grocer's son to get the epileptic to whitewash over the graffiti. Which he did.

Cotta made it his habit every evening to search his garret at the ropemaker's for scorpions. Ever since one restless night when he had turned on the light and seen a huge insect crawling into a crack in the wall by the window recess, he no longer went to bed without first shining a light in every chink and beating every crease in the tapestries with a whisk broom. When he finally did fall asleep, he often dreamed of stings, bites, wounds – the many weapons of subtropical fauna.

During the day he strolled along the shore until the heat forced him back under the shade of the cliffs, waited for the cool of evening in the Bay of Balustrades along with the other idlers of the town of iron or sat in Arachne's parlour, following the almost indiscernible growth of a bird-filled sky on her loom. At night he wrote letters to Rome, to his family, to Cyane. He would wait here in Tomi for Naso to return from the mountains. He compared the deep-gouged bays of the Black Sea with the rocky shores of Sicily and the thorny hedges of its valleys with the groves of Rome. . . . Whatever he wrote, he would seal it and take the envelope to Fama's store the next morning, stick it in the postbag that lay ready for the next docking of the *Trivia*, adding it to its collection of letter upon mildewing letter.

Like every other inhabitant of the coast, Cotta sensed a great, overpowering weariness in everything he did. The August heat had settled on Tomi like a nightmare from which no one could escape, weighing even upon the animals, slowing the motion of every living thing. Many smelters let the fires in their furnaces go out and now spent their mornings getting drunk in the brandy cellar, where Phineus iced down his rotgut. Others dozed under awnings in the Bay of Balustrades and did not return home for days on end. During the hours of the afternoon, all that could be heard in town was the sound of cicadas – no voices, no hammers. The squares lay dusty and deserted in the white light.

It was on one of these blazing-hot, stagnant afternoons when the cry of *a ship*! wrenched Tomi out of its lethargy. *A ship*! But it was not the long-awaited *Trivia*. The frigate that slipped out of the glare of the sea into the shadow of the mountains flew the flag of Greece. It had not been seen on this coast for years. Its red sails hung like bloody battle robes from the yard-arms and gaffs. A wedge of smoke from the stack of its auxiliary engine ascended into the calm as it manoeuvred to dock – and was still lying over the bay long after the ship was moored to the jetty.

Whoever had legs to walk now joined the crowd running down to the sea. As if to spur one another to greater haste as they ran, people called out the name that shone in weathered golden letters on the bow of the frigate, a name as likely to elicit mistrust and bitterness as hopeful anticipation in the towns along the Black Sea coast – *Argo*! It had sailed out of the Bay of Tomi many years before, had long been considered lost – but the *Argo* had returned.

Like everyone else, Cotta hurried through the streets to the jetty and now saw Lycaon sitting on the steps of the harbour-master's office. From the ropemaker he learned that this frigate was the boat of a Thessalonian navigator who called himself Jason. Even with its sails reefed, the obsolete three-masted battleship, re-rigged now for service as a freighter, had an eerie look to it. Black armoured bulwarks recalled its earlier vocation, as did the gun-deck portholes ornamented with iron dragon heads and a burning steering-wheel painted on the smokestack. But it was the deep red of its sails that had made the *Argo* as notorious as it was unmistakable. For Jason those sails commemorated long-forgotten battles at sea and all the blood that had thickened the water beneath his ship's keel.

Following no schedule, the frigate vanished and appeared quite unpredictably in the harbours of the Black Sea coast, often leaving confusion, arguments and rancour behind. For the Thessalonian carried more with him than simple merchandise to be traded for bars of iron, pelts and amber. He also had on board a permanent gang of emigrants: unemployed labourers, impoverished farmers, the inhabitants of the ghettoes of Thessalonica, Volos and Athens. . . . To all of them Jason promised a golden future on the Black Sea and relieved them of their last penny for a stifling berth below deck on the *Argo*.

Once they reached the dilapidated piers of Odessa and Constanta, the fire-gutted docks at Sevastopol or some other desolate stretch of coast, Jason's passengers recognised the futility of their hopes. By then, however, they lacked the money and the energy to return to Greece. And so they left the ship to seek the shadow of their fortune among the ruins of bleak towns.

From Constanta to Sevastopol, the Greek emigrants were loathed as *dragon's teeth* sown by Jason. They disturbed the peace of backwaters, holing up in caves and pits and raking the gravelly beaches for mother-of-pearl and amber. Hunger often drove them to steal from the locals. They dragged off and slaughtered even the mules, then fled from the wrath of those they had robbed, ever deeper into the mountains or the wastes of the Crimean peninsula, turned savage, led the lives of stone-age men.

People cursed Jason the Thessalonian for this human freight he had snared, just as they revered him for the magic of his wares, for the news and novelties he brought with him, the reflected splendour of great distant cities beyond their reach, all of which he spread out on board his ship and offered for sale or barter.

This time, too, the hostile and greedy smelters, farmers and fishermen of Tomi crowded up the gangway onto the deck of the *Argo*, while Jason stood at the helm and cried his wares through a bullhorn – muslin, spices, music boxes, all the wonders of his cargo. And this time too, wretched men stood at the railing of the quarterdeck, beckoning to the customers thronging on board and besieging them with questions about the wealth and delights of Odessa, to which no one had an answer. As if gazing at an omen of their own future misery, other emigrants stared silently at the high menacing cliffs shimmering in the heat, at the ruins of the town, which seemed to have merged with the mountains. But in most of those faces there was only relief that this desolate spot was not the promised destination, that Odessa and all their hopes and future still lay hidden below the horizon and that the *Argo* would soon carry them away from this wilderness of ravines.

Between shouts in praise of his wares, Jason still found breath enough to bellow over their heads the latest from the civilised world, including such stale items as the death and deification of the emperor, but he concluded with sensational news – met with incredulous amazement – that for a colossal carnival parade last spring, the successor to such omnipotence had had fifteen battleships of the Roman navy drawn overland! from the Tyrrhenian Sea to Rome, rolling them in cradles down the grand avenues of the capital under full sail, thus demonstrating that every bearer of the name Augustus could turn even the stones of the earth into a sea and the sea into a mirror of his triumph.

The *Argo* spent only a few hours in the harbour of the town of iron before Jason set sail again for Odessa, but the effect on lethargic Tomi was at least as intense and enduring as that caused by the arrival of the projectionist, a festival or a storm. All fatigue and exhaustion seemed vanquished. Shouting and running filled the narrow streets. Every man a pillager, they stormed their own houses, snatching up anything that might be of value, and dragged it aboard the *Argo* to sell or trade. Smelters and blacksmiths gasped their way up the gangplank in such haste and so weighed down with iron, that many of them were still feeling woozy as they bartered. Although most of them left the frigate under a load hardly any lighter, with every hour the *Argo* sank lower into the water beneath the weight of rusty bars, gratings, rails and crossbeams.

The weight came, it seemed, not from the metal, but from the satisfaction that the fruit of their labour, stored for months and years in smithies and sooty sheds, had finally served some purpose, been unloaded and put to further use, the satisfaction that their torment at furnaces and in the darkness of the mines had at last been given a meaning by trading it away: iron for silk and muslin, iron for aromatic oils, sugar-loaves and pain powders, iron for news of an elegant and mad world.

When at last the cool of evening let the traders breathe somewhat more easily, the jetty seemed a market of shadows. The colours of all the lovely things gradually faded, leaving behind motion and shouts. A sea made of silver lay in the dusk.

Torches flared here and there in the long procession of bearers, mules and carts creeping from the harbour into the black streets of town and returning again and again to the jetty. The inhabitants of Tomi were so busy transporting their newly acquired goods that hardly anyone noticed Jason's command readying the *Argo* for sail. The Thessalonian preferred to spend nights on the open sea rather than in the risky harbours of a coast where the greed for ship-borne riches was great.

As the lines slapped the water and Jason set his sails and got up a head of steam, people threw sacks of bread and jerky up to the ship, relieved that none of the Greek emigrants had disembarked to remain in Tomi. Under a cloud of smoke that eclipsed the moon, and strung with garlands of light, the *Argo* slipped into the darkness.

It was late that night that Tomi quietened down. Load after load was dragged from the jetty into the stone houses, where everything was once again touched, checked and admired. But out of all the diverse merchandise, both useful and frivolous, that Jason had left behind in exchange for the smelters' iron and amber – one item alone of all the loads carried that night would so transform life in Tomi that ultimately it seemed the sole purpose of the Thessalonian's trip had been to bring its small burden to the town of iron.

It was a black wooden crate, which was now tied to Fama's mule, something the grocer had ordered years ago and then forgotten, a machine made of metal, glass, light bulbs and mirrors capable of casting a glowing, magnified copy of anything laid under its polished eye onto the nearest white wall – yellowed photos, scraps of newspaper, even a hand held out nervously . . . anything.

Fama called this wonderwork an *episcope*. True, its pictures did not move like those of the projectionist, but it could take the most worthless things of life and transfigure them, lending them such beauty that they became precious and unique. If one gazed long enough at the reflections on the wall, one saw the inner life of things become visible – a flickering, a pulsing and fluttering that made the motions of the outside world seem clumsy and trivial in comparison.

What did it matter if the brandy dealer claimed the images flickered that way simply because the generator was not running true as it pounded and hammered in a cellar closet to produce electricity for the grocery's lights and cooling coils. . . . Objections like that did not bother the audience, which grew larger every time the projector was set up in Fama's backroom.

When a swineherd spread the rumour that the festering wound on his hand had healed within hours after he had shown it to the machine, most visitors brought pocketbooks and sacks full of items they wanted laid under the eye of the episcope and projected on the wall: wrought-iron or clay replicas of ailing limbs and hearts, photos of miners who had become ill from working the tunnels, dowsing rods for fnding new veins of iron, bristles and claws of infertile livestock or lists of wishes scribbled full with longings, letters to nowhere.

Fama was happy to indulge the curious and superstitious crowd. To be sure, she demanded no entrance fee from her visitors, but along the path to the backroom she very cleverly set out the oldest and most rancid items she had in stock, so that hardly anyone left her store without having bought at least a can of vegetable oil, a bag of walnuts or a dusty box of pralines.

Within a few weeks the backroom of her grocery – a cool, dark storage space at the far end of rows of shelves, lockers, vats and stacked crates – became a grotto shrine. Rows of candles and tallow dips burned along the walls; several shelves whose wares had been sold off were used for the bouquets and lockets placed there in remembrance of some comfort received, a pain eased, a desire fulfilled. The generator never stopped hammering at night now. At dawn or in the small hours of night – whenever a visitor entered Fama's store, a magic blue light fell through the door opening onto the grotto, the reflection of ecstasy.

When their business with Jason proved that even the low-grade iron of Tomi still had some trade value, several smelters rekindled the fires of their furnaces, and some of the idlers left the Bay of Balustrades to return to the dark perspectives of the mines. Others, however, fell under the spell of the grotto's miracles and apparitions. Before the arrival of the *Argo*, they had languished in the August heat, but now they sat enthralled by the train of strange images in Fama's back-room, numbing themselves on Phineus's rotgut as they watched and forever dragging in new materials for putting the machine's miraculous powers to the test. Even when the desired effects failed to appear and the stench from the diesel and the rapid fluctuation of garish light and darkness made their eyes water, the sheer expectancy of it all – the various sufferings and longings gathered there – ensured an atmosphere in which something beyond their understanding seemed possible at any second.

Of them all, however, it was Fama's son who was ensnared the worst by the projector's spell. Under Fama's guidance, he had become so familiar with the gadgetry of the projector – he kept its reflectors free of dust, was handy at changing bulbs – that in the end Fama left the episcope's operation entirely to him. For the first time in his life, the epileptic lad learned what it meant to be a part of the human race. For the first time, people crowded around *him*, stretched out their arms for him to take whatever they wanted placed under the machine's eye, bribing him with small change and sweets to keep an image shining on the wall for as long as hope for a miracle demanded it. Battus grasped their hands, arms, presents, squealed and babbled in delight.

For two days and nights he was in absolute control of the machine, and when the grocer tried to get him to go to bed he set up a howl, resisted her with such force, that she ended up laying a mattress down for him under the table where the episcope stood, even brought his meals to him in the grotto the next day, because nothing could bring him to part from his machine. She finally gave up trying to get her teenage son back out into the fresh air or even behind the grocery counter.

Battus never left the grotto now. He took care of nature's call in a nook of the room, behind a folding screen in which he had torn a hole so as not to lose sight of a single image even while squatting there over a tin pail. If he was alone in the grotto or the other image addicts were so drunk or exhausted that they had no further wishes, he would use the machine for some choice items from his own collection, things he had found back when he rummaged the town of iron's garbage dumps for bits of coloured glass, buttons or dried mice still in their traps. Sometimes he would sink into a light, restless sleep, from which he would start up the moment anyone tried so much as to touch his episcope. He spent all of August and the first days of September like this, never seeing any light other than the glow of tungsten filaments, and he held on stolidly even as his audience, the believers in miracles, gradually strayed off and the town of iron began to forget its holy shrine.

As candles and tallow dips burned low, went out and were not replaced, as the grotto slowly reverted into a storage room and lost its radiance, the epileptic boy sat watching the world's objects appear and disappear on the wall, apparently as enslaved to his unquenchable need for endlessly new disembodied images of light as he was to the violent force that sometimes seized him, shook him, threw him to the floor and made saliva foam from his mouth.

After weeks of heat, the drought eased only by dew, the first rain of autumn came rushing down one September night – a warm, heavy rain that was sucked up by the thin soil of the terraces, until the cracked, infertile crust was sated and turned into mud that slid from the walled nests of gardens and fields and crept down to the sea.

That night Fama suddenly started up in fright from her sleep – it was quiet. She could hear the ring of silence. From outside came the rush of rain, but her house was as silent as the inside of a mountain. The hammering and pounding of the generator had stopped. The grocer got up, threw a shawl over her shoulders and hurried down the stairs to her shop. The door to the backroom stood open. Except for an almost imperceptible soft glow, there was no light. As Fama entered the darkness scented with tallow and candlewax, she saw her son crouching motionless as usual beside the machine, beside that cold, black piece of iron. A grey light, or so it seemed, still glimmered on Battus's face and hands, the reflection of vanished images, scarcely brighter than the pale blur of a rock in the darkness.

Fama screamed – because even before she gently brushed her son's brow in terror, she knew that the poor disturbed creature, whose birth and life were agony to her, had turned to stone.

It took five men, roustabouts as strong as the butcher, to move Battus from the backroom into the store. The wheel on their barrow broke under the weight, so they had to carry him like some bagged animal in a sling of leather belts and twine. Their panting breath and their faces flushed with exertion made the stone look even paler and colder.

All attempts to bring the epileptic back to pliant life were in vain. To comfort the wailing grocer with some glimmer of hope, Thies the German rubbed the rigid figure with salves and aromatic extracts. At the suggestion of a herdsman, Tereus poured pig's blood over the stone, and a well-meaning neighbour wanted to start up the generator so that they could once again bathe the transformed boy in the redemptive light of the projector.

But while the neighbour was kneeling in the cellar closet, tugging and yanking on the drive belt, Fama flew into such a desperate rage that she began to bang away at the episcope with a hammer, cursing Jason and the *Argo*. Then she ran to Arachne's cliff and hurled a sack of smashed metal and glass into the waves.

And so in the end, Battus, a stone among stones along this coast, stood in the shop amid kraut kegs, scythe handles and bonbon glasses. Black with congealed pig's blood and shiny with the German's salves, he intruded into the world of the living like an idol smeared with sacrifices.

When Fama had given up the last hope that the stone could ever be awakened to life again, she closed her shop for seven days of mourning, opening neither to the shouts of customers nor to the worried knocks of women who came to console her. She cleared the backroom, scrubbed the stone floor with vinegar-water and ashes – the customary cleansing in rooms where people died – and then nailed the door shut with oak pegs. At night people could hear her through her closed shutters, praying. At the feet of the petrified boy, she placed candles in a semicircle, lights that were to burn day and night from then on, and adorned him with crêpe, floral wreaths and finally with a garland of the fresh, stinging nettles that grew among the elderberry bushes in her yard. Battus, who his whole life long had had to grab, to touch everything to assure himself that it really existed, forever burning his fingers on nettle garlands like this one, was himself now protected from all obtrusive curiosity.

On the morning of the eighth day, Fama pushed her sliding shutters up, unveiling to the town of iron her monument to her son. At first the inhabitants of the coast approached the petrified boy in disbelief or fear, some even on their knees, but then with growing nonchalance – once no further misfortune or miracles occurred – until finally a farmer from the plateau near Limyra tore off the nettle garland and convinced himself with his burning bare hands that the grocer's son had solidified into ordinary limestone. Stupid gravel! he shouted in the brandy cellar afterward, there was more than enough stupid gravel in the waste dumps. What was supposed to be so grand about a human being meeting his end by turning to stone in a gloomy grocery store instead of to dust in a dark grave?

And so the epileptic's fate gradually receded into the workaday world, into the pallor of memory, became a legend and then was forgotten, like the fate of everyone destined or condemned to live out his or her life along the coast of the Black Sea. So what if a grey statue stood there among the kegs and crates, if the flames from a wreath of candles shone into the draughty depths of the grocery store like golden-red arrows pointing to an indelible memory – to the customers Battus's statue was nothing more than a heavy piece of inventory in their way, as much a part of the store as the iron clothes-horse beside the door, where on some days now long coats wet with rain hung on the hooks. In the little dirty puddles that formed under the coats, Battus's reflection appeared, a quivering face, distorted by the fall of each delicate drop, as if with the rain life itself had returned to the epileptic's crumbling features.

The period of drought was over. To be sure, the autumn was mild, sunny, even hot – something summers in the past had seldom been – but rain was falling again now, in thunderstorms at night, in quickly passing showers, and in such abundance that the parched colours of the coast gradually began to merge as a deep, dark green. Even the ravines and slopes lay under what looked like drifts of green shadow. Moss blossomed on the rocks and roofs of Tomi. The snakes and spiders vanished.

Cotta spent the first weeks of autumn in seclusion at the ropemaker's, so secluded, in fact, that not a word was wasted on his presence around the tables in Phineus's cellar. For weeks now, his garret had looked like the messy lodgings of some smelter.

Since Echo's disappearance the signs of neglect became more apparent at the ropemaker's with each passing day. No one bothered now with the ivy and weeds growing in the crevices of the walls, the roots clawing and tearing gaping cracks to make way for organic life inside the stones. If a shutter stood open and banged in the wind, it banged until it broke from its hinges or the wind abated. In the halls and storage rooms, the dust from the drought mixed with the sand trickling from the walls to form soil that grew fertile in the moist air and sprouted pale green blades of grass on the chests, planks and boxes. One room upstairs was made uninhabitable by a swarm of hornets that hung the menacing lantern of their nest between the beams of the ceiling. It did not matter to the ropemaker. Foot by foot, he abandoned his house to nature's resolute advance.

On many nights Cotta heard Lycaon leave the house, and next morning he would see him return from the slopes exhausted and bruised. But until the day the epileptic turned to stone, wrenching Cotta from his lethargy, he would have dismissed these nocturnal excursions as the quirk of an ageing eccentric, even if Lycaon had once again run off into the mountains wearing the moth-eaten wolf's costume from his safe, a howling carnival fool. . . .

Like many fugitives of the state who conformed to the language and customs and, in time, even to the mind-set of the subjugated, barbaric societies in which they sought refuge from merciless Rome, Cotta, too, had so completely adapted himself to life in the town of iron that he was hardly distinguishable from its inhabitants now. He dressed as they did, imitated their dialect, and sometimes even managed to accept the incredible enigmas of these shores with the lazy indifference of a native. He wrote no more letters to Rome. It took Battus's turning to stone, however, to demonstrate to him that the place he occupied was neither in the town of iron nor the eternal city, but rather that he had stumbled into some middle world, where the laws of logic no longer seemed valid, but where there were apparently no other laws either – to sustain him and keep him from going mad. Battus intruded not only into the world of the living, but also impalpably into Rome's world of rationality – clear reason that found expression in every palace of the capital, in every rank of soldiers in battle, but which in Fama's grocery store was nothing but a collection of empty sentences and phrases.

These days, when he slept or simply dozed off for a few minutes, Cotta was tormented by dreams from the *Book of Stones*. Characters and phantoms from Echo's retelling of the stories Naso had read to her from the flames pursued him and would not let him go. He heard Echo's voice speaking to him from the darkness, about a paradise of ravines and slopes, about the tawdry pomp of organic life – a meteor that blazed and faded – about the incorruptible dignity of stone. . . . Megalithic structures grew up around him, halls that reverberated with the gentle voice of the vanished woman. Their architecture rose ever higher and vaster, until the sky above him was only a chaos of pale streaks and he realised that the walls of the labyrinthine building closing in around him were made of blocks and masses of petrified heads, arms and legs, of the stiff bodies of the people he had known, loved or feared in his life. But when he awoke from this labyrinth, he could not escape the tight embrace in which it held him fast – there in Fama's store stood Battus, grey and cold, a dire warning, decked out in lavender and saxifrage, that the border between reality and dream was perhaps lost forever.

Sometimes Cotta would give the ropemaker a furtive once-over as the old man emerged from his workshop. What a relief to find Lycaon as taciturn and sullen as ever, and without the least sign of bristles, fangs and claws – just a stooped, grey-haired man on his way to the well to wash his face and hands.

For the ropemaker, Battus's turning to stone was nothing more than a rare case of some disease he had picked up, some incurable form of lockjaw the epileptic had caught from that rabble aboard the *Argo* or while rummaging through trash on the beach, not worth talking about and perhaps the best thing that could happen to the fool, since he was finally free of the agonies of epilepsy. Lycaon had no desire either to see or touch the petrified grocer's son, he had seen enough stone in his life. . . . Lycaon was the same as always.

One moonlit night as Cotta lay awake and thought he heard a wolf howling high up the slopes, he could not bring himself to check the workshop. Maybe the old man's bed was empty. He did not calm down until the howling was lost in a deep thunderous rumble, the distant noise of sliding rocks or mud that was audible in Tomi sometimes by day as well as now. The soil on the steep slopes, saturated by autumn rain, loosed itself from its rocky bed, and riven with channels and brooks, plunged downward, covering upland valleys in a new layer of silt that smelled of the resin of shattered trees, of the fresh blood of wild animals, of moss and earth. The soil began to turn green again and blossom.

Two shepherds and most of their herd had been killed in a gorge by one of these avalanches. Thies discovered the accident when panicked sheep, smeared with blood and muck, stampeded towards him along a mule track. Thies fetched miners and amber-hunters to help him unearth the crushed bodies and bury them under little domes of stone there on the broad ridge of the slide. The sheep carcasses were brought back to the town of iron on mules and roasted for the funeral meal over two large fires out on the mole. What could not be fitted on grills and skewers Tereus pickled or smoked.

These days, when Cotta could no longer stand his narrow garret and walked the streets of the town of iron, gazing up at the ravines and cloud-hung peaks, it sometimes seemed to him as if the source of all his dreams and fears, both past and present, lay somewhere deep in those rumbling mountains. And what lay deepest within them was named Trachila. Since the horrors of carnival he had avoided the slopes of Trachila, always finding new excuses for not searching out the exile again in his last dangerous, inaccessible refuge. But whatever secrets still might lie hidden up there among the collapsed doorways, vacant-eyed windows and overgrown foundations – they could not be stranger or more upsetting than the statue in Fama's store.

One October morning radiant after a night's rain, when the last towers of a cloudbank were crumbling at the rim of a sea-blue sky and the air was scented with wet foliage, Cotta left the ropemaker's house convinced that only one person could keep him from going mad and lead him out of his confusion and back to the compact clarity of Roman reason: Naso.

Surely the mysteries of this coast had caused the exile the same torments – which meant that over the years of exile Naso must have had just that much more experience dealing with those mysteries and solving them. Whatever his reasons for beginning his search for the poet and the charred masterpiece – whether as an enterprise of ambition, adventure or boredom – on that October morning Cotta was forced to recognise that he now had no other choice: he *must* find the exile.

And so he headed into the mountains, under the gaze of a sleepy cow that lay on some straw in a terraced field, chewing its cud and staring after him until he had vanished. Of all the many paths his imagination had rifled through in the file of possibilities when he was still aboard the *Trivia*, only one remained to him now: the path to Trachila.

The landslides had not spared a single upland valley. Like primaeval monsters clad in uprooted pines and heather, flows of gravel and mud had come down out of the cloud-hung heights, creeping over meadows, deserted huts and the entrances to abandoned mine shafts.

Steep slopes that had cast aside their vegetation like a mummer's costume and were left lying as barren bluffs below the ridges; abysses, where sheep once grazed; dry brook beds filled with dirt instead of water, which now flowed around the slides and leapt in muddy, erratic cascades toward the sea coast – the higher Cotta climbed, the worse the devastation. The mountains, which he thought he knew well by now, had been transformed into a strange wilderness that constantly forced him to make arduous detours around new barriers, entangled him in painful tussles with thorny underbrush and lacerated his hands with knives of splintered stone.

Cotta – a wanderer, a reptile, an insect, a dark moving point losing its way in chaos, vanishing for minutes on end in ravines and craters, re-emerging, climbing higher, disappearing and returning. But no matter how baffling the path he took, Cotta's companions, carrion birds circling high above him, seemed to know where he was at every moment of the climb. They drifted in easy loops above his exertions – griffon vultures, the same kind that flocked in the wake of a thundering avalanche, gliding above the scene of the catastrophe and waiting for silence in the depths below, for the water to run off or the dust cloud to move on and reveal a carcass.

When Cotta stopped to wipe the sweat from his brow and looked up at his companions, he screamed curses at them, but his words died away far below them. If they sailed around a pinnacle, rustling as they settled upon it, he threw stones at them. Watchful and impassive, the scavengers followed each movement the bruised wanderer made. His stones fell wide of their mark with a soft plop.

One of the miners who helped Thies unearth the bodies of the two shepherds from the mudslide and bury them had told his tale in Phineus's cellar – how when they found the poor fellows, one of the victims had had no eyes, no face, but that you could still feel a bit of warmth in the arms and legs. Wedged in among the fallen rocks, battered, unable to use his broken limbs to defend himself against the hunger and incredible strength of the birds, the shepherd had probably still been alive as they pecked his eyes out of his head. Always took the tenderest, softest parts first.

After five hours of climbing, Cotta had wandered far off the obstructed path that had led him to Trachila months before. He could only surmise his goal now from the position of the sun. When a pain in his shoulder began to make throwing stones at the vultures difficult, he noticed that even without his threats they came no nearer. They finally began to mount higher and higher, until they spotted some other prey in the distance. Often hidden by scudding tatters of clouds, they began to circle above one particular ridge, closing their loops ever tighter, and Cotta thought it was not just some random spot above which the scavengers were hovering, but Trachila. From the course of the birds' flight he realised just how lost he was. A labyrinth of ravines, valleys and gorges separated him from Naso's final refuge. And so he entered the labyrinth.

By afternoon the sky contained neither clouds nor birds. Cotta approached the ruins of Trachila by working his way up through one flank of a mountain, which brought him to a plateau gashed with the weathered remains of a mining operation. The mouths of mine shafts yawned from the cliffs above him, at the foot of a waste-dump stood the frame of a conveyor belt overgrown with brambles, up-ended tipcarts lay beside a section of railway track that ended in a shallow pond – and in the rubble, gondola cars for transporting ore still stood in a row along their snapped cable. . . . Cotta was standing among the remains of a copper mine that once belonged to the ghost town of Limyra. The town's fate was still remembered only too well in Tomi and its story still told, because, they said, *all* mining towns would end that way some day.

Over the centuries Limyra's miners had hollowed out a chain of mountains, exhausted every vein of ore and then dug their tunnels away from the mountain town, further and further toward the coast, until they reached rock as barren as gravel and Limyra found itself sucked into ruin. Prosperity vanished along with the copper, and with prosperity, peace.

When all the granaries had been emptied and all the livestock slaughtered, the remaining inhabitants began to attack one another and fight for crusts of bread – until one August night the flank of a mountain carved with endless layers of tunnels collapsed, burying the almost deserted town beneath it. Above the mountains hung a huge golden-red dust cloud, which was finally parted the next day by winds from the south and then crept away toward the sea like a multifingered weather front.

A rust-eaten bus sometimes followed an ancient road hewn in the rocks and mounted the pass to the rubble-heaps of Limyra, bringing with it a horde of copper-hunters. In the course of the trip the bus became a rumbling archive of all knowledge about the ghost town. As the diggers sat there on the benches of the bus shouting above the roar of the motor to exchange their experiences, as they excavated mine shafts with shovels and picks, grubbing for bronze pots, jewellery and weapons, for copper cables and tools, and as they returned at last to the coast in the overloaded vehicle – during those days and hours, Limyra arose once more.

It was as if the copper-hunters drove their shafts not simply into the rubble of a catastrophe, but into time itself. Every patinaed clasp recalled women who should have worn such jewellery to the grave and for all eternity. The blood of forgotten battles dripped from jagged blades, blackened with decay, that were once daggers and axes. The meat of extinct animals was still stewing in pots without bottoms. The past rose like smoke from every shaft.

The copper-hunters opened graves as dispassionately as they cleared debris from sheepfolds or the bedroom of a citizen surprised in his sleep by a rockslide. Whether buried by the avalanche or by human hands long before the catastrophe, *everything* was brought into the light of day, because no matter how many uses the items may have once had in the world of Limyra, they were now important for only one thing: the value of the copper. Cables, statuettes, bracelets, amulets to protect miners from accidents lurking deep in the earth – there in the debris of the excavated town, the diggers melted down everything they found into flat bars that banged together at each pothole on the trip back, a sound like the rumble of rolling stones.

Cotta had heard about these expeditions from Phineus, or mention was made of them in Fama's store, but he had never actually seen the battered vehicle, which belonged to a mechanic from Constanta. The bus appeared in the town of iron only once a year, in the weeks between the dog days of summer and the first storms of autumn, and by then it was usually filled with loudmouthed passengers. Before every trip to Limyra the mechanic drove along the coast of the Black Sea through every village and back-country farm he could get to, until he had sold the last seat on his bus. This year, however, the people of Tomi had waited for him in vain.

Cotta cooled his bruised hands and sore feet in the turquoise water of the pond, waded out along the submerged tracks up to his knees and then sat down in exhaustion, leaning against one of the overturned lorries and staring into the depths below, staring up across the ridges to the sky, whose light was slowly fading now. He would not reach Trachila – or Tomi – before nightfall.

As he hovered between the imperial, indisputable reality of Rome and the incomprehensible mysteries of the town of iron, nothing seemed more frightening to him than spending a night alone in these mountains, but he resigned himself to it at last and began to prepare for the ordeal, unlaced his pack, built a windbreak of stones and rubble across the entrance to a caved-in mine, gathered brush for a fire and opened two rusty tin cans from

Fama's store with a mallet. He could find neither a can opener nor a knife in his pack. With hands dripping olive oil, he ate soggy fish, canned corn and bread.

The sun set. A blue, velvety darkness rose from the sea, robbing things of their colour, chasing the animals of the day into caves, dens or the crowns of trees where they slept, and luring those of the night out of the shelter of their hiding places. But whatever moved now through the deep dusk, it scurried, crept, and flew so cautiously and softly that Cotta sensed only peaceful silence around him.

Wrapping himself in a blanket, he lay down on the sandy ground inside the black maw of the mine shaft, which only a few yards behind him was blocked by boulders and splintered shoring. He lay unmolested in the night, below him the wide, flat sea and the invisible coastline, and he had the feeling that his shoulders, his back, his whole body was clinging to the vault of some vast room and that he was no longer looking *up* at the stars, but down into bottomless deeps filled with billions of hovering sparks.

Nothing disturbed Cotta's rest that night. Until dawn he lay snoring in the mine entrance, through which the breath of the mountain sometimes brushed past him, its musty draught impeded by the cave-in. Watched over by summer dreams – which he was never to recall – he did not see the moon rise or set, nor hear the howls that rose from a ravine under the moon and then fell silent only when its light died.

Here in the middle of the last of the exhausted mines of Limyra, Cotta was protected by his dreams; he was as safe here as if he were in the gardens of Sulmona, where the enclosing stone walls, stairways and marble statues gave back the sun's warmth each night. He heard chinking glasses, the conversations and laughter of small garden parties coming from terraces enveloped in clouds of blossoming bougainvillaea, gentle sounds that lost themselves in the olive and orange groves. Here in the vast stony wasteland of the Black Sea coast he was a larva embedded in sand, moss and linden-green lichens, waiting to awaken. He woke shortly before dawn. His first thought was of Naso, who – he was sure – slept night after night like this in these mountains, a Roman who had exchanged not only the columned halls of the empire, but also the stone roof of his last refuge for this open sky. He no longer feared the wilderness.

The tumbledown copper mine was hours behind him by the time the October sun rose above the ridges, bathing the lifeless stony wastes above the timberline in implacable light. He moved persistently toward his goal, as if this one night had given him years of experience with the mountains. This morning, too, the vultures were circling again above the cliffs beneath whose shadow Trachila must lie.

In the face of Cotta's determination obstacles lost their power. He moved ahead so steadily that it came as a shock when at noon he encountered the first token of Trachila – the smashed statue of a dog that had blocked his way once before. He had reached Naso's last home – and yet, there was hardly a ditch that matched his memory of the landscape. The cliffs rose up so white and shiny against the weathered grey of the mountains, like some newly opened quarry. Where once there had been ridges worn down by erosion, there was now a maze of gaping black crevices, and immense boulders lay in the midst of scree draped across the slopes like the canvas of tents.

As Cotta surmounted the last rise still separating him from the ruins of Trachila, the vultures moved in on him, so close that he could hear the rush of their wings, but no cries. They cast their silent spell in circle after circle above Naso's refuge. And then, among the splintered branches of a battered pine tree, Cotta saw the prey they had divided among them with their hatchet beaks. There it lay – eyes gone, flanks ripped open, hide hacked, gutted and covered with iridescent swarms of flies – the carcass of a wolf.

Trachila lay beneath stones. Fleeing the hostility of the town of iron, Rome's poet had sought seclusion in this brutal place, but not even ruins could endure here.

The hamlet's crumbling walls, the exile's house, the well – almost anything that served as a reminder of human presence – had been crushed or swept away by an avalanche. A path littered with debris pointed back up to a bulwark of cliffs and overhangs. The avalanche must have come from those walls up there – a storm of stones raging down into Trachila and on through Trachila. The path disappeared into the blue depths of a ravine. There was hardly a fragment of wall or foundation that had withstood its force. Half a gateway arch stuck up above the rubble like the arm of a drowning man. Cotta saw what remained of the overgrown thicket of brambles and ferns under the shadow of a huge boulder wedged in the gorge at the entrance to Naso's garden. The thicket still concealed the menhirs, now free from their coating of slugs. The mulberry tree was untouched as well, hung with a profusion of blue-black fruits.

Suddenly overwhelmed by a sense of hopeless abandonment, Cotta moved past the wolf's carcass and towards the archway. Swarms of flies rose up from the blood-caked hide, an iridescent burst of buzzing hailstones. He threw his hands to his face, running through this horrible shower with a cry of disgust. But only the vultures retreated to greater heights before his cry. Deaf and blind to some Roman's despair, the flies fell back out of the sweep of upward motion, pattering down onto the carcass to suckle in the sweet putrefaction.

A bright, metallic sheen lay over the rubble of Trachila. For a moment Cotta thought this shimmer was the afterglow from the swarms of flies – as if with their buzzing ebb and flow they had shed the silk of their wings and left it behind in the autumn air as drifting, glistening flecks of light. But upon reaching the spot where the exile's house had stood, he realised that the glitter all came from the rubble in the avalanche's path, a wintry sparkle that lent the same hue to the ruptured cliffs above him. In some places where the slide had carried off the mountain's rock, the sheen was tinged with black, dulled by oxidation, but in other spots it was bright and radiant – like the carafes, silverware and vases in the vitrines on the Piazza del Moro, when on lovely afternoons sunlight fell through treetops and open windows onto the glass cabinets of the salons.

Ore. The rocky debris that had buried the ruins of Trachila or carried them away beneath it was galena and silver ore – a terrifying wave of riches scouring all life from the slopes on its way to the depths below: stunted firs, scabs of grass, wolves and their prey. . . .

But at least one resident of Trachila must have survived the catastrophe, because dozens of cairns still lined the path of the avalanche, were perched atop boulders waving tattered rags or lay among shattered trunks of trees fragrant with resin. Some of them, protected by erratic blocks, had escaped the slide unscathed. Most of them, however, had been erected from the debris of the disaster and placed like emblems of triumph along the crests of petrified rivers of rubble.

Still dazed by the sight of Trachila, Cotta noticed thin wisps of smoke drifting from the shadows of a ravine, and suddenly came wide awake. Barely fifty steps away, in the cleft of a rock, smoke was rising from the cast-iron stove in the exile's house. Pythagoras was squatting beside the open door. Across his knees he had spread an unruly blue cloth. He seemed to be writing on it. And there, next to the old man – shunning the silvery light of the slopes and leaning on a cairn as if it were a reading desk, one arm lifted in a casual gesture – stood Naso, the poet of Rome.

Naso was gazing at the fire in the stove, apparently speaking to his servant. Cotta knew the lilt of that voice, but could not understand a word, heard the blood ringing in his head, heard the gusty wind snatch sentence after sentence from the exile's lips and bear them off up the slopes. Pythagoras's hand, however, skimmed over the blue cloth in great haste, as if to capture the words before they were scattered.

Time slowed now, stood still, fell back into the past. A moulding orange rolled across the dock of the town of iron. The *Trivia* rammed its way through violent seas. Flakes of ash flew from a window on the Piazza del Moro, and encircled by the blazing gems of two hundred thousand torches, a thin figure stood before a bouquet of microphones in the Stadium of the Seven Refuges. And now time snapped back, from the thundering oval into the ruins of Trachila.

I have found Naso, I have found the poet of Rome – exiled, missing and presumed dead. As if a suffocating weight had been lifted from him, relief swept over Cotta amid all this rubble and devastation – the last refuge of the man who had once been the most famous person in the capital. The sight of these two men beside the smoking stove, the sight of the poet veiled in smoke, striking the same casual pose as the orator in the stadium, tore him from the town of iron's embrace back into the reality of Rome. And so he rushed toward the exile, shouting, waving his arms, laughing, stumbled over a rock and did not feel his bruised ankles or a tendon almost ripped by a sprain. He had found Naso at last.

Cotta ran – it was less than fifty careless strides across the silver ore, but they did more damage to his feet than all the obstacles on the path to Trachila – reached the ravine, stumbled out of the brilliance of the slopes into the shadow of the cliff, was robbed of sight for a few moments by the abrupt change in light, heard loosened stones rolling behind him, gasped his greeting – and was alone.

Granted, the stove stood smoking before him, its firing door sprung from the hinges, a gaping crack in its cast-iron jacket. A gust of wind had rekindled the old embers hidden deep in the ashes between two charred logs. Granted, a piece of blue cloth with writing on it fluttered and snapped in the wind. But the rag was not spread over Pythagoras's knees, it was merely entwined in a squat cairn that from a distance might be taken for a seated man. And it was not the poet of Rome leaning against the other cairn but the trunk of a pine tree stripped of its bark by falling stones. Probably intended for firewood, its sawn-off branches lay scattered about the stove. Only one branch, as thick as a man's arm and badly scarred by futile blows with an axe or knife, had not been hacked off, but was still planted firmly in the trunk, pointing towards Cotta and, beyond him, into the depths. There the sea glistened. Cotta was alone.

The acrid smoke blown his way by the shifting wind, forced him from his frozen position. The pain in his foot was so acute now that tears came to his eyes. With a groan he hobbled over to the blue rag, and propping himself on the stone monument, lowered himself to the ground, where he sat leaning against the cairn. Whenever the wind veered from the west to the south for a few seconds, the cloth fluttered in his face. He did not even lift a hand to fend it off. The fire grew smaller, went out. The stove turned cold. Cotta stared at this piece of trash cast aside by the avalanche and felt a new force rise up from within him, which began to shake him, at first gently, then ever more violently. The snow of ashes fell from the dark hole of the firing-door, fine, white ashes. There was no doubt, he must have gone mad.

Mad. Strange – the stones were still here, he could pick them up and fling them away. And the pain in his sprained ankle was still there, too, and so were half of an archway in the rubble, his pack and the sheen of the slopes. He had gone mad, and still the world had not abandoned him, but patiently endured beside him – its last inhabitant. The sea stayed with him. The mountains. The sky.

And then the cramp shaking him wrenched open his mouth. Was it a roar, a laugh, a sob – he did not know. He heard his voice far in the distance, he was outside himself now, somewhere high up in the shimmering rocks, watching a madman crouching in the ruins of Trachila – far below, beside that cold stove, a battered man. A fluttering blue cloth brushed the tears from his eyes, slapped his mouth. Again and again. Until he finally stopped sobbing, screaming, laughing. And then it was wondrously still.

In this stillness he returned from the heights of the rocks into his heart, into his breath, his eyes. The tormenting conflict between

Rome's reason and the Black Sea's incomprehensible realities dissolved. Times and seasons laid their names aside, intermingled, fused. The epileptic son of a grocer could turn to stone now, could stand as a crude statue among kegs of sauerkraut, human beings could become beasts or limestone, tropical forests could blossom into ice and melt away. . . . Regaining his self-control, he grabbed the cloth slapping him, and read its fragments of text scribbled in charcoal, Armenian bole and chalk. He would find blurred traces of such texts on all the other cairns as well:

> *. . . stingers*
> *of silver*
> *. . . the thunder . . .*
> *. . . unprotected*
> *the heart . . .*
> *the butcher's wife*
> *. . . a nightingale*

Cotta spent two days in the debris of Trachila. He pulled the blue swatch of cloth from the cairn and used it to bind his swollen ankle. He gathered silver ore and built a windbreak across the ravine for the night, got a roaring fire going beside the stove and slept wrapped in the glow of its embers. Fighting down his nausea and with flies buzzing around him, he covered the wolf's carcass with gravel and stones, making a futile attempt to arrange them in a dome. In the end, the wolf simply lay under a crude heap of stones. For hours the flies searched for ways to crawl inside. The carrion birds disappeared.

Over the next two days he also entered the thicket of Naso's garden, an oasis under the shade of the cliff, an island in rivers of rock. He found the inscribed columns, hewn blocks and menhirs just as he remembered them from his first visit on that night in April – sunk into the earth, atilt or toppled, more like neglected gravestones than memorial markers. Protected from the summer's heat by a leafy roof of laurel, fern and sloe, a new generation of slugs had taken possession of the menhirs, merging above the texts into pulsating, glistening mantles. The engraved words were left revealed in only a few places. The tiny lichens in those grooves apparently still retained the smell of vinegar, an odour of death that kept the terrifying space free for words. It was as if the slugs were *besieging* each individal letter, waiting until the last reminder of their doom had evaporated, so that they could then creep patiently, resolutely over all the characters on the stone, burying word after word beneath their bodies.

Cotta hobbled through the world of Trachila's debris like a survivor in the ruins of a razed city – aimless and confused at first, but gradually regaining his composure until he was even willing to rummage in the rubble for whatever might still be usable. . . . But nothing was left in Trachila except a cracked cast-iron stove and words scribbled on rags, words hewn in stone. And so he reviewed the archive of faded symbols, cairn by cairn, untangled the banners from the stones, read aloud in the silence what was readable – meaningless, jumbled texts – and stuffed the rags in his pack. For among the many ravaged inscriptions and words, names he recognised fluttered in the wind, names of inhabitants of the town of iron.

After two days his supplies ran out and his teeth turned violet from the watery fruit of the mulberry tree. Perched atop pinnacles and ridges, however, were unread stone markers, those he could not reach because of his sprained ankle. Hunger drove him to return to the coast. He was determined to come back here before the rains washed the last letters from the rags.

Using a forked branch for a crutch, Cotta climbed step by painful step back down to the sea the next morning, a stormy October day.

He reached the Bay of Balustrades by dusk. There the brandy dealer found him. He had brought two mules and large baskets to the beach to gather gravel ground smooth by the breakers. Phineus could see the Roman was exhausted, and so he untied the baskets from the packsaddle of one mule and offered him a ride. Half asleep, huddled and tottering on the mule's back, Cotta arrived at the ropemaker's house after sunset. It was as he had expected – the windows and doors stood open. Lycaon's house was deserted.

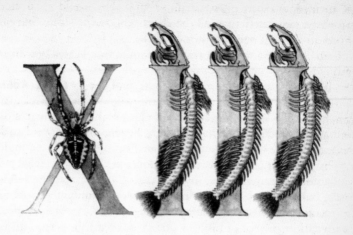

Tomi was like a city at war. As moraines and avalanches destroyed farms and pastures, more and more mountain people fled to the coast with their livestock. Upland valleys sank under rubble. On many days seismic waves rattled the dishes in Tomi's cupboards. In the Bay of Balustrades, ledges and balconies broke off, and the waves reared up so high that although the walls of the harbour basin were still intact, the boats had to be pulled onto land. It was as if the mountains, veiled in autumn rain, were shaking off all life, gathering it on the coast and holding it captive in the narrow strip between rock and tide. The town of iron was livelier than it had ever been.

The refugees found shelter in caves and ruins, laying makeshift roofs of branches, reeds or tin over the crumbling walls. In their misery they planted lupins and shared stone floors with pigs and sheep when they slept. The nights were bright with flickering fires and noisy with the barking of sheep dogs and the drunken shouts of the homeless who took refuge from the rain in Phineus's cellar. Many of these mountain people had never been to the coast. Weighed down with amulets to protect themselves from the anger of the spirits to whom they attributed their misfortunes, they bemoaned their fate in an unintelligible dialect. They flung offerings from the cliffs into the oncoming waves – amber, clay figurines and hair woven into wreaths. And when the sea grew calmer at last, they sang breathless, monotone verses out on the mole.

Hardly a day went by without fights and brawls between these barbarians from the mountains and the locals. Now many smelters kept their shutters closed during the day, too, and if refugees passed through their street, they emptied their pisspots or threw stones and garbage over the walls.

Only the brandy dealer seemed pleased with the throng of unfortunates growing day by day. Fama's store and the brandy cellar were among the few places where mountain people and residents of the coast could not avoid one another. Phineus softened the misery of his new guests, soaked it in vermouth and gin and in payment took whatever they had been able to salvage from their valleys and pastures. The bare stone storerooms of his house slowly filled with undressed hides, wood carvings and minerals. The inner courtyards became a pig wallow. On rainy days he sank up to his shins in the mire.

Phineus no longer left his shop even at night. He slept in a wooden hut that stood next to the bar and looked like a dog house. Separated from the racket and fumes of the carousers by a curtain of coarse linen, he lay in his hut on a steel-frame cot and until he fell asleep tried to imagine the faces of the shadows that scurried and tumbled across the curtain.

But when a fight broke out at the bar or the bartender had to get rough with a drunk and drag him swearing and cursing to the stairs, the brandy dealer would burst from the thin husk of his dreams, rip back the curtain, sit there naked and pot-bellied in his dirty sheets, pull out a crowbar he kept under his mattress and start banging on the steel cot frame until the din brought the cellar to silence for a few moments. Not saying a word, he would then point the crowbar menacingly at the alleged perpetrator of the rumpus, fling the curtain closed again and fall back into the rumpled sheets with a loud sigh. This farce was repeated almost every night now.

Since his return from Trachila, Cotta lived alone in the ropemaker's house, every nook and cranny of which he explored, searching out its secrets but finding nothing more than junk, dusty tools and running yards of rope. Evening after evening, he bolted the iron shutters and gate as if he expected an attack in the night and then lay awake for hours, sweating with rage at the noise from the ruins.

Sometimes he was awakened by a shout or a bottle smashed against the cobblestones, but if he got up to peek out from the dark security of a window recess, all he could ever see were herdsmen staggering along the slaughterhouse wall, still in their pelt coats despite the sticky November air. Bellowing sentimental ballads, they would suddenly stop and double over to vomit. . . . But no one, not even the crudest semi-conscious drunk, so much as approached the ropemaker's house at night, let alone tried to push open the gate. Cotta was the guardian of a house people shunned. What was more, as if by tacit agreement the smelters came to regard him as the new owner. The house was slowly receding into its thicket. Ivy enveloped the walls, darkening one window after the other, until many of the shutters could no longer be opened and disappeared under the shiny hearts of the leaves. Cotta's lame foot seldom hurt now, but it was so sensitive to weather that he could not wear shoes when it rained or the moon changed. On those days he went barefoot.

The inhabitants of the town of iron seemed as little moved by the ropemaker's disappearance as by the news of Trachila's destruction. . . . If someone needed yarn, twine or rope, he entered Lycaon's workshop through the door that opened onto the sunlit street and, with the Roman looking on, quickly rummaged through the dusty chaos until he found what he wanted and paid with a handful of coins, which Cotta then tossed into a tin box as nonchalantly as Lycaon had thrown money into his safe. People noticed that the Roman stood at the windlass some mornings now, too, and from the rope-walk came the familiar groan of the winch.

The only thing new and peculiar about Lycaon's house was the maze of banners Cotta had hung on hemp cord, rows of garlands that stretched across the workshop and out onto the covered porch – the rags he had loosened from the cairns in Trachila and brought back to the safety of the coast. Like the countless slogans and precepts displayed on banners and notice-boards in the streets of the capital (constant reminders to the citizens of Rome of their many duties), the little faded flags of Trachila dangled their scribblings from lines of cord crisscrossing the ropemaker's house.

Cotta tried to bring some order to the tatters. Each cord was associated with an idea, with a name and everything that could be tied in with that name – *Arachne* . . . *Gulls* . . . *Silk*. . . . But where to hang all the names of plants and stones that he deciphered from the bleached fabric? On Echo's cord? Or on the petrified epileptic's? The game, begun as a makeshift device for sorting out his bundle of rags, sometimes held him fast for days.

Arachne knew nothing. When he showed Arachne a piece of cloth that bore her name, she only clapped her hands and wriggled her fingers in unintelligible signs.

Phineus laughed and wiped the bar with the scribbled rag before handing it back to the Roman.

Tereus had trouble even reading his name, gave a silent shrug and bent back down over a vat full of brine.

Only Fama remembered. Mourning for her son had made her talkative. She needed listeners. To pacify an impatient audience, she doled out chewing tobacco and cordials while she told endless stories describing her misfortune – even to the refugees from the mountains, who pressed against the shelves, fingering their amulets, staring at the statue of her son, at the flickering candles, and listening stupidly to her tales. . . .

Fama remembered: whenever the exile's servant came down to the coast for supplies, he collected rags like these from homes in Tomi – aprons, frayed clothes, things kids had outgrown – and used them for those strange stone men he set up, like road signs, in the mountains.

Pythagoras had found his way to the shores of the town of iron on the *Argo* – a cold, stormy summer it was, long before Naso's arrival. An inventor, a scholar, he had fled a despotic regime at home somewhere in Greece. *Samos*, that was his home. And he was forever carrying on about the power of time, which would not only crush the despot of that island, but also transform all authority of man over man and turn humankind into one happy community. But the letters and newspapers that found their way to him over the years refuted that.

For a decade or more the Greek lived on the beach of a narrow bay cut deep in the coast south of the Cape of Tomi – in a stone house built as a refuge for fishermen to wait out bad weather if they got caught in a storm on the way home. For a long time the hermit's only company were fishermen forced by heavy seas to beach there. Sometimes they brought him back to Tomi on board their boats, where he was popular since he only appeared like a harbinger of good weather once people had ridden out a storm. It became the custom to give him gifts. Panting under the heavy load of his visit, he would follow mule tracks back to his solitude. There he sat among driftwood and kelp and wrote in the sand, so that the waves would lap up his words and symbols and force him to start over again with something new and different.

He hung three wind harps in the crown of a pine, the only tree in the bay, and from the sound of their swelling and fading harmony he could tell when to expect a storm – and visitors – from the sea. In the last years of silence and solitude, he began to talk to himself, and toward the end babbled crazy stuff when he came to the town of iron, giving speeches at the slaughterhouse door about the abomination of eating meat, until Tereus would appear at the open window and pelt him with sheep hearts and intestines.

Pythagoras claimed that in the eyes of cows and pigs he could see the gaze of forlorn, transformed human beings, just as he could see a beast of prey lurking in the drunken stare of a smelter. He claimed that in the course of its wanderings his own soul had occupied the armoured bodies of both lizards and officers and that bullets had released him from these shabby incarnations, claimed he had seen cities like Troy and Carthage rise from the stones and sink back to dust. He had been given up for mad, when one bright blue summer day, the *Trivia* pulled into the harbour of Tomi and, to the gaping amazement of the crowd on the mole, an exile disembarked. Naso strode down the gangplank escorted by two border guards, signed his name to a stack of carbon-copy forms in the harbour-master's office and was still sitting among his baggage on the dock, not saying a word, when the schooner cast off hours later and a stiff breeze blew it out of sight.

Pythagoras recognised his own pain, indeed his own fate, in the despair of this exile, and did not return to the beach that day. Talking incessantly, he helped the Roman move into a vacant house assigned to him on a deserted street. He stayed with him in those first days of exile and in the weeks and months that followed, finally accompanying him to the desolation of Trachila after hostility in the town of iron forced the exile to that last refuge. When Tomi finally realised that the gentleman was as harmless as his servant, neither of them wanted to return to the house on the coast. Trachila was a safe spot.

Gradually Pythagoras discovered *all* of his own thoughts and feelings in Naso's responses and stories and came to believe that in this correspondence between them he had found a harmony worth communicating to others. And so he no longer wrote in the sand, but began to leave inscriptions behind wherever he went – at first only in Phineus's brandy cellar, where he carved the tables with his fingernails and a pocketknife, later he wrote on the walls of houses with clay shards and on trees with chalk, and once in a while even scribbled on runaway sheep and pigs.

Battus, Fama sighed, as always wiping the tears from her eyes when she mentioned her son, Battus sometimes came home from his expeditions on the slopes with rags just like those Cotta had brought, although she had forbidden him again and again to go off like that, on account of his epilepsy, and had made him kneel on firewood as punishment.

So what if this piece of cloth – Cotta smoothed it as he laid it across her counter – had her name on it? That meant nothing. Because Pythagoras's veneration of the poet brought him to a point where he tried to preserve everything Naso said, every sentence, every name. Up in Trachila, he was out of reach of the mockery and protest of the smelters, who had fought back against the graffiti on the walls of their homes and gardens with buckets of water, dogs and stones. Up in Trachila, the Greek could abandon himself to his passion, and he began to make a monument of *every* word Naso uttered, erecting stone cairns clear up where glaciers began, even on the steepest pinnacles and rock chimneys – each a symbol that he, Pythagoras of Samos, was no longer alone in his thoughts and opinions about the world.

December came and snow had not fallen once in Tomi. Each time a line of heavy rain moved in, the steady, mild wind, sometimes gusting to a gale, broke it up and a new impenetrable layer of cloud came in from the sea. But between these recurrent periods of iron-grey skies, some days were so sunny and warm that blankets and pillows were spread on garden walls for airing, fishermen caulked rows of upturned boats out on the jetty and sometimes even launched them, rowing out into the bay until a cloudbank billowed up and chased them back into the harbour. The coast remained green.

Cotta waited. The rumblings from the mountains ebbed and then returned, refugees kept pouring in from the mountain valleys with reports of casualties, scattered herds and buried huts. For the moment it seemed pointless to risk another trip to Trachila. And so hardly a day went by that he did not spend hours in Fama's store. A glass of tea at his side, he sat on a footstool next to Battus's statue, browsed through the yellowed, mildewed magazines from the *Trivia*'s last delivery, lent Fama an occasional hand, rolling kegs or stacking crates – and returned again and again, because the grocer's conversation was so congenial it was as if he had never been a stranger here.

As she went about serving her poverty-stricken customers from the mountains, inspecting the wool, opals and rancid-smelling hides the refugees offered her in trade, she bemoaned her own bizarre misfortune, cursed the rigours of life on this coast and to illustrate the truth of her tale of woe, named the names of people in Tomi, whose sad stories she unfolded in long, elaborate and often contradictory accounts. Cotta sat on his footstool, listening without asking any questions, but at times his face took on the same stupid expression Battus's had when he tried to follow his mother's lamentations. The inhabitants of the coast despised these refugees from the mountains, it seemed, not so much because they were destitute or had coarse, foreign ways as because even the most ragged of these poor homeless people reminded the locals of their own past.

In bits and pieces Cotta learned from Fama's lament that not only the Greek servant's life story resembled that of his master, but that along the coast of Tomi *all* biographies were alike in one point at least: whoever made his or her home in the ruins, caves and weather-beaten stone houses of Tomi had come here as a stranger from somewhere else. With the exception of a few grubby, draggletail kids, there was no one in Tomi who had lived here since birth, no one who had not been tossed up on this coast as a refugee or an exile after a long, roundabout journey.

To hear Fama talk, the town of iron was moribund, little more than a camp for transients, for people who landed here at the end of an unhappy chain of events and reversals of fortune and lived here among the ruins as if in a penal colony, until time or chance freed them from this wilderness or they simply vanished like Echo, like Lycaon, like so many others who had shown up here at some point, camped in the ruins for a while and then disappeared.

The deaf-mute weaver, for example, had arrived on Tomi's shores on the ship of a purple-dyer, a Greek, who searched the reefs for murexes, nondescript sea snails from whose mucus he derived the colour of emperors, a deep red worth its weight in sapphires to him in the harbour towns of Italy. But the dyer's boat ran into a storm outside the Bay of Balustrades, struck a reef and sank. Clinging to a cork buoy, the deaf-mute was washed ashore. Five or six people were saved in the disaster, but only Arachne stayed behind in the town of her rescue.

Or Tereus! According to Fama's tale, avalanches following a sudden thaw had forced the butcher and his Procne from their upland valley – just as rockslides were forcing out shepherds and farmers now. For months Tereus had holed up in Tomi, waiting in vain for a berth on a ship to Byzantium, but in due time he started taking money to slaughter livestock in a spill-pond by the brook, and he killed and carved up his victims with such dexterity that little by little people left all the butchering to him. He forgot about Byzantium, made one of the ruins habitable again – and stayed on. . . .

And then Phineus. Fama was proud of the fact that in all the years since his arrival in Tomi, she had never spoken to him once. She called him a scoundrel, someone even the horseflies avoided. He had come to town with the Lilliputian one August – sitting up on the box of Cyparis's wagon, selling whisky and spouting tongues of flame from a mouth full of alcohol. He could play the clarinet and produced a basket full of snakes that he wrapped around his neck or tattooed arms. After the third performance, a superstitious swineherd, who wanted to rid Tomi of these sinister reptiles, set fire to the actors' tent and burned the snakes to death. Phineus demanded that the residents of Tomi compensate him for his loss, banging with a crowbar on gates and walls and bellowing his threat to kill the arsonist so loudly that at last people tossed him his money from their windows and offered him a vacant house to stay in until the show left town.

But Phineus stayed behind when the Lilliputian packed up his projector that August and moved on. Encouraged perhaps by the timidity with which people had tried to pacify his anger, he took over the vacant house, filled it with what possessions he had rescued from the fire (sooty bundles, demijohns as big as mules' stomachs) and assembled a still from pieces of glass he kept in a trunk – and within one day had transformed himself from a vagabond showman into the brandy merchant of Tomi.

True, for some time after his transformation, he spoke about moving on, about long journeys, the oases of Africa, trade winds and dromedaries, but all the while he was digging his way deeper into the rocky earth under the town of iron, using gunpowder and chisel to enlarge the cave beneath his house into a cellar, where he stored sour wine and sugarbeet schnapps and served it to his customers any time of the day or night. Of all the brandy dealer's enterprises, it was the cellar in particular that aroused Fama's envy – her hatred – and formed the basis for years of acrimony. Because after a while Fama's customers, who used to sit around the molasses keg in her store and drink syrupy liqueurs, switched to Phineus's cellar when they wanted a drink. Dust settled over her row of garish liqueur bottles.

When Cotta sat there on the footstool next to stony Battus and listened to her, Fama was often reminded of the good times and company – gone now, won over to Phineus. Then she would grieve for the noisy market days, the shouts, weep for Battus, who used to burn his fingers on the nettle garlands of the liqueur shelf. She spoke with growing bitterness about a world that, try as you might, you could not hold onto and keep as it once was. Things came, and things went.

With Battus's death, the heart of her own story had turned to stone as well, and now Fama's sole criterion for judging the fate of Tomi's inhabitants was whether the weight of misfortune that others bore was heavier or lighter than her own. The only person with whom she never compared herself was Thies – the German, the mixer of salves, the gravedigger. Years before, a draught horse had kicked him in the chest and crushed the ribs on his left side so badly that they had had to be pulled from his flesh like broken arrows. Since then, an unprotected heart beat in his breast. A stumble, a bump, a fist – any blow that struck his sunken and scarred chest might kill him.

Thies had arrived in the town of iron on a stretcher. He came lurching down the street, borne by migrant herdsmen, who had found him bathed in blood and lying in the gravel on the road to

Limyra and decided to bring him to the sea to die. In those days there had been a hospital down by the harbour – though only the foundation, overgrown with wormwood and broom, was visible now – an infirmary run by the mine, where mangled miners waited on crutches or coughed coal dust and blood from their lungs.

Thies lay strapped to an iron bed in this hospital for seven months, sinking sometimes into a deep coma for days at a time. A flower bed of silver tubes sprouted from his chest, dripping pus and fluid from his wounds, and when his dressings were changed he gave off such a stench that it was finally decided to carry him down a short stairway to the mole once a week and remove the bandages and dress his wounds there in the brisk wind. His screams on bandaging days could be heard in houses on the outskirts of town, and far up the rubbled slopes. His roar of pain was so loud that Fama would flee inside her store, crouch there, hands pressed to her ears, and wait for the screams to diminish to whimpers and finally fade away. But what every inhabitant of Tomi expected – and at times longed for, so horrible was that roar of pain – did not occur: the invalid did not die, he got well.

Thies was the last veteran of a defeated, scattered army, which at the height of its fury had literally set the sea on fire. Even now the thunder of artillery rolled through the gravedigger's night-mares, and although that sound had died away long ago, to him it was so painfully loud that he forced his mouth wide open to prevent his eardrums from bursting. Then he would see destroyers and hospital ships sinking into the deep and carpets of flaming oil moving toward the coast. Constanta, Sevastopol, Odessa – the most prosperous cities of the Black Sea coast – vanished once again, and then again, behind a curtain of fire. And in every dream Thies had to enter a warehouse somewhere in the middle of one of those ravaged, conquered towns, had to open its heavy double doors and endure a ghastly vision of humankind:

The residents of an entire neighbourhood had been crammed into this windowless stone room and asphyxiated with poison gas. The doors held as they rushed them in grim desperation, in the agony of death – a gasping wave of humans struggling to breathe, searching the cracks and joints of the door in vain for the least draught of air. The strong ones crept up over the bodies of the weak, higher and higher, but the gas vapours calmly obeyed the laws of physics and climbed with them and in the end transformed the strong ones, too, into merely another tread in the stairway for the strongest, who agonised their way to death at the crest of this wave of humankind, smeared with blood and faeces, mutilated in the battle for one single moment more of life.

Each time, the struggle had ended long before he arrived, the victims lay there open-mouthed and frozen in their convulsions. Thies opened the door – and saw humankind in ranked order come tumbling out at him from a cloud of stench. Then he woke up. Then he screamed. Then Proserpina, his fiancée, had to hold him and calm him, tell him again and again that those doors were the past, that they stood open now, forever, that the blackness all around him was only night in Tomi and not death, only the town of iron, only the sea. Again and again she had to tell him.

One afternoon in the middle of war – almost everything that could be destroyed or lost had been, the contested terrain was reduced to wasteland by battle – Thies was so overcome by the horror that he broke away from his unit as it marched through ravines and over passes on its way to destruction. He did not know why he was struck by the horror at that particular moment, why it was he could not advance one step further with his column, but suddenly he sat up on the box of his supply wagon, yanked the reins around, began whipping his horse like a madman and raced back over the pass to the valley below. No one bawled an order at him. No shot was fired. Only a few weary, haggard faces turned to stare at the deserter and then back at their route of march.

Thies sped ahead, whipping and urging his horse on, even as he heard his cargo – ammunition boxes, rolls of barbed wire, signal poles – tumble to the road behind him and the lurching wagon threatened to burst apart. Hurtling downhill, he had the sense that his transport column was still very close, that *he* was not moving at all, but that instead stones and bushes, the blue, green and black of the depths below were racing toward him. Lined with debris, corpses and carcasses, the road unrolled before him.

Then that overhanging rock was thrust into his path, forcing him to swerve to avoid it. He pulled so violently at the reins that his horse threw back its head and reared up, sending the wagon into a skid. He lost his grip, reins and whip were flung from his hands, and Thies was unseated. Pitching headlong towards the horse, he grabbed hair as he fell, the flax of its tail, hung on tight.

Straining, sweating, panicked and frightened by the whip, the horse gave a kick, threw all the force of its hind legs against the invisible weight clutching at it – against a marauding beast, against a tormentor, against Thies's chest. Sensing the drag give way at once, it took off at a wild gallop.

Before the blood gushed from his mouth and pain robbed him of consciousness, Thies saw a whirling white sky, saw a thundering structure of axles, beams and planks slide past above him, an ugly building, and saw, too, the spokes of the wheel speed merrily by, a strange fence that he tried to grab hold of and that tore him away with it.

For Thies the world was far away when they found him. Dragging wreckage at the end of its shaft, a horse had left erratic tracks in the barley of a terrace field far below. They caught it later only with difficulty. Thies lay in his black tranquillity and did not notice when they lifted him up or where they carried him. It took seventeen days before the first sounds of an alien world pierced his bloody veil: the hammering of blacksmiths, the plaintive braying of an ass, voices, a name – Tomi.

Although Thies always suffered worse from homesickness for the chalk-white dunes of Friesland than from the effects of his wounds, although sometimes he would sit working on his salves and with open eyes dream of birds above islands lost under the incoming tide, of lowland meadows alive with cows and herring gulls, he never showed any intention of returning to his homeland. After all the deaths he had seen, all the mad destruction he had lived through, he believed that the road back to the coasts of his birth was forever lost. Nothing could ever again be as it once was.

He was awarded a pension as a disabled veteran after a tedious and protracted correspondence, delayed for years by ship's post and endless winters. With the money he bought a fallow field where he began to grow sleep-inducing plants and medicinal herbs. Bit by bit he learned how to make and dispense the remedies that had healed his own wounds, mixed salves, pounded murky crystals into powders, sold tinctures in little dark blue bottles. And at last, in a remote village, he found a woman who wanted to share his life in the town of iron. But Proserpina, his fiancée, stayed with him reluctantly – and only intermittently. Year after year she tried in vain to convince him to travel with her to see the splendours of Rome, and after days of arguing would sometimes leave him. Yet she always returned to his silent house, fragrant with the odour of myrrh and aloe.

But as passionately as Proserpina tried to win her fiancé's favour, her love could not alter his sullen, melancholy nature. For the truth was that, after being battered by war and hooves and rising again from his coma with an unprotected heart under his scars, Thies lived only for the dead. However efficacious his medicines and tinctures proved to be, he remained profoundly convinced that there was no help for the living, that there was no form of cruelty and degradation that every one of them – whether out of hunger, rage, fear or simply stupidity – might not commit *and* have to endure. They were all capable of anything.

Only in the faces of the dead did he sometimes think he saw an expression of innocence, which touched him and which he tried to preserve with bitter oils, until he had to cover the awful decay with earth and stones. Thies the gravedigger knew nothing more defenceless, nothing more helpless than a corpse. And so he washed each body given to him for burial, as tenderly as he would a baby's, perfumed it, dressed it in fine clothes, bedded it in its box and erected above the grave his elaborate dome of stone, an emblem to the knowledge that death was all.

When Thies sat in Phineus's cellar, alert but taciturn, the brandy dealer sometimes managed to draw him into conversation. Then he would talk about a coastline as endless and flat as a becalmed sea, about the black and white cows and sunken forests. Once he had even opened his shirt to show his scars to a table of drunks. They could see his heart beating there. *If* Thies did speak, however, he always worked one particular sentence into what he had to say – a maxim, so Fama claimed, that Naso had brought with him from Rome. It eventually became so characteristic of Thies that people would secretly count along and place bets on how often he would use his adage this time. Thies sensed their mockery, and yet the platitude came to his lips again and again, because it contained everything that he had experienced, everything the world had shown him: *Man is a wolf to man*.

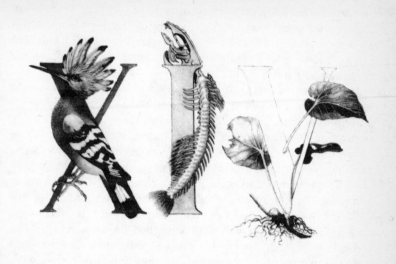

No snow fell that winter. No hoar frost glazed the branches. Protected from the wind by walls or rocks, bushes of pale yellow flowers blossomed.

When the sun had passed its imaginary southern solstice and the days were beginning to grow imperceptibly longer, a gust of wind shattered the window in Cotta's attic room and tugged so violently at the shutters that the window frame broke from the masonry. The garret became uninhabitable. In the damp weather the mildew crept relentlessly across the wall hangings – across the flocks of birds, the wide sky, the paradise of forests and low rolling hills – and forced Cotta to escape to the dry corners of the workshop. And so he made his bed among dusty hawsers, winches and spools, abandoning the upper storey to hornets and smoky brown ringdoves attracted as if by magic to the broken glass and open windows and colonising the ropemaker's house room by room. Along the walls, ant armies moved and fought soundless battles for wisps of dove down, the undigested seeds in their droppings and the shimmering shell of a desiccated rose beetle.

Whenever Cotta returned to the decaying house from Fama's store, from her stories and complaints, he would pace – often until late into the night – among the hanging garlands of banners still crisscrossing the rooms like decorations for a ragamuffin ball, and compare the grocer's gossip with the fragments and names on the faded tatters from Trachila.

But whatever Fama chose to talk or complain about, he thought he recognised most of it in these scribblings as he wandered a labyrinthine path through the ropemaker's house – Thies's unprotected heart, Phineus's snakes. Much about these inscriptions remained enigmatic, but one evening he nevertheless came to the conclusion that the stone markers of Trachila contained little more than the grocer's chatter – the lives, legends and rumours of the coast, which Naso and his Greek servant had collected, taken to the mountains and recorded in a curious, childish game they played with what had been told them. The stained and frayed banners that hung here from clothes-lines and fluttered in the wind on cairns above the timberline – they were the town of iron's memory.

The mountains seemed calmer during weeks of monotonous rain that held people captive in houses, caves and tarpaulin-roofed ruins. The thunder of mudslides and avalanches was fainter and further away now, and some days it could not be heard at all. The poorest refugees began to prepare for the return to their devastated upland valleys – life could hardly be more miserable in the ruins of their farmsteads and villages than in the muck of the town of iron.

Sometimes, when the rain would let up for a few hours or give way briefly to dripping silence, they would stand in groups outside their shelters staring at the clouds and routinely ended up arguing whether that narrow band of paler grey on the horizon was in fact a sign of a change for the better, the signal for them to depart to their buried homes – or only just another shimmer of deceptive hope. Sometimes they were still standing there in the mire of the gutters – gesticulating, cursing, shouting at one another – long after the low clouds had closed dull ranks to advance once again and rain swept down on them, as heavy and steady as ever.

The outskirts of town were veiled in fog and mists, the black cliffs above the Bay of Balustrades were invisible, the seas hidden except for the line of waves breaking at the shore, the mountains concealed in clouds. Sagging above the stone and slate roofs, the sky seemed to hesitate to reveal the terrible upheaval of the coastal mountains, the result of the great stirrings in stone that had caused the avalanches and mudslides – all of which would become apparent one bright January day.

In the rain, human time seemed to stand still, but it flew for plants. The air was so warm and heavy that spores germinated in just a few crumbs of the poorest soil, seeds burst open and nameless sprouts unrolled their leaves. Awakening after only an hour's nap, people felt as if threads of mildew had been spun about them. Whatever required no more than moisture, warmth and this grey light, flourished in rank growth. When a fire went out, lush weeds crept from the ashes. Firewood sprouted. At first it was only stealthy, transparent roots, then came little green fingers and deceptive blossoms, and finally sinewy arms plated with mossy bark – the wilderness was reaching out to grasp the town of iron.

Although Tomi's ancient colour of rust gradually vanished under green that sparkled with rain, the rust itself kept eating away in secret, its pace disastrously accelerated by the damp. Iron shutters loosened beneath the blossoms and ivy, crumbled like cardboard and disintegrated. Wrought-iron fences buckled. The decorations of metal lilies, and spear-shaped leaves, even the railings on the footbridges across the brook broke loose. Gratings rotted like plaited grass.

It was impossible to tell if a weather-cock or a gable ornament was still in place or had long since fallen apart under the embracing branches. The rioting green mimicked the forms it enclosed, playfully, mockingly at first, but then, obeying its own law of form and beauty, went on relentlessly to obliterate all signs of human handiwork.

Early in January a plant crept deep into the ropemaker's house – a blue bindweed that began to ramble happily among Cotta's garlands of rags. As if to decorate the tatters from Trachila, it guided ringlets of tendrils along the clothes-lines, now pinning a brooch or medal of trumpet flowers on the chest of a ragged shirt, now framing a piece of silk-lining with a wreath of leaves, gradually binding and weaving the garlands together into a single canopy, a swaying sky – and Cotta accepted this as calmly as the ivy on the walls or the moss on the stairs.

Perhaps he would never have untangled this web of rags, twine and blossoms, would have forgotten the faded scribbles just as he was slowly forgetting Fama's gossip and even Rome itself, if that wild woman – a barefoot creature, disfigured with scratches and open sores – had not come wandering down the streets of Tomi one January morning, bringing with her not only the ultimate destruction of the sky in the ropemaker's house but also the collapse of Cotta's world.

The strange woman came out of the clouds. Wrapped in what was once a shawl, she came out of the shoals of a fog that had lifted from the sea that morning like a school of silvery fish, taking wing and gliding above the roofs of Tomi and its rubble-filled slopes. The whole coast lay under a white, steamy silence. The rain had stopped.

Her unblinking eyes fixed to her path, the strange woman stumbled towards the sea and seemed not to realise that she was no longer surrounded by a wasteland of abysses but by houses, that she was no longer walking through ravines and gorges but through streets. She was heading for the sea. She took no notice of the town of iron, of the world of men, and was herself hardly noticed at first – there were so many ragged people, so many wretched souls nowadays.

When she reached the mole, she stood leaning against an upturned boat, staring with relief into the emptiness. She had been standing there motionless for hours, as if glued by caulking tar to the boat's planks, making occasional crude, unintelligible sounds if a wave crashed foaming on the harbour mole – when several children, who had been breaking open seashells on the jetty, finally noticed her. They quickly realised how defenceless the woman was. They began throwing pebbles at her, came closer, pulled at her rags, jumped back laughing, poked her with sticks and branches, and screeched with glee when the strange woman reacted to their pokes with frightened cries. She did not even try to shoo away the flies nibbling at the sores on her cheeks, but suddenly she made a grab for a piece of bread that Itys, the butcher's son, held out to her at the end of a stick.

Perhaps the woman was mute and used flying fingers to speak, like the deaf weaver. And so ten or more little hands made signs to her. Fists, flailing arms and fingers twisted as if for a shadow game leapt out at her, when a piercing scream froze this maze of meaningless signs and all the arms dropped in fright like the leaves of a mimosa.

But it was not the stranger who had screamed, it was Procne, the butcher's fat, out-of-breath wife. As if her scream had focused the attention of the whole town on one human tragedy, Tomi turned its gaze to the ghastly stranger. Smelters, women dressed in black, refugees, miners, they all came running.

Procne had been in the slaughterhouse stuffing sausages, and through an open window she spotted her son standing too near the water with a gang of excited children. She called him, but that did no good, so she ran down the stairway to the mole, panting all the way, to drag Itys back under her watchful eye – and suddenly there was that woman, staring at nothing, and Procne recognised the disfigured, fly-covered face. It was Philomela, her sister.

Procne's scream was followed by terrified silence, the silence by the drum of running feet. Sensing an entire town running towards her, the strange woman turned away from the sea and toward Procne, but apparently she did not recognise the face buried in the fat and opened her mouth for a moan. And now the curiosity-seekers saw that she was mute for a very different reason from that which made the weaver speechless. Instead of a mouth, the woman had nothing but a seeping, black, scabby wound. Her lips were torn, her teeth knocked out, her jaw broken. The moaning woman, who let Procne take her in her arms now, had no tongue.

That was Philomela? The people of Tomi gathered on the mole recalled a pretty face, a girl not twenty years old, who had cleaned intestines and plucked chickens over steaming vats in the slaughterhouse, but who was in every way the opposite of Procne, her clumsy sister encumbered in her fat. Philomela, who had been treated no better than a milkmaid in her sister's house, had fallen to her death in the mountains, years ago, though it was true her body had never been found. . . . Philomela . . .?

That morning Tomi also recalled the rumours that had spread along the coast at the time, but then dried up when the butcher threatened trouble, and all that was left – or was allowed to be left – was the simple chronicle of an accident.

Tereus had packed a mule with meat for a camp of amber-hunters and headed into the mountains with Procne's sister, who sometimes accompanied him on these trips. But that same day – it was early evening, a summer thunderstorm had passed and mist was rising from the sea, just like today – the butcher came running down the slopes, badly scratched and out of breath, weeping and shouting that his mule had shied, slipped off the narrow track and fallen into the depths, pulling his sister-in-law with it.

Weary as he was, Tereus would not rest even for an hour, but hurried back into the mountains with help – a hard climb, what with all those ropes, torches, and lanterns.

They searched for the girl two days and nights, but all they found at the bottom of a dark ravine, its floor scored by deep cracks and crevices, was the mangled carcass of the mule – and sausage, salt meat and slabs of bacon scattered everywhere. Jackals howled with hunger from the cliffs and vainly tried to find a way down to this heaven-sent feast. The men had to use ropes to salvage what they could from the shadows. Philomela, so they said, must have fallen down one of those black gaping crevices at the bottom of the ravine, forever out of reach in the depths below.

And now here she was, had come like death itself to the town of iron – a mutilated victim, coerced into silence, who whimpered in Procne's arms and apparently was unable to comprehend a simple question, a comforting word. She would permit no touch except that of Procne's red, swollen hands, and if so much as the shadow of a man fell across her she cringed with fear.

The town of iron understood that Procne's sister had lost not just her tongue and her beauty, but her mind as well, and that all questions were pointless that morning. But they asked their questions nevertheless, a hundred times or more, each turning helplessly to the others – and the last person asked himself, muttering softly, determined not to speak aloud the only answer possible, the one name at the tip of every tongue. They glanced furtively about, looking for the butcher in the crowd. But Tereus was not among the curiosity-seekers. His boat was missing too.

Philomela was safe in Procne's arms, and yet so close to infinity – white, salty infinity. She seemed to respond to human voices in the same way she heard the squawking gulls, the pounding surf. But then the brandy dealer pushed his way up to the two women, forced Philomela to look at him. He opened his mouth wide, stuck out his tongue, wrapped his hand around it, and with one horrible gesture tried to wrench the mutilated woman's memory back to the most horrible moment of her life. And shouted *who*? *Who*? Only now, and for no more than a heartbeat or two, did

Philomela seem to return from far away to this world of reason and cruelty, to realise that people were around her, and she stared at them, horror in her eyes – and saw the overgrown ruins of the town of iron rise up, saw villages tumble from the cliffs, saw all this strange green along the coast, and shining in the sun amid the chaos, a white wall, where in happier days the projectionist's pictures had scurried over its peeling whitewashed surface.

Noticing Philomela's momentary awakening, Phineus feared she would sink back again to where he could not reach her, leaving no sign or clue behind, and so he roared his question again and again as if she were hard of hearing – who had tortured her? – until at last Thies tried to pull the two women away from the raving man.

Then Philomela looked straight into the brandy dealer's eyes, silencing him and forcing him to turn away, and she lifted her arm, slowly, as if her weariness were infinite, and pointed to the butcher's house, to a blank wall framed in ivy and wild grape.

The coast lay deep in twilight when that same evening Tereus sailed into the harbour of Tomi under a light west wind and moored his boat to the jetty. He had taken advantage of the calm seas that day to set nets and baited hooks in the bays. A silent town received him. The streets and squares were as good as deserted. For the first time in weeks, the sky revealed stars.

Tereus wearily carried home his catch, two baskets of fine fish, some of which still squirmed or beat frantically with their fins, squandering what little life they had left.

The butcher did not notice how on both sides shadows fell back from him into the darkness of doors, niches and archways. The lights were out in many houses, allowing the shadows to watch from black windows as the beast walked the streets.

The butcher's own house was as dark and breathless as the town. Tereus pushed open the gate, set his fish baskets down on a stone bench and called a greeting into the gloom. Light flared in the windows. Then two shadows glided out of the house and disappeared among the ruins. Procne pulled her sister along with her into the night.

And then, almost mechanically – like a clock with gears that fling doors open and shut, counterfeiting the passage of time as little porcelain Jack pops out and vanishes again – Tereus appeared at the door of his house, brightly lit now and casting its glow out into the front yard and the riotous shrubbery of the street.

In his arms – still glistening with the dull sheen of fish scales – he held his son. He carried him carefully down the steps to the well. But from the way Itys's head rocked in his father's embrace with every step he took, from the way his naked feet dangled and slapped together, the town of iron knew, even before it saw the child's blood-drenched shirt, that Itys was dead.

Tereus did not cry out, did not weep. Tereus, who could outbellow any terrified animal fighting for its life as he pulled the rope tight around its neck, walked down the steps to the well now, so hesitantly, so helplessly, pressed the little body to him, laid it gently on the stones grooved by ropes that drew the buckets. But when he slipped off the dead boy's shirt and blood and water ran from the gaping knife-wound, they all heard it – everyone hiding close by and watching as if spellbound heard the butcher groan, heard a voice transformed by pain, as strange and awful as the mutilated woman's moans.

Tereus washed his son for burial, pressed his brow against the sharp edges of the wound, and the town, frozen there in the darkness, realised that this death was not merely an act of helpless, blind revenge for Philomela's mutilation, but also the culmination of a decade of despair. Procne had lifted her son out of time and laid him back into her heart.

Tereus carried Itys back into the house, leaving his little bloody shirt behind at the well. He laid his son in his bed, covered him with a starched white cloth, picked up an axe and left the house forever. Those who saw him now – how he struck his axe blindly at dark corners and bushes, how he let the light of his lantern glide slowly across the rubbish in ruined houses and ripped the blankets from refugees crouching by their fires and then carelessly stepped over the flames without a word – knew the butcher was looking for Procne in order to kill her. But not a hand or voice was raised to calm or console him. Like a hundred eyes impassively watching in the jungle as a prowling beast stalks its prey, Tomi watched the butcher track down a woman who had no chance.

There was not a door in the town of iron that could have held against his axe. Protected only by darkness, Cotta sat huddled in a window recess of the ropemaker's house and followed the light of Tereus's lantern as its restless flicker leapt from street to street, disappeared into the blackness of a shed or cave, re-emerged, broke through a garden thicket and cast mad shadows across walls and façades.

Whenever the light stood still, Cotta thought he could already hear the noises of discovery, feet running, stones rolling. . . . But the silence held. Then he heard a smothered voice outside the workshop door, like the angry, muffled cry of someone who has been gagged, but was afraid to risk any move or a light. Now the door opened cautiously, and he recognised the ashen white of a bare arm – Procne, pulling her distraught sister behind her into the hiding place. She whispered calming words to Philomela, laid a hand over her mouth.

Philomela resisted following her into the darkness, wanted to stay where she was, wanted to sleep. The two women dropped to the floor near the wide-open door, two shadows against the dark grey of the courtyard. Cotta said nothing, at first out of helpless surprise, but then for fear that a single word, a footfall close at hand might frighten the women, make them flee or scream in terror – and summon the axe and flickering light into his house. He leaned silently back into the darkness of his nook, until he felt the rustling wind behind him forcing its way through the broken window.

Although the mutilated woman now sat propped against the large, warm body of her sister and had fallen fast asleep, no longer in need of calming words, Procne kept up her incessant whispers, as if years of silence had to be broken at last, as if by evoking each lost day she could provide Philomela's despoiled memory with a new history.

Cotta was so tired that at times he heard Procne only from a great distance, soft and strangely melodious. The three of them crouched there in the night, bound together solely by this incessant voice resounding in the depths of Philomela's dreams and the Roman's exhaustion, a voice so marvellously soothing, so captivating that in time Cotta no longer listened to the words or sentences, but only to its sweet tone, which let him forget Tereus and every threat. And so, hour after hour of night passed.

It was shortly before dawn, the light above the eastern sea promised that all fog and clouds were tattered and fleeing. Cotta nodded off for a second, then awoke to that gentle voice, to a *song* that seemed to fill the ropemaker's house, a melody so enchanting it was as if Procne's beauty, her youth and lost happiness had returned, transformed now into pure sound. But as Cotta lifted his head to locate this transformation in the darkness, he saw the butcher. Saw the dull sheen of his axe in the doorway. Tereus had at last found the woman who murdered his son.

What happened now was merely the fulfilment of what had long stood written on the ragged banners of Trachila.

The song broke off. Tereus lifted the axe to do what grief and hate commanded. Sprang at his victims. But the two women did not raise their arms to end off the blows – instead, two startled birds spread their wings. Their names were recorded in the archives of Trachila: swallow and nightingale. Beating their wings madly, they flew across the workshop. Yet even before they shot through the broken window into the open air and were lost in the blue night sky, the curved handle of the axe had become yet another beak, Tereus's arms had turned into wings, his hair to brown and black feathers. A hoopoe lifted in easy, billowing flight and sailed off in pursuit of the two escaping birds as if gliding on the echo of Procne's voice.

That morning the sun rose out of a glistening sea, bathing a strange, transformed mountain landscape in its clear light. Freed from fog and clouds and advancing rain, encircled by fractured ridges, by the debris of obstructing avalanches and toppled cliffs, a new mountain towered into the sky. Even beyond the timberline, its flanks were draped with luxuriant folds of green and its peak was wreathed in fern. Thrust upward toward the stars by unrelenting pressure from the depths of the earth, the mountain rose from the subtropical jungle of the coast and on up to regions of dead, deep blue, icy clouds. All the sounds of the heaving earth, the thunder of cascading rocks, even the soft trickle of sand had ceased. A weary silence lay over the ravines and slopes.

Cotta sat alone in the workshop, amid the tatters of his sky. With a child's thoughtless glee he rummaged in the rags of the canopy, loosened the scribbled banners from the bindweed's blossoming tendrils and leaves, and read some of the inscriptions aloud to the empty room, the way someone sorting through junk repeats the names of things one last time before parting with them and tossing them out.

It was right there in the tatters: Tereus was the hoopoe and Procne the nightingale, Echo was an echoing voice and Lycaon a wolf. . . . And what flapped in the wind from the cairns in Trachila or now slid through Cotta's hands – riddles no longer – were not only past lives of the town of iron, but future destinies as well. And the name of the massive, snow-capped peak he could see shimmering brightly through the broken window was also recorded on the rags: *Olympus*. Mightier than anything that had ever risen above the Black Sea, the mountain now cast its shadow over the coast of the town of iron.

It was late morning before Tomi hesitantly stepped out from under this shadow and Cotta left the ropemaker's house. The sun climbed to its zenith, the blazing white epitome of fire. Phineus was spreading ashes over his bed of beets, and he tapped a finger on his brow when he spotted the Roman coming down the street – he was crazy, must have gone crazy. Cotta strode along muttering in deep conversation with himself. Around his neck he wore a rope of plaited tendrils, tatters and twine, the ragged garlands trailing behind him like the tail of a kite.

Cotta did not hear the words people shouted to him, did not notice a single wave of a hand. He heard the squabble of laughing-gulls, the breaking waves, even the song of birds and the rustle of palm fronds in the wind – but no human voice, not now. His eyes saw only the scenes promised by the inscriptions on his rags. The slaughterhouse was merely a mossy rock on which a flock of hooded crows was sharpening beaks, the streets were mountain paths through the thickets of blossoming brambles, the inhabitants had been transformed into stones, or into birds, wolves and empty echoes. Above Arachne's cliff, a huge swarm of gulls took flight with a roar. Freed from the threads of moulding tapestries, the birds hurled themselves into a sky of cloudless blue.

His high spirits growing with every step and sometimes bursting from him in a giggle, Cotta moved through chaotic debris towards the slopes of Trachila and climbed the new mountain. Here Naso had walked. *This* was Naso's path. Banned from Rome, from the realm of necessity and reason, the poet had finished telling his *Metamorphoses* beside the Black Sea, transforming this barren craggy coast, where he froze and ached with homesickness, into *his* coast, transforming these barbarians, who harassed and drove him to the forsaken world of Trachila, into *his* characters. And in telling *every* story to its conclusion, Naso had freed his world of human beings, of their rules and regulations. And then no doubt he had himself entered his landscape devoid of humans – an indestructible pebble rolling down the slopes, a cormorant sweeping above the foam-crested breakers, a swatch of triumphant purple moss perched atop the last crumbling wall of a town.

His Greek servant had written down his tales and erected a monument to every word he spoke – but that was meaningless now and at best a game for madmen. Books mildewed, burned, turned to ashes and dust. Cairns toppled back down the slopes as formless rubble, and even letters chiselled in basalt vanished under the patience of slugs. Reality, once discovered, no longer needed recording.

One thing drew Cotta into the mountains – the only inscription he had not yet discovered. He would find it on a banner buried in the silvery lustre of Trachila or on the boulder-strewn flanks of the new mountain. He was sure it would be a small banner – after all, it carried only two syllables. When he stopped to catch his breath, standing there so tiny under the overhanging rocks, Cotta sometimes flung those syllables against the stone, and answered, *here*! as the echo of his shout came back to him. For what reverberated from the walls – broken and familiar – was his own name.

AN OVIDIAN REPERTORY

With three exceptions all the passages printed in *italics* in this repertory are taken from Ovid's *Metamorphoses* (quoted from the translation by Rolfe Humphries).

The exceptions are: fragments from Ovid's *Epistulae ex Ponto* under the entries for *Augustus I, Augustus II* and *Cotta Maximus Messalinus* (quoted in free translation from the original). The spelling of the names and the summary of the stories in the *Ancient World* are taken from Ovid's mythology.

Characters in The Last World

Actaeon

At the Byzantium Fair, Cyparis ★, a travelling film projectionist, commissions a scenery painter to decorate the canvas cover of his horse-drawn wagon. By morning's end, a painting in deep reds has taken shape. It depicts a stag being ripped apart by a pack of dogs. When Cyparis asks about the meaning of the picture, the painter tells him the story of a hunter who is transformed into a stag and then pursued by the hunt. He calls the hunter Actaeon.

Alcyone

Leading female character in a melodrama that Cyparis ★ the projectionist beams on the walls of Tomi's slaughterhouse. The door

Characters in the Ancient World

Actaeon

Hero from Boetia. While pursuing a stag, he stumbles into a rocky grotto where he surprises Diana, goddess of the hunt, bathing with her nymphs. Diana, outraged that a mortal has seen her naked, sprinkles the hunter with spring water and transforms him.

. . . Once pursuer, he is now pursued, fleeing his old companions. He would cry 'I am Actaeon: recognise your master!' But the words fail, and nobody could hear him, so full the air of baying. . . . And surely he would rather see and hear the dogs than feel them. They circle him, dash in, and nip and mangle and lacerate and tear their prey, not master, no master whom they know, only a deer.

Alcyone

Daughter of the wind god Aeolus, wife of Ceyx ★, queen of Trachis. Tries in vain to deter her husband from a pilgrim voyage he wishes

of Fama's * grocery store is decorated with a poster of the Roman character actress, Antonella Simonini, who became famous even beyond the borders of the Augustinian Empire for her role as Alcyone.

to take to the shrine of Apollo of Claros. Sailing the coast of Asia Minor, Ceyx perishes in a storm together with all his companions. Alcyone waits many long months on the rocky shore of Trachis for her husband's return and hurls herself from a cliff into the sea when she sees Ceyx's corpse drifting in the waves.

. . . She leaped into the sea – a marvel that she could – and never fell, but seemed to skim the surface, like a bird on new-found wings, and as she flew, unhappy, her mouth, a slender bill, made sounds like one complaining, sorrowful.

Arachne

Deaf-mute weaver of Tomi, who lives in a dilapidated house built for the lighthouse keeper of the town of iron. The signal fire has been extinguished for years. She weaves into her tapestries stories she has read from Naso's * lips. When the sea in the Bay of Tomi turns sulphurous yellow one morning, she is the only person who can explain its colour to the bewildered inhabitants of the coast. With her fingers she tells them: it is simply wind-borne pollen from forests of stone pine. What is stone pine? they ask her. Arachne came to the coasts of Tomi in much the same manner as this sulphurous yellow veil – aboard the ship of a purple-dyer searching the reefs for sea snails. The boat sailed out of the bay and sank. Clinging to a cork buoy, the deaf-mute woman was washed ashore and was the only one of the

Arachne

Daughter of the purple-dyer Idmon of Colophon, famous for her artistry as a weaver. Provokes Minerva, the virginal goddess of war, science and art, saying: *I, Arachne, weave more beautifully and skilfully than the goddess herself.* And indeed, Arachne's flawless tapestries, depicting the amorous adventures of the Olympian gods, surpass what Minerva can weave. She angrily rips Arachne's tapestries to shreds and strikes her with the shuttle of her loom. Arachne is so humiliated that she tries to hang herself.

. . . Minerva at last was moved to pity, and raised her, saying: 'Live, wicked girl; live on, but hang forever, and, just to keep you thoughtful for the future, this punishment shall be enforced for always on all your generations.' As she turned, she sprinkled her with hell-bane, and her hair fell off, and nose and ears fell off, and head was

few people rescued who stayed in the town of iron.

shrunken, and the body very tiny, nothing but belly, with little fingers clinging along the side as legs, but from the belly she still kept spinning; the spider has not forgotten the arts she used to practise.

Ascalaphus

Amber merchant from Sulmona, who returns to Rome from the Black Sea carrying with him the post from Tomi, including Naso's ★ will – a tinted postcard of the town of iron. Addressed to Cyane ★, the postcard contains the exile's one remaining wish: Fare well.

Ascalaphus

Demon of the underworld; reveals that Proserpina ★ has eaten a pomegranate while in Hades and so dooms her to a life in the world of shades. As punishment for his betrayal, she turns Ascalaphus into a bird.

. . . And she, in anger, turned him into a bird, of evil omen, dashing hell-water in his face, to give him a beak, and feathers, and big round eyes, and wings all sulphur-coloured, a head enlarged, and talons, and a dull way of moving, so he barely shudders his feathers, sluggish, a bad omen to mortals, the foul screech-owl.

Augustus I

Emperor and Hero of the World; chooses a rhinoceros – a gift of the procurator of Sumatra – as the heraldic emblem of his reign; every day, for hours on end, observes this rhinoceros from a bay-window in his palace – and when disturbed from doing so by an informant who wishes to report about a scandalous speech given by the poet Publius Ovidius Naso ★, dismisses him with an angry wave of his hand. Officialdom assumes responsibility for interpreting this wave of the hand and ultimately construes the annoyed gesture to be a sentence of banishment for the poet.

Augustus (63 BC to 14 AD)

First Roman emperor; son of Atia, Caesar's niece; from a family of wealth but not of high rank. Originally named *Octavius* by his father, he is renamed *Octavianus* by his great-uncle Julius Caesar, who makes him his heir; after Caesar's assassination in 44 BC, he calls himself *Gaius Julius Caesar*; after 38 BC, *Imperator Caesar Divi Filius*; after 27 BC, *Augustus*; after 12 BC, *Pontifex Maximus*; after 2 BC, *Pater Patriae* – and is declared a *god* four weeks after his death.

During his reign, Brutus's head is cut off and laid at the feet of a statue of Caesar, Antony and

Cleopatra commit suicide, Jesus of Nazareth is born, Ovid is banned to the Black Sea, and the Romans are defeated in the Battle of the Teutoburg Forest.

. . . Augustus, the father of his fatherland, Caesar, belongs to all men – a fraction of that common property belongs to me as well. . . . When I see him, I see Rome, for he matches the city in majesty and character. . . . All things come to his ears, nothing that happens in this world is hidden from him.

Augustus II

Adopted by Augustus I * as *Tiberius Claudius Nero* and named his heir; retains the rhinoceros as the heraldic emblem of his reign; revokes no laws, lifts no decree of banishment; so zealously emulates his divine predecessor in every question and decision of power that at last he assumes his name as well and has himself adored as *Julius Caesar Augustus*. Decrees that fifteen battleships of the Roman navy be rolled in cradles from the Tyrrhenian Sea to Rome in order to demonstrate that *every* bearer of the name Augustus can turn the stones of the earth into a sea and the sea into a mirror of his triumph.

Augustus (42 BC to 37 AD)

Second Roman emperor; son of Tiberius Claudius Nero and Livia Drusilla of the Claudianus family; at first named for his father; adopted by Augustus I * after the latter falls in love with Livia Drusilla and makes her his wife. Succeeds his step-father and guards his inheritance as *Tiberius Gaius Julius Caesar Augustus*.

. . . When Caesar appears, even the gladiator leaves the arena unharmed – such strength is he given by the very sight of that face. . . . But I, O Caesar, have guided my poem from the beginnings of the universe even into your own days.

Battus

Son of Fama * the grocer and a miner; suffers from epilepsy and a compulsion to grab, touch, and name everything to assure himself that it really exists. Fama nails garlands of nettles to the shelves to

Battus

Messinian shepherd; sees Mercury, the messenger of the gods, driving off a herd of stolen cattle, but when given a cow as a bribe, swears he will hold his tongue. Mercury departs, but returns dis-

keep him away from her wares, but the epileptic is forever burning his fingers on them because he is incapable of learning from his pain; he turns to stone at the end of his life.

guised as a stranger and tests the shepherd. Battus breaks his oath.

. . . And Mercury laughed: 'You rascal, would you betray me to myself, in person?' And with the word, he turned him into stone, the kind called touch-stone, to this very moment, as if the stone had been the guilty talker.

Ceyx

Leading male character in a melodrama that Cyparis * the projectionist beams on the walls of Tomi's slaughterhouse one April evening. But unlike the role of Alcyone *, which proved lucky for its portrayer, the role of Ceyx was a disaster for the Neapolitan actor Omero Dafano. He committed suicide after a terrible review of his performance as Ceyx was published in the Roman film magazine *Colosseo*.

Ceyx

Son of the Morning Star, husband of Alcyone *, king of Trachis; refuses to let his wife's pleas deter him from a pilgrimage to Claros; killed in a storm at sea, his body drifts back to the rocky shores of Trachis. There Alcyone discovers him and casts herself into the sea in her grief.

. . . And through the pity of the gods, the husband became a bird, and joined his wife. Together they suffered, and together loved; no parting followed them in their new-found form as birds. They mate, have young, and in the winter season, for seven days of calm, Alcyone broods over her nest on the surface of the waters while the sea-waves are quiet. Through this time Aeolus keeps his winds at home, and the ocean is smooth for his descendants' sake.

Cotta

Cotta is one of many: in the years of Augustus's reign, increasing numbers of Rome's subjects and citizens leave the great city to escape its apparatus of power, the omnipresent surveillance, the forest of flags and the monotonous bawling of patriotic slogans. Many of them are also fleeing the draft,

Cotta Maximus Messalinus

Youngest son of the orator Valerius Messalla Corvinus; poet and orator, friend of Ovid; is mentioned several times in the works of the historians Pliny and Tacitus – for instance, that he represented Tiberius's position in the senate and was later defended by the emperor himself against charges of lese-

or simply the boredom of a citizenship whose every ludicrous duty is prescribed. Somewhere on the uncivilised borders of the empire, far from the symmetry of a well-ordered life, they go looking for a life free from supervision. Both in the jargon of the government press and in police files, travellers of this sort are called *fugitives of the state*.

majesty. Dies, it is presumed, after taking poisoned medicine. Six of Ovid's letters from the Black Sea (*Epistulae ex Ponto*) are addressed to him.

. . . Cotta, I hope these good wishes I send will reach you, that they come true for you. . . . Are you surprised that I am still writing? I surprise myself sometimes and ask what good it all is. Perhaps common folk are right when they say poets are crazy – I am after all a good example; I am still writing, sewing seed on barren ground. . . . I once put my hopes in my friends – well, they will forgive me for that. I shall never make that mistake again. . . . I have long since grown indifferent to all suffering. I have come here. And here I shall die, . . . for most people I was already dead as my star sank.

Cyane

Wife of the exile Naso ★; a shy, beautiful woman from one of the important families of Sicily; tries to maintain their home on the Piazza del Moro in hope of a speedy pardon for her husband. To no avail. The estate falls into ruin. The fountains sink back into their basins. The surface of the ponds is covered with pine needles and leaves. In the second year of his exile, Cyane flees from the relentless deterioration to the muffled plush velvet of dark apartments on the Via Anastasio, and in her letters to the Black Sea she reports about life in a house whose windows have long since been nailed shut.

Cyane

Sicilian water nymph; blocks the path of the god of the underworld and attempts to prevent him from abducting Proserpina ★; the enraged god flings his royal sceptre into her pool, splits open the earth and rides down into the world of shades with his stolen bride.

. . . Cyane grieved for both violations, girl and fountain, and in her silent spirit kept the wound incurable, and, all in tears, she melted, dissolving, queen no longer, of those waters.

Cyparis

Dwarfish projectionist from the Caucasus, who not only shows films but also sells Turkish delight and stone alum and makes a stag dance on its hind legs to march music. Cyparis loves his audience. When, after tedious preparations, the projector magnifies the face of a hero to gigantic size and the slaughterhouse wall becomes a window onto jungles and deserts, the Lilliputian sits hidden in the darkness and watches the spectators' faces in the blue reflected light. At times he thinks he recognises in their pantomime the power of his own unrealisable longings. Sometimes during the show he falls asleep and dreams of trees, of cedars, poplars, cypresses, dreams that he bears moss on his skin. Then his toenails crack open, and roots that creep from his crooked legs begin to bind him deeper and deeper to the spot. The protective rings of years form around his heart. He grows.

Cyparissus

Handsome youth from Cea; beloved by Apollo, the god of poetry, music, augury and medicine. Kills his tame stag by accident.

. . . One summer noon-day, when the heat of the sun held hot around the seashore, the deer was lying, tired, with his body on the grassy ground, under a tree's cool shadow, and Cyparissus shot him, by some ill luck, with pointed arrow, and as he saw him dying from the wound, wanted to die himself . . . and prayed the gods, as a last boon, to let him grieve forever. . . . His limbs were green in colour, and the hair over his snowy forehead, bristled, roughened, like any bush, rose, tapering toward heaven. Apollo spoke in sorrow: 'I shall mourn you as you shall mourn for others, an attendant on all who mourn their dead.'

Deucalion

Character in a story that Echo ✶ tells. She explains to Cotta ✶ that it is taken from the *Book of Stones*, a work apparently written by the exiled poet Naso ✶. In that book, Deucalion is the last man, a survivor of doomsday, of a flood that destroys everything except him and his beloved Pyrrha ✶. The loneliness of survivors, Echo says, is surely the worst punishment of all.

Deucalion

Son of the Titan Prometheus, husband of Pyrrha ✶, with whom he survives the great flood by which Jupiter ✶ drowns all humankind. As the waters recede, their raft is stranded on the slopes of Mount Parnassus. There they seek solace in a silted temple and are given instructions to cast stones behind them. Without understanding the meaning of this oracle, Deucalion and Pyrrha follow its advice.

. . . The stones the man had

*thrown turned into men. . . . Hence
we derive the hardness that we have,
and our endurance gives proof of what
we have come from.*

Echo

Cotta's * close friend, his lover for
one night and his victim; suffers
from a scaly patch of skin that
shifts about her body. Whenever it
disappears under her clothes, Echo
is a woman of captivating beauty;
but when the scales return to her
face, any touch, indeed a simple
gawking stare, causes her such
pain that those who love her with-
draw and avoid her. And Echo is
loved, though in secret, by many
inhabitants of the coast; by cover
of night both herdsmen and smelters sometimes seek her out in her
cave, and there in Echo's arms are
transformed into babies, into lords
or animals. Her lovers know that
Echo's impenetrable privacy pro-
tects them from any reproach, any
shame, and in exchange they leave
amber, hides, dried fish or pots of
oil behind in the debris of her cave.

Echo

Nymph, who keeps Jupiter's *
wife Juno busy with long conversations while the god is sport-
ing with his lady friends. As a
punishment for Echo's being in
league with her faithless husband,
Juno takes away her ability to
speak: she can only repeat the last
words addressed to her. Echo lives
an unhappy life until she meets
Narcissus, a beautiful youth with
whom she falls in love but who is
incapable of loving anything
except his own image. Narcissus
rejects the nymph, who flees grief-
stricken into the wilderness:

*. . . spurned and hiding, ashamed,
in the leafy forests, in lonely caverns.
But still her love clings to her and
increases and grows on suffering; she
cannot sleep, she frets and pines,
becomes all gaunt and haggard, her
body dries and shrivels till voice only
and bones remain, and then she is voice
only for the bones are turned to stone.
. . . But all may hear her, for her voice
is living.*

Fama

Owner of Tomi's grocery shop;
widow of the former owner; a
migrant miner is the father of her
epileptic son, Battus *; in her
desperation, she tries at one point
to put the misbegotten child out of
its misery with an extract of cyclamen and daphne blossoms; she is

Fama

Goddess of rumours.

*. . . There is a place at the world's
centre. . . . From here all things, no
matter what, are visible; every word
comes to these hollow ears. Here
Rumour dwells, her palace high upon
the mountain-summit. . . . Day and
night the halls stand open, and the*

so devoted to him, however, that when she does in fact lose Battus, she becomes talkative, dependent on her listeners and their consolation; tells Cotta * the life stories of Tomi's inhabitants.

bronze re-echoes, repeats all words, redoubles every murmur. . . . Rumours in thousands, lies and truth together, confused, confusing. Some fill idle ears with stories, others go far-off to tell what they have heard, and every story grows, and each new teller adds to what he hears.

Hector

Title of the first part of a heroic trilogy shown by Cyparis * during Holy Week in Tomi. The film depicts the fall of Troy and the defeat of Hector, its most valiant defender, who is dragged around the walls of his own fortress until at last his gruesome death is apparent from the trailing pack of dogs tussling over the wide-strewn scraps of his flesh.

Hector

Son of Priam and Hecuba, the last king and queen of Troy; the most famous of all Trojan heroes; in the tenth year of war, he is killed by Achilles and dragged naked around the city walls; his father is slain as well, his mother is carried off by the Greeks.

. . . 'Farewell, O Troy, we are taken!' the Trojan women cry, and kiss their land, and leave the smoking ruins. Last of all, most pitiful, came Hecuba, hauled away from where the Greeks had found her, at the tombs of buried sons, trying to give their bones her farewell kisses. Only Hector's ashes she could redeem, and bore that rescued dust in her bosom with her, leaving, at his tomb, locks of her thin grey hair and the stain of tears.

Hercules

Title of the second part of a heroic trilogy shown by Cyparis * in Tomi. The film shows the life of the invincible warrior Hercules, who perishes at last at his own hands; he dies after slipping on a magic shirt whose poisoned fabric immediately fuses with his own skin, begins to burn on his body like boiling oil and cannot be cast off again except at the price of his

Hercules

Son of Jupiter *, king of the gods, and Alcmena, a mortal; besides many other deeds, he accomplishes twelve labours in the service of the king of Argos; battles with the river god Achelous for the beautiful Deianira, wins her; kills Nessus, a centaur who tries to abduct his wife; is poisoned by a shirt soaked in Nessus's blood, which an unsuspecting Deianira

very life. Hercules tears his own skin and flesh from his bones along with the shirt, lays bare his bleeding sinews, his shoulder blades, the red cage of his ribs, and inside it, lungs burning out, his heart. He falls.

gives him in the belief that it will renew their love. Mad with pain, Hercules flings Lichas ★, who has brought the shirt, into the Euboean Sea and then burns to death on a pyre he has built for himself on Mount Oeta.

. . . So Hercules put off the mortal body, thriving, and in his better part becoming greater, more worthy of veneration, and Jove raised him through hollow clouds to the bright stars, a rider in the chariot drawn by the four heavenly horses.

Jason

Thessalonian navigator, whose freighter, a rerigged battleship, pays unscheduled, unpredictable visits to the harbours of the Black Sea coast, often leaving confusion, arguments and rancour behind. For the Thessalonian carries more with him than simple merchandise to be traded for bars of iron, pelts and amber. He also has on board a permanent gang of emigrants: unemployed labourers, impoverished farmers, the inhabitants of the ghettoes of Thessalonica, Volos and Athens. To all of them Jason promises a golden future on the Black Sea and relieves them of their last penny for a stifling berth below deck on the *Argo*. Once they reach the dilapidated piers of Odessa and Constanta, the fire-gutted docks at Sevastopol or some other desolate stretch of coast, Jason's passengers recognise the futility of their hopes. By then, however, they lack the money and the energy to return to Greece.

Jason

Son of King Aeson of Iolcus; builds a ship, the *Argo*; is sent by his uncle Pelias, who has usurped Aeson's throne, to the east coast of the Black Sea to retrieve the golden fleece from King Aeetes. Good winds bring Jason and his crew to Colchis; with the aid of Medea ★, daughter of Aeetes, he carries out all the tasks demanded of him, recovers the golden fleece and sails back to Iolcos with Medea, whom he has made his wife.

. . . They suffered much, but came at last with Jason, their brilliant leader, to the muddy waters where Phasis meets the sea. They went to the king, claiming the golden fleece . . . and heard the dreadful terms, enormous labours. And the king's daughter burned with sudden passion, and fought against it long, and when her reason could not subdue her madness, cried: 'Medea, you fight in vain.'

And so they leave the ship to seek
the shadow of their fortune among
the ruins of bleak towns.

Icarus

Subject of a tapestry Cotta ★ sees
in the house of Arachne ★, the
deaf-mute weaver; the scene: vast
emptiness, woven in tones of blue,
white and silver threads, a view
onto a sea lying peacefully in the
sun, a bright summer sky dotted
with clouds, a gull or two above
the gentle swells, but no coastline,
no island, no ship. In the far
distance, just below the razor-edge
of the horizon, two grey wings –
their span as wide as a condor's,
lifted straight up, helpless – disappear into the water like the arms
of a drowning man. The jets of
spray from the impact rise like
white lances above the wings, and
from overhead lost feathers, down
and delicate quills come drifting
and tumbling, permitting a slower
descent to the sea than the heavy
body that bore such pinions. *Icarus*
– the name of the fallen creature
sinking beneath the lustre – is one
of the deaf-mute's many finger
signs that Cotta sees as they fly up
out of her hands, but does not
understand.

Itys

Son of Tereus ★ the butcher and
his wife Procne ★, nephew of Philomela ★; during one of Cyparis's ★ shows, he mutilates a finger
by sticking it into the whirring fan
that cools the projector's bulbs.
The blades disperse the boy's

Icarus

Son of Daedalus, an architect from
Attica, an inventor and murderer.
Daedalus, jealous of Perdix, his
nephew and pupil, slays him and
flees to the court of king Minos of
Crete; there he builds the labyrinth
of Cnossos for the tyrant, designs
for him new battleships and other
armaments – but in the end decides
to flee from Minos's protection
and brutality; he builds wings for
himself and his son; they fly away
from the palace at Cnossos and
across the sea. But Icarus, carried
away by his enthusiasm, climbs
higher and higher:

   . . . nearer the sun, and the wax
that held the wings melted in that fierce
heat, and the bare arms beat up and
down in air, and lacking oarage took
hold of nothing. Father! he cried, and
Father! until the blue sea hushed him.
. . . And Daedalus, father no more,
called 'Icarus, where are you! Where
are you, Icarus? Tell me where to find
you!' And saw the wings on the
waves, and cursed his talents, buried
the body in a tomb.

Itys

Son of Tereus ★, king of Thrace,
and Procne ★, daughter of the king
of Athens; nephew of princess
Philomela ★; Itys senses his
approaching doom when he hears
Procne cursing his father.

   . . . Her son came in, young Itys.

blood over the Lilliputian's projector in a thousand tiny droplets: an evil omen, Proserpina * says. And indeed, the very next year, Itys meets a tragic death.

She looked at him with pitiless eyes; she thought: How like his father he is! That was enough, she knew, now, what she had to do. . . . But when the little fellow came and put both arms around his mother, and kissed her in appealing boyish fashion, she was moved to tenderness. . .

Jupiter

Mummer's mask in Tomi's carnival parade: a man bent low under the weight of a vendor's tray on which he carries an electrical device, a battery encrusted with saltpetre petals feeding the wreath of rhythmically flashing light bulbs that encircles him.

Jupiter

God of celestial light, king of the gods, lord of the Silver Age; son of Saturn and Rhea, brother and husband of Juno, brother of Neptune and Dis *; together with his brothers, casts his father into the underworld; they then cast lots to divide dominion over the cosmos among them; heaven and earth fall to him.

. . . Easily seen when the night skies are clear, the Milky Way shines white. Along this road the gods move toward the palace of the Thunderer.

Lichas

Missionary of the Old Believers of Constantinople, who arrives in Tomi every year around Easter, coming from the Bosporus aboard a fishing cutter; in the twilight of Tomi's neglected, mildewed church, he reads out an endless litany of tortures endured by members of his sect slain under Roman rule. On Good Friday, he interrupts the showing of a film about the death of Orpheus *, screaming that the sufferings and agonies of the crucified Lord of this world ought to be remembered on such a holy day and ringing the church bell until

Lichas

Servant; he brings Hercules * a shirt drenched in centaur's blood, which is intended to kill him. Hercules, near death from the agony of the poisoned shirt, flings Lichas into the Euboean Sea.

. . . Lichas, hurled through the air by Hercules, grew colder, the blood, by fear, made rigid, and the body all stone and hardness.

Cyparis * is forced to stop the show.

Lycaon

Ropemaker of Tomi; rents Cotta * an attic room, unheated and hung with garish wall hangings; occasionally employs Echo * as his housemaid; sleeps in a corner of his workshop among yarn winches and reels of rope and goes barefoot even on icy days; in his safe he keeps – along with crumpled paper money, blackish silverware and an army pistol – a stone-grey, moth-eaten wolf's pelt.

Lycaon

Aracadian tyrant, decides to kill Jupiter *, a visitor in human form, while he sleeps; but first tries to test the god's omniscience by serving him human flesh to eat. Jupiter burns down the tyrant's palace; Lycaon flees.

. . . He fled in terror, reached the silent fields, and howled, and tried to speak. No use at all! Foam dripped from his mouth; bloodthirsty still, he turned against the sheep, delighting still in slaughter, and his arms were legs, and his robes were shaggy hair, yet he is still Lycaon, the same greyness, the same fierce face, the same red eyes, a picture of bestial savagery.

Marsyas

Charcoal burner from a mountain valley near Limyra; one of Echo's * suitors; after her disappearance, he waits for her in vain all night, gets drunk and wrecks her home; his howls and strange music rob Tomi's residents of their sleep; at dawn Tereus * throws him into a water trough; Procne * pulls him out and saves him from drowning. In a drunken stupor, in a tangle of heavy dreams, he lies on the mossy stones beside the trough until afternoon; the only person up and down the coast of Tomi who feels any sadness at Echo's disappearance.

Marsyas

Satyr, a virtuoso on the flute, whom Apollo, the god of poetry and music, skins alive because Marsyas plays more beautifully than he in a musical competition to which the satyr has challenged him. Apollo hangs Marsyas head-down from a tree:

. . . flaying him, so the skin all left his body, so he was one great wound, with the blood flowing, the nerves exposed, veins with no cover of skin over their beating surface, lungs and entrails visible as they functioned. The country people, the woodland gods, the fauns, his brother satyrs, the nymphs, and even Olympus, whom he loved through all his agony, all wept for him with every shepherd looking after his flocks along those mountainsides. The

fruitful earth drank in those tears, and
turned them into water, and sent them
forth to air again, a rill, a stream, the
clearest of all the running Phrygian
rivers, named Marsyas, for the victim.

Medea

Title figure of a tragedy by
Naso ★, acclaimed in all the
theatres of the empire and making
a celebrity of the poet. Cotta ★
thinks he recognises her among the
costumed fools in Tomi's carnival
parade – a gigantic woman, her
torso made of wood and straw and
splattered with red paint, who uses
the two thin arms sprouting from
her gut to fling a cardboard skull
high into the air, again and again,
and gives shrill shrieks each time
she catches it. In Naso's tragedy,
Medea slaughters her own brother,
dismembers his childish body and
hurls the chopped-off head against
the rocks of a coastal cliff.

Medea

Title figure of a lost tragedy by
Ovid; daughter of King Aeetes of
Colchis, granddaughter of the sun
god, famous for her powers of
magic; falls in love with Jason ★,
helps him obtain the golden fleece,
marries him, follows him to Iolcus; there she kills Jason's uncle,
the woman Jason once loved and
the children from their own mar-
riage; flees to Athens, where she
becomes the wife of King Aegeus
and tries to poison his son Theseus;
flees again. Among her many
magical powers, she has the power
to reverse the course of time and
restore all living things to their
youth.

. . . And all the while the brew in
the bronze cauldron boiled and
frothed white; in it were root-herbs
gathered from Thessaly's lonely vales,
and seeds and flowers, strong juices,
and pebbles from the farthest shores of
oceans east and west, and hoar-frost
taken at the full of the moon, a
hoot-owl's wings and flesh, a were-
wolf's entrails also, and the fillet of
fenny snake, the liver of the stag,
long-lived, the eggs, the head, of the
crow whose years run for nine genera-
tions. All of these were in the caul-
dron, and a thousand others, things
without names, out of the world of
mortals, and the barbarian woman
stirred them well, mixing them, top to

bottom, with a branch of olive, dry and dead, and the old dry branch, stirring the brew, turned green, and green leaves sprouted along its length, and suddenly it was loaded with olive fruit: wherever the scum spilled over and the hot drops fell on the ground, the ground turned green, soft grasses grew and flowers broke into blossom.

Memnon

Refugee from Ethiopia; superstitious gardener at Naso's ★ villa on the Piazza del Moro; the morning after Naso's important speech, he trims hedges and grafts a wild cherry tree in the garden – and interprets a great swarm of pigeons flying over the estate and darkening the sky to be an omen of good luck. In truth, this flock of pigeons, their shadow whisking over the house, the gardens, the whole neighbourhood, embodies the colour of the Black Sea.

Memnon

King of Ethiopia; son of Aurora, the goddess of dawn, and of Tithonus, who has been transformed into an immortal cicada; Memnon is the last ally of Troy slain by Achilles; as his body burns on the pyre, Aurora weeps and begs Jupiter ★ to ease her grief.

. . . So Jove assented and Memnon's pyre crumbled from leaping flames to ashes, and the hue of day was darkened by black and rolling smoke, as rivers send fogs that admit no sunlight. The dark ashes whirled high, and in the air they massed and thickened, took on a form, a heat, a spirit, lightness from the wings of fire. It was like a bird at first, then a bird really, and its pinions whirred, and there were countless sisters whirring with it, all from that heavenly source, and round the pyre three times they flew, three times their noisy clamour rose up to air.

Midas

Title figure of a comedy by Naso ★ that leads to a scandal in Rome. The play deals with a Genoese shipping magnate, an absolute fanatic about music, who is so mad with greed that everything he

Midas

King of Phrygia; Bacchus, the god of wine and intoxication, gives him the ability to change everything he touches to gold.

. . . He hardly dared believe it! From an oak-tree he broke a green twig

touches turns to gold. In the last act the shipping magnate is sitting caked in filth and wearing ass's ears, an emaciated skeleton in a golden desert. In his long monologue, names known all over town are dropped as well, hidden within palindromes and spoonerisms – of board chairmen, congressmen and judges. After three triumphant performances, a senator from Liguria, who owns docks in Genoa and Trapani, has the comedy closed down. A troop of mounted police wielding steel truncheons prevents the audience from entering and the actors from leaving the theatre; both actors and members of the audience are wounded. They lie, bleeding and moaning, in their golden costumes and evening finery on the steps of the theatre until they are dragged away. The scandal gives rise to fully unexpected personal repercussions for Naso – even lottery vendors, fish and soft-drink dealers, money changers and illiterates now know his name; he becomes *popular*.

loose; the twig was golden. He picked a stone up from the ground; the stone paled with light golden colour; he touched a clod, the clod became a nugget. . . . His mind could scarcely grasp his hopes – all things were golden, or would be, at his will! A happy man, he watched his servants set a table before him with bread and meat. He touched the gift of Ceres and found it stiff and hard; he tried to bite the meat with hungry teeth, and where the teeth touched food they seemed to touch on golden ingots. . . . Midas, astonished at his new misfortune, rich man and poor man, tries to flee his riches hating the favour he had lately prayed for. No food relieves his hunger; his throat is dry with burning thirst; he is tortured, as he should be, by the hateful gold.

Naso, Publius Ovidius

Poet of Rome; his love poems make him well-known, his tragedy *Medea* makes him famous, but not until his comedy *Midas* does he become *popular*. Amid political uproar, myths cluster around him. If for some he is an eccentric poet, others revere him as a revolutionary, fear him as an enemy of the state or despise him as a luxury-seeking opportunist. At the end, the only thing certain is

Naso, Publius Ovidius

Poet of Rome; born 43 BC, the son of a country squire in Sulmo; studies rhetoric in Rome; makes a Grand Tour of Asia Minor and Greece. After serving briefly as a civil servant, he abandons his chances of a career as a senator and (supported by his father's wealth) devotes himself to literature; following his abandonment of political life and the early death of his brother, a talented orator,

that the poet is to be banned to the Black Sea; despairing of his fate, he burns the manuscript of his masterpiece, of which his readers know only the title and fragments he has read in public: *Metamorphoses*. After lighting his beacon fire, the poet disappears to barbaric shores. Rome mourns or celebrates, puzzling over what mistake it was that led to Naso's exile: where had his journey to the end of the world begun? Though perhaps not the only reason for his fall, Naso's carelessness as one of eleven orators at the opening ceremony for a new stadium certainly was a contributing factor. For at the signal from the emperor, looking bored now after seven speeches and giving his nod for the eighth orator from a distance so great that Naso could see only the depth of pallor on Augustus's face, but no eyes, no features . . ., at his weary, indifferent signal, then, Naso stepped forward that night to a bouquet of shiny microphones and with that one step left the Roman Empire behind him. Because he did not mention – because he forgot! – the one directive more important than all others, he forgot the litany of greetings, the genuflection before senators, generals, before the emperor himself beneath his canopy, he forgot himself and his own fortunes. He stepped up to the microphone without the slightest bow, and simply said: Citizens of Rome.

the family in Sulmo buries all hopes for further social advancement – and is surprised by Ovid. He has great success with his first love poems and ultimately becomes a celebrated poet. What a sensation, then, when in 8 AD this renowned and socially prominent man is banned, without trial, by order of the imperial government to Tomi on the Black Sea, to the end of the world. The real reasons for his banishment (which, since there was no sentencing by a court nor any fine imposed, was legally comparable to being expelled from school) have been the subject of books down to the twentieth century. At the time, the official reason given is the shamelessness of Ovid's erotic poetry; the explanations attracting the most adherents at present, however, either have to do with Ovid's being involved in a scandal centring around the granddaughter of Emperor Augustus – or suggest that as party to some political intrigue of Agrippa Postumus (one of Augustus's direct heirs) he had to be removed from Rome. All attempts to appeal against the imperial edict are futile. Ovid dies in Tomi in 17 or 18 AD; his grave is unknown.

WORKS: *Amores* (Love Poems), *Ars amatoria* (The Art of Love), *De medicamine faciei feminae* (How Women Use Cosmetics), *Medea* (a lost tragedy), *Remedia amoris* (Remedy of Love), *Heroides* (Letters of Heroes' Wives to their Husbands), *Metamorphoses* (completed, except for final corrections, but not yet published when Ovid is forced into exile; in despair and grief over his departure from Rome, Ovid burns a copy of the manuscript), *Fasti* (A Calendar of Roman Feasts, uncompleted), *Epistulae ex Ponto* (Letters from the Black Sea), *Tristia* (Laments).

Almost everything that posterity claims to know about Ovid's life is taken from the fourth book of his Laments, which contains his autobiography and is considered the first poetical self-portrait in European literary history. And indeed, speaking of his own importance, Ovid anticipates history by ending his *Metamorphoses* with an author's postscript.

. . . Now I have done my work. It will endure, I trust, beyond Jove's anger, fire and sword, beyond Time's hunger. The day will come, I know. So let it come, that day which has no power save over my body, to end my span of life whatever it may be. Still, part of me, the better part, immortal, will be borne above the stars; my name will be remembered wherever Roman power rules conquered lands, I shall be read, and through all centuries, if prophecies of bards are ever truthful, I shall be living, always.

Orpheus

Title of the third part of a heroic trilogy shown by Cyparis ★ during Holy Week in Tomi. The film was to show the martyrdom of a poet who was stoned to death by women wrapped in the hides of panthers and deer, then was skinned and hacked to pieces with

Orpheus

Son of Apollo, the god of poetry and music, and the muse Calliope; the most famous singer of antiquity; loses his wife Eurydice when she is bitten by a snake, but procures her release from the god of the underworld; loses Eurydice a second time, because on the way

axes and sickles. The film is interrupted, however, during the first scene by Lichas *, an Old Believer.

out of the underworld he disobeys the order not to turn and look back. Introduces paederasty among the Thracians and is torn to pieces as a misogynist by a band of frenzied women.

. . . They bayed him down, as in the early morning, hounds circle the doomed stag beside the game-pits. They rushed him, threw the wands, wreathed with green leaves, not meant for such a purpose; some threw clods, some branches torn from the tree, and some threw stones, and they found fitter weapons for their madness. Not far away there was a team of oxen ploughing the field, and near them farmers, digging reluctant earth, and sweating over their labour, who fled before the onrush of this army leaving behind them hoe and rake and mattock and these the women grabbed, and slew the oxen who lowered horns at them in brief defiance and were torn limb from limb, and then the women rushed back to murder Orpheus, who stretched out his hands in supplication, and whose voice, for the first time, moved no one. They struck him down, and through those lips to which the rocks had listened, to which the hearts of savage beasts responded, his spirit found its way to winds and air. The birds wept for him, and the throng of beasts, the flinty rocks, the tree which came so often to hear his song, all mourned. The trees, it seemed, shook down their leaves, as if they might be women tearing their hair.

Philomela
Barefoot, mutilated stranger, who arrives in the town of iron from the mountains one January morn-

Philomela
Daughter of Pandion, king of Athens; sister of Procne *; she is raped by Procne's husband,

ing; Procne ★ recognises her as her sister, long presumed dead. Philomela, apparently unable to comprehend a simple question or a comforting word, whimpers in Procne's arms and cringes with fear if so much as the shadow of a man falls across her.

Tereus ★, who is so enraged by her wailings that he mutilates her.

. . . The double drive of fear and anger drove him to draw the sword, to catch her by the hair, to pull the head back, tie the arms behind her, and Philomela, at the sight of the blade, was happy, filled with hope, the thought of death most welcome: her throat was ready for the stroke. But Tereus did not kill her; he seized her tongue with pincers, though it cried against the outrage, babbled and made a sound something like 'father,' till the sword cut it off. The mangled root quivered, the severed tongue along the ground lay quivering, making a little murmur.

Phineus
Whisky seller and snake charmer who arrives in the town of iron with Cyparis ★; moves into a tumbledown house after someone sets fire to his tent and basket of snakes; settles in Tomi as a brandy dealer. He speaks about moving on, about long journeys, the oases of Africa, trade winds and dromedaries, but all the while he digs his way deeper into the rock earth under the town of iron, using gunpowder and chisel to enlarge the cave beneath his house into a cellar, where he stores sour wine and sugarbeet schnapps and serves it to his customers at any time of the day or night.

Phineus
Son of the king of Ethiopia; vainly attempts to prevent the hero Perseus from marrying the beautiful Andromeda; Perseus taunts him and defeats him in battle by holding up to him the magical, snaky head of Medusa.

. . . As he struggled to turn his eyes, his neck grew hard, his tears were changed to marble, and in marble still the suppliant look, the pleading hands, the pose, the cringe – all these were caught and fixed forever.

Phoebus
Mummer's mask worn by Tereus ★ in Tomi's carnival parade: under trappings of gold

Phoebus
The *bright one*: cognomen of Apollo, the god of poetry, music, augury and medicine – *and* of the

confetti and chrome chips, the butcher drives a whitewashed ox-cart through the streets and swings a burning whip; Cotta * thinks the costume is meant to be a caricature of the sun god and his fiery wagon. The butcher is trying to be Phoebus.

sun god Sol; both are given this title in the *Metamorphoses*. Under the name Phoebus, for example, Apollo flays Marsyas *, falls in love with Cyparissus * and transforms a snake that is about to swallow the cut-off head of Orpheus *.

. . . And here a serpent struck at the head, still dripping with sea-spray, but Apollo came and stopped it freezing the open jaws to stone, still gaping. And Orpheus' ghost fled under the earth, and knew the places he had known before, and, haunting the fields of the blessed, found Eurydice and took her in his arms.

Under the name Phoebus, Sol turns pale at the sound of Medea's * bewitching songs and mourns Caesar's death.

. . . And the sun's visage shone with lurid light on anxious lands. Firebrands were seen to flash among the stars, the clouds dripped blood, rust-colour blighted the azure Morning-Star, and the Moon rode in a blood-red car.

Procne

Wife of Tereus * the butcher, mother of Itys *, sister of Philomela *; sickly, but uncomplaining, she accompanies her spouse through their ugly life; Tereus beats her often, without a word and without anger, as if she is an animal entrusted to him for slaughter, as if the sole purpose of each blow is to numb what scant will she has left, to numb the disgust she feels for him; her only protection against Tereus is a

Procne

Daughter of Pandion, king of Athens, sister of Philomela *, wife of Tereus *; slays her son Itys * in revenge for Tereus's rape and mutilation of her sister.

. . . Without more words, a tigress with a young fawn, she dragged the youngster with her to a dark corner somewhere in the palace, and Itys, who seemed to see his doom approaching, screamed, and held out his hands, with 'Mother, Mother!' and tried to put his little arms around her.

growing corpulence; the once slender woman seems to be gradually disappearing into fat that she pampers with salves and essential oils. When it is revealed that Tereus has raped and mutilated Philomela, she goes mad, lifts her son out of time and lays him back into her heart.

But she, with never a change in her expression, drove the knife home through breast, through side, one wound, enough to kill him, but she made another, cutting the throat, and they cut up the body still living, still keeping something of the spirit, and part of the flesh leaped in the boiling kettles, part hissed on turning skewers, and the room dripped blood.

Proserpina

Fiancée of Tomi's mixer of salves and gravedigger; Proserpina lets the cattle dealers leer at her like a cow, lets the amber-hunters ogle her like a gem, is Fama's * comment, behind her hand. Year after year she tries in vain to convince Thies * to travel with her to see the splendours of Rome, and after days of arguing sometimes leaves him, but always returns to his silent house, fragrant with the odour of myrrh and aloe. But as passionately as Proserpina tries to win the favour of her fiancé, her love cannot alter his sullen, melancholy nature.

Proserpina

Goddess of the underworld; daughter of Jupiter * and Ceres, the goddess of agriculture and grain; loved by Dis *, the lord of the underworld, who abducts her; she finally obtains permission to return to the world above for the fruitful half of the year.

. . . But Jupiter, holding the balance even between the husband and the grieving mother, divides the year in half, so that the goddess may be with both and neither; and her bearing is changed, her sorrow alternates with sunlight, the cloud and shadow vanishing.

Pyrrha

Character in a story that Echo * tells. She explains to Cotta * that it is taken from the *Book of Stones*, a work apparently written by the exiled poet Naso *. In that book, Pyrrha is the last woman, a survivor of doomsday, of a flood that destroys everything except her and her beloved Deucalion *. The loneliness of survivors, Echo says, is surely the worst punishment of all.

Pyrrha

Daughter of the Titan Epimetheus wife of Deucalion *, with whom she survives the great flood by which Jupiter * drowns all humankind. As the waters recede, their raft is stranded on the slopes of Mount Parnassus. There they seek solace in a silted temple and are given instructions to cast stones behind them. Without understanding the meaning of this oracle, Pyrrha and Deucalion follow its advice.

Pythagoras

Greek emigrant; the town of iron considers him to be Naso's ★ crazy servant; hangs wind harps in the crowns of a pine and in the sound of their harmony he hears approaching storms and hail showers; believes in the transmigration of souls, claiming that in the eyes of cows and pigs he can see the gaze of transformed human beings; so he gives speeches at the slaughterhouse door about the abomination of eating meat, until Tereus ★ the butcher pelts him with sheep hearts and intestines. Recognises his own fate in Naso's despair, his own thoughts in Naso's words, and believes that in this correspondence between them he has found a harmony worth communicating to others; begins to leave inscriptions behind on the tables in the brandy cellar and on the walls of houses and gardens and finally makes a monument of every word the exile utters – stone cairns that have inscribed rags fluttering about them, symbols that he, Pythagoras of Samos, is no longer alone in his thoughts and opinions about the world.

Pythagoras

Learned man from Samos; born circa 570 BC; leaves the island ruled by Polycrates around 532 BC and, at Croton in lower Italy, founds a religious–scientific society, whose political activities are finally met with force of arms; although now an old man, Pythagoras moves to Metapontum on the Tarentine Gulf; dies there circa 497 BC. Since he refused to write down any of his doctrines in order to prevent his wisdom from being passed on to the uninitiated, his ideas are known only generally from the teachings of the *Pythagoreans* (e.g., the transmigration of souls, the spherical shape of the earth, some laws of physics and mathematics, etc.). In book XV of the *Metamorphoses*, Naso ★ has this learned man deliver a long speech describing the religious and philosophical background for all metamorphoses.

. . . *All things are always changing, but nothing dies. The spirit comes and goes, is housed wherever it wills, shifts residence from beasts to men, from men to beasts, but always it keeps on living. . . . Nothing is permanent in all the world. All things are fluent; every image forms, wandering through change. Time is itself a river in constant movement, and the hours flow by like water, wave on wave, pursued, pursuing, forever fugitive, forever new.*

Tereus

Tomi's butcher; standing in the shallows of the brook, he smashes open the skulls of bulls; when his axe lands with a crack between the eyes of the fettered beast, every other sound is so inconsequential that even the rushing torrent seems to halt for a moment, transformed into silence. Rapes and mutilates Philomela *, the sister of his wife Procne *. In her despair, Procne kills their son Itys *, the only creature to whom Tereus can show tenderness. Procne flees with her sister, and Tereus searches all night for the woman who has murdered his son, discovers the two sisters at dawn in the ropemaker's house, lifts his axe to slay Procne – and Philomela flies away as a swallow, Procne as a nightingale; the axe-handle becomes yet another beak, Tereus's arms turn into wings, his hair to brown and black feathers. As a hoopoe he follows the two escaping birds.

Tereus

King of Thrace, who victoriously defends Athens against a barbarian horde, in return for which Pandion, King of Athens, gives him his daughter Procne * for a wife; falls in love with his sister-in-law Philomela *, rapes her and then rips out her tongue to prevent her from betraying him. Nevertheless, the bloody deed becomes known; Procne kills her son Itys * out of revenge, chops him up with Philomela's help, roasts and boils the pieces of his corpse and serves them up for Tereus to eat.

. . . *High in the chair sat Tereus, proud, and feasting, almost greedy on the flesh of his own flesh, and in his darkness of mind, he calls: 'Bring Itys here!' and Procne cannot conceal her cruel joy; she is eager to be the herald of her bloody murder. 'He has come in,' she answers, and he looks around, asks where the boy is, asks again, keeps calling, and Philomela, with hair all bloody, springs at him, and hurls the bloody head of Itys full in his father's face. . . . With a great cry he turns the table over. . . . Now, if he could, if he only could, he would open up his belly, eject the terrible feast: all he can do is weep, call himself the pitiful resting-place of his dear son. He draws the sword, pursues them, both Pandion's daughters. They went flying from him as if they were on wings. They were on wings! One flew to the woods, the other to the roof-top. . . . Tereus, swift in grief and lust for vengeance, himself becomes a bird: a stiff crest rises upon his head, and a huge beak juts forward, not too unlike a sword. He is the hoopoe, the bird who looks like war.*

Thies

Mixer of salves and gravedigger of Tomi; comes from Friesland and is tossed up on the shores of the Black Sea by war; receives money by ship's mail, a disability pension, and is known to the inhabitants of the town of iron as *Moneybags*. A draught horse once kicked him in the chest and crushed the ribs on his left side so badly that they had to be pulled from his flesh like broken arrows. Since then, an unprotected heart beats in his breast. However efficacious his medicines and tinctures prove to be, he remains profoundly convinced that there is no help for the living. Only in the faces of the dead does he sometimes think he sees an expression of innocence, which touches him and which he tries to preserve with bitter oils, until he has to cover the awful decay with earth and stones. Although Thies suffers worse from homesickness for the chalk-white dunes of Friesland than from the effects of his wounds, his fiancée Proserpina ★ cannot convince him either to travel to Rome or return to his homeland. After all the deaths he has seen, all the mad destruction he has lived through, he believes that the road back to the coasts of his birth is forever lost; nothing can ever again be as it once was.

Dis

The Roman name for Pluto, the Rich One; son of Saturn, brother of Jupiter ★ and Neptune; god of the underworld and lord of the shades; he is given this realm when his three brothers cast lots after overthrowing their father: Jupiter becomes lord of heaven and earth, Neptune lord of waters and seas. Dis falls in love with Proserpina ★ and abducts her; the reason for this, however, lies in a complaint that Amor, Venus's son, makes to his mother: whether in heaven, on earth or in the seas, Amor has conquered everywhere – only the realm of shades is still without love. And so the god of love took up his weapons.

. . . And Cupid, searching through his quiver, found the sharpest shaft of all, and sent it flying from the bow bent at his knee, and the barb struck deep in Pluto's heart.

I would like to thank the jury of the *Elias Canetti Foundation* of the city of Vienna, who awarded me a fellowship that made it easier for me to write this book.

I would like to thank Brigitte Hilzensauer for her advice – for which I frequently asked. And I thank my Johanna for her steadfast company through the Last World.

C.R.
Vienna, Summer 1988